MURDER UNDER
A RED MOON

ALSO BY HARINI NAGENDRA

The Bangalore Detectives Club

MURDER UNDER A RED MOON

A Bangalore Detectives Mystery

HARINI NAGENDRA

PEGASUS CRIME

NEW YORK LONDON

MURDER UNDER A RED MOON

Pegasus Crime is an imprint of
Pegasus Books, Ltd.
148 West 37th Street, 13th Floor
New York, NY 10018

First Pegasus Books cloth edition March 2023

ISBN: 978-1-63936-370-4

10 9 8 7 6 5 4 3 2 1

Printed in the United States of America
Distributed by Simon & Schuster
www.pegasusbooks.com

For Venkatachalam Suri and
Dhwani Nagendra Suri,
always

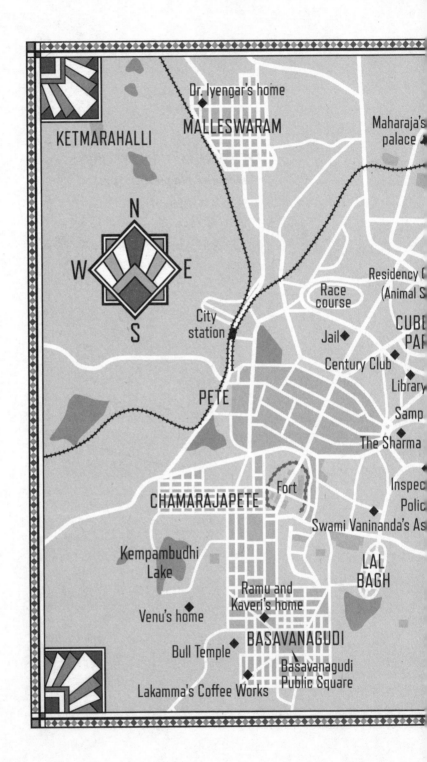

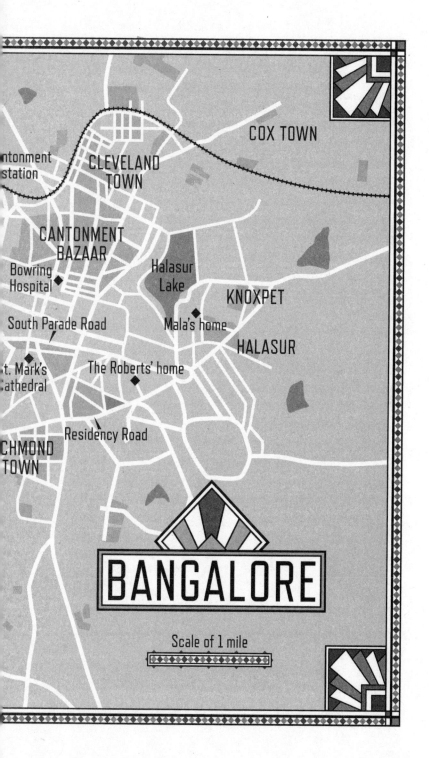

This story takes place in 1920s Bangalore, so a few of the words may be unfamiliar.

If you don't know them, **Kaveri's Dictionary** on page 275 will tell you what they mean and how to pronounce them. It also explains a bit about the geography and history behind this book.

And please peruse Recipes for a mid-afternoon meeting of **The Bangalore Detectives Club** on page 279 for some delicious Indian recipes, adapted to modern times and inspired by the food in *The Bangalore Detectives Club*.

1

The Ugliest Dog in Bangalore

Bangalore, September 1921

Mrs Kaveri Murthy's emerald green velvet blouse showed off her strong shoulders, developed through hours of swimming in the Century Club pool.

Not bad, she thought, as she inspected the pleats in her peacock blue chiffon sari that flared out from her waist. So what if she didn't wear a smart *cloche* and a flapper frock with high heels? She was a well-known and respected detective. At just nineteen years of age, she could hold herself with the best of the English and Indian society who would be at the animal show today.

Kaveri adjusted her gold chain, admiring the delicate locket in the shape of a magnifying glass. Her husband Ramu had given it to her a couple of weeks after she solved her first case: the murder of Ponnuswamy, a local pimp, in the lawns of the Century Club. The locket hung a couple of inches below the scar on her neck, reminding her of her encounter with a desperate murderer a few weeks ago. The scar was fading, but memories of that frightening evening remained fresh in her mind.

The large grandfather clock on the wall chimed, bringing her back to the present. Half past ten already? Kaveri rushed out of her shed towards the main house, pausing briefly to grin at the large sign hanging outside the shed.

THE BANGALORE DETECTIVES CLUB

Although it had been up for several weeks now, it still gave her a deep sense of satisfaction.

The word seemed to be spreading – last week, a man from Majjigepura, the village of buttermilk, had come to her, seeking help to find his missing flock of goats. From his story, Kaveri deduced that his untrustworthy cousin was the culprit. He had sent her a huge tin of goat ghee in gratitude, which her mother-in-law Bhargavi promptly claimed so she could massage her aching knees.

The broad smile on Kaveri's face dulled, as it always did when she thought of Bhargavi, who disapproved of most things she did. She wished she could avoid her today, but to her dismay, Bhargavi had insisted on meeting her at the animal show. She had sounded *very* mysterious.

'Bhargavi *athe*? I am leaving now,' Kaveri said, dragging her feet as she finally went into the house. She expected to see the dour expression that had been ever-present on Bhargavi's face since Kaveri had solved a murder and attained local fame as a woman detective. That sour look had pushed Kaveri to spend much of her time in her shed over the past few weeks, working with her mathematics textbooks. Calculus and algebra were her refuge, an ordered path to certainty that calmed her when confronted with unpleasantness.

But Bhargavi surprised Kaveri by giving her an approving nod. 'Remember, come to the Dewan's tent after the dog show, Kaveri. I will be there.'

'After the show? Aren't you coming to see the dogs compete?' The question was out of her mouth before Kaveri could swallow it. When she saw Bhargavi's smile turn into a frown, she cursed her inability to stop interrogating people when she felt things didn't make sense.

'Of course not. You know how I hate dogs – nasty, smelly creatures. I will see you at the tent,' Bhargavi responded in a curt voice.

Why does she want to meet me after the show then? Kaveri shook her head and ran down the stairs, thankful to be away from her mother-in-law's disapproving presence.

She pushed all thoughts of Bhargavi and her dislike for unruly creatures – dogs and her daughter-in-law included – out of her mind as she approached her beloved Ford. Their gardener had polished the car with a piece of soft leather just that morning, and she couldn't help but admire how it shone in the light. Kaveri's mood lifted as she got into the car, thinking of the stunned look on the traffic inspector's face when she had gone in to take her test a few months back. Ramu had told her with glee that she had been a major topic of conversation in the traffic room – only the second Indian woman in Bangalore to possess a driver's licence.

Kaveri drove slowly along the roads, enjoying the feeling of the breeze on her hair as people on the streets gaped at the young woman in the driver's seat. It was nearly noon when she arrived at the Residency Grounds, and the animal show was in full swing when she turned into the private enclosure. She handed her premium ticket to the gatekeeper before driving beneath the arch and parking.

A large cloth banner hanging above the arch announced the presence of 'The Horse, Dog and Animal Show, Bangalore, 1921' in the three official languages of Mysore: English, Kannada and Urdu.

The wisps of clouds, remnant from last night's rains, were scattering and it could not have been a brighter or more glorious day. A military band, resplendent in full regalia, began to play a lively selection of music.

Tents with striped bunting in red and gold protected folding tables from the scorching heat of the afternoon sun. A stout Anglo-Indian lady wearing a frilly pink lace frock and a wide-brimmed pink hat manned a large table, loaded with jars of jams, preserves and chutneys. Kaveri's steps slowed as she took in another table crammed with trophies and prizes for the dog show. Out of the corner of her eye, she noticed the gold bangle for 'Ladies' Pet Dog' donated by Messrs Barton and Son, the jewellers who had crafted the Mysore Maharaja's silver throne. Miss Roberts, whose brother was Ramu's supervisor at the Bowring Hospital, would certainly be angling for that one!

An usher, resplendent in the Maharaja's colours of red and gold, hurried up to Kaveri. 'This way, madam. Are your dogs coming in a separate vehicle?'

'No, I've come to watch the prizegiving ceremonies,' she said with a smile for the fresh-faced young man who looked so eager to be of help. The usher changed direction, escorting her to a large spectator tent.

Kaveri looked around as she stepped inside, trying to spot her friend Mrs Reddy. There must have been scores of people in there, dressed in their best French chiffon saris and frocks. The air was thick with perfume, and Kaveri didn't recognise a single face in the crowd.

She lifted up a loose flap of the tent to squint past the haze of sun and dust from the arriving cars, and saw a number of well-dressed men and women accompanied by dogs of all shapes and sizes, from small brown terriers and snow-white Pomeranians to massive Afghan hounds. Excited yips and barks filled the air outside. She peered out at the crowd, shaking her head. How on earth would she find Mrs Reddy, much less talk to her in this chaos?

'Pardon me,' a distinguished-looking Indian gentleman said as he moved past. He wore a well-cut grey morning suit with a marigold blossom in his lapel, and he held on to a large greyhound the size of a small pony. The dog bared its teeth, generating a deep threatening rumble as it looked at the press of people.

'It's far too crowded, Shanthi. Shall we move to the neighbouring tent?' A woman Kaveri assumed to be his wife took his arm as they exited the tent. Kaveri looked after them, wondering absently if she should get herself a deep purple sari like the woman was wearing, with a crochet lace border in maroon.

'Kaveri? There you are, my dear,' a familiar husky voice boomed from the back.

Kaveri turned and found herself enfolded in the familiar embrace of Mrs Reddy. She was wearing a stunning sari in rich red colours. As always, it had been wrapped carelessly around her ample curves. Mrs Reddy had the most exquisite taste in textiles, but lacked the patience to dress up – and Kaveri only loved her all the more for it. She hugged her back tightly, feeling a wave of affection for the woman who had taken the place of her mother in this unfamiliar city when she had moved to Bangalore a few months ago.

'Ah, Kaveri. How nice to see you.'

Kaveri frowned inwardly at the sound of a nasal voice she recognised all too well.

'Miss Roberts!' She pasted a polite smile on her face, turning and extending her hand to Dr Roberts' sister.

She had to be nice to the woman – Dr Roberts was Ramu's supervisor.

The older woman was neatly clad in a grey silk frock with a modest high neck and long sleeves, the hem extended a few inches below her knees.

'I didn't expect to see you here,' Mrs Reddy said. 'I thought you would be in the other tent, where the pet owners are.'

'Oh, I never intended to stand there all day with my dog, dear,' Miss Roberts drawled. 'Prissy, my fox terrier, is so hairy, you know. She sheds all over my frock, and you know how difficult it is to get good clothes cleaned by native servants.'

Kaveri caught Mrs Reddy's eye before looking away. 'I hear they have some nice prizes today,' she offered, trying to change the subject.

'But the tickets, my dear! Two rupees! So expensive,' Miss Roberts complained in her grating tone.

'It is for charity, after all,' said Mrs Reddy mildly, catching the eye of a bearer circulating with a tray of lemon sherbet. 'The proceeds go to the cantonment orphanage.'

Kaveri took one of the drinks and tried to take delicate sips, even though her throat was parched. As she gave up, draining the remainder in one unladylike thirsty gulp, the usher opened the tent flap and a man began to beat a large drum, signalling the entrance of the judges, followed by the dogs with their handlers. Kaveri clapped politely, but curiosity stirred inside her when she saw the couple she had seen a short while back re-enter the tent, accompanied by an elderly British pair.

Her attention was diverted when the announcer picked up a megaphone. 'Ladies and gentlemen. Thank you for attending the animal show. We thank Messrs Barton and Sons, jewellers to His Majesty the Maharaja of Mysore, and Mr and Mrs Sharma of the Sampangi Mills for donating the prizes today.'

Mr Sharma acknowledged the crowd's applause with a polite smile, but his wife had turned back, striking up a whispered conversation with a young woman standing a few feet behind them. Head bent, she wore a grey sari, and her body was hunched into itself, looking sulky. Kaveri looked on with interest. Mrs Sharma seemed to be speaking to the younger woman firmly, almost like a mother to an errant daughter. But surely Mrs Sharma was too young to be her mother?

Kaveri felt eyes on her, and when she looked up, she noticed that Mr Sharma was staring at her. He nudged his wife and whispered something in her ear, and Mrs Sharma turned, caught Kaveri's eye and gave her a slight wave. The young woman behind them shot Kaveri a hostile glance and stepped back, limping slightly as she moved further into the shadows.

Who were these people? They acted like they knew her, but Kaveri could not remember ever meeting them before.

As the prizes began to be announced, Miss Roberts looked on eagerly, but her face soon became pinched. Her brother's new greyhound, Tommy, came third and she muttered about the lost opportunity to snag an ornate Travelling Clock from Messrs Barton and Sons. Her fox terrier fared even worse, getting only an honourable mention. She began to look decidedly irate, speaking under her breath about rigged, deceitful contests. Kaveri exchanged pained looks with Mrs Reddy. How were they to get rid of this wretched woman?

'And now, ladies and gentlemen, the moment I'm sure you've all been waiting for!' The announcer, a portly man with a pink face and a white bristling moustache that looked exactly like a toothbrush, waved his arms with a flourish. 'The Ugliest Dog Prize!'

Kaveri burst out laughing. 'Is that really a category?'

'Shh!' a large woman in front said with an imperious frown, as a series of decidedly strange dogs were paraded past the avid audience.

'It's an audience favourite,' Mrs Reddy whispered into Kaveri's ear. 'A lot of people place private bets on the winning dog.'

Kaveri took in the parade of mutts, tiny and massive, hairy and smooth-skinned, with odd gaits, droopy flaps of skin, sticky dribbles of drool and flatulent emissions. She hoped no one had told the dogs that they were being given prizes for being ugly. Peculiar they certainly were, but each had a distinct presence and personality.

A bristle of anticipation went through the crowd.

'And the winner is . . . Gunner Sherrin's chum, with his dog Putta. The young man in question gets a silver cigar case.' The British announcer was still at his megaphone, shouting out the winners as the crowd stepped back from him.

Kaveri giggled again. *Putta* meant small in her language, Kannada, and the dog in question was not small in the slightest. He was enormous, with a huge body and an even larger head that seemed almost too big for his torso. One raggedy ear showed the side effects of a scrap with some other dog, and he panted with exuberance, drooling a little on the red carpet, which was already showing signs of wear. His owner stepped forward to receive the prize.

'Why can't they call out the dog owner's name? Imagine calling him Gunner Sherrin's chum.' Mrs Reddy looked irritated.

'Well, you know, some of these natives have such difficult names to pronounce.' Of course, that was Miss Roberts, again.

Really, this was a bit much. It was only last week that Miss Roberts had launched into a tirade about the inability of the stockist at her favourite condiment store in Bangalore to pronounce Worcestershire. If Mrs Roberts could expect the poor Indian shopkeeper man to know that it was 'Wooster' sauce, surely she, who had been in India for some weeks now, could learn to pronounce Indian names with some attention to accuracy.

Just then the winner walked by them, holding Putta by the leash.

'Congratulations!' Mrs Reddy told him, trying to change the topic. 'What is your name?'

'My name? It's Palanivel,' the man responded, looking at them doubtfully. 'Er, why?'

But Miss Roberts was there again, thrusting herself into the conversation. 'I say, my good man. What's that there?'

'It's no good to me,' Palanivel said mournfully, holding up the silver cigar case tucked carelessly into his shirt pocket. 'I don't even smoke cigars.' He patted the dog absently. 'But this here's a fine dog, and a perfect sweetheart. He's just a pup, really, less than a year old. Well trained even though he's a bit of a *bhayandanguli*, gets afraid easily. Still, he's going to be massive when full grown, I'm sure one look at him will be enough to scare anyone. I don't suppose any of you are looking for a guard dog?' He squinted at them hopefully, the stench of alcohol on his breath making them recoil.

Miss Roberts soldiered on. 'Not the dog. But I would like to buy the case from you.'

'You would? And how much would you be paying me then, madam?' The man's face brightened. As they haggled over the price, Kaveri and Mrs Reddy used the opportunity to make their escape out of the tent.

'Phew. I thought we would never get rid of her.' Kaveri shot Mrs Reddy a pleading glance. 'Are you going straight back home after this? My mother-in-law said she would meet me at the Dewan's private hall. A welcome lunch has been arranged there for the Indian attendees.'

'And you want me? For moral support?' The older woman cast her a shrewd look, walking alongside her towards the hall. 'You should find a way to get on your mother-in-law's good side, Kaveri. A house where the women are pulling in different directions is never pleasant.'

'I *am* trying – you know that. But it's so hard, especially when she disapproves of everything I do,' Kaveri said as they set off to the large white hall, a few yards to the back of the pavilions. 'Though perhaps today will be different. She said she wants to bring a friend to meet me. A friend who requires my help.'

'Really? Perhaps it's the start of a new mystery.' Mrs Reddy gave Kaveri a hopeful grin. 'After all, you are now Bangalore's most famous detective.'

Kaveri's mouth twisted into a wry smile. 'Women and crime? She doesn't think they go together. Not in genteel homes like ours.'

2

Good Women Are Malleable, Like Gold

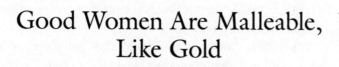

As they entered the Dewan's hall, Kaveri looked up at the unique structure of the octagonal dome and wondered how to estimate the surface area of such an unusual shape. Lost in thought, she was startled to hear her name being called loudly, as Bhargavi came bustling up to them. Suddenly, the large hall felt a bit cramped.

'Ah, Bhargavi. How nice to see y—' Mrs Reddy began, then stopped to look at a woman in her mid-twenties who was hurrying up to them, beaming expectantly at Kaveri.

'Ah, there you are, dear.' Mrs Reddy smiled at the stranger. 'This is my cousin – she wanted to meet your famous daughter-in-law,' she explained.

Bhargavi's lips thinned as she turned to greet Mrs Reddy's cousin – a plump-looking, cheerful young woman.

'You must be so proud of your daughter-in-law,' the young woman gushed to Bhargavi, squeezing Kaveri's hands in a tight, sweaty grip. 'I have heard so much about her, and how she solved the famous murder case of the missing milkman last summer.'

A mother and daughter who were standing nearby overheard the word 'murder' and their ears pricked up. They started to whisper, heads together, and moved closer to the group of women, unashamedly eavesdropping. Bhargavi bristled, but Mrs Reddy seemed oblivious to her pointed glare, and turned towards the mother and daughter to include them in the group.

'Did we hear you say murder?' The daughter, who towered over her petite mother, leaned in towards Mrs Reddy, her eyes glinting avidly. Kaveri looked at Bhargavi nervously. She knew from experience that such avid interest was like a red rag to a bull for Mrs Reddy, and she also knew that Bhargavi considered public discussions of murder and detection crass.

More women began to gather around them. Encouraged by the receptive audience, Mrs Reddy began to tell the tale of Kaveri's last encounter with murder, elaborating it with relish. The women oohed and aahed as their gold and diamond bangles clanked on their wrists, and the scent of jasmine from the garlands woven into their hair grew stronger in the heat of the midday sun.

Bhargavi let out a frustrated sigh, and looked away into the crowd.

Out of nowhere, Kaveri's stomach rumbled audibly, causing Bhargavi to look her way. Their breakfast of *idlis* this morning suddenly seemed a long way off.

'Shall we go get a plate of vadas and some coffee?' Bhargavi suggested.

Before Kaveri could answer, she was being expertly manoeuvred through the crowds and towards one of the interconnected rooms that led out of the main hall. Bhargavi maintained a grip on Kaveri's wrist as she towed her alongside her, but she didn't seem to be moving towards the snacks. Instead, Kaveri saw Bhargavi casting searching glances around her, as though she were looking for someone.

The air was thick with incense smoke, making Kaveri nauseous. Beads of sweat formed on her forehead, rolling down towards her nose, and she stifled an urge to sneeze. Why had Bhargavi brought her here, to this hot and crowded room, when she looked as irritated in the heat as Kaveri felt?

Bhargavi's gaze finally settled on a figure at the far end of the hall, and she folded her hands in a reverent *namaskara*, lips parted in awe. Kaveri peered into the distance, where she could see a tall, heavy-set man in saffron robes perched on a red velvet throne-like chair atop a small platform. She could hear the crowd around her saying 'Jai Swami Vaninanda – long live the holy man! Glory be to him.'

Kaveri hadn't realised that Swami Vaninanda would be at the event today. The priest had moved to Bangalore a few years back and seemed to be steadily growing in influence. He was frequently covered in the newspapers, and rumoured to have the ear of several people in the Maharaja's court. Someone must have invited him to the Dewan's hall today and Bhargavi had probably seized on this as the perfect occasion to introduce Kaveri to him.

No wonder she had been so coy about her reasons for wanting to come with Kaveri to the event today. She was probably afraid of what Ramu might say if she had mentioned it in advance. Kaveri grimaced at the memory of a recent argument that had erupted when Bhargavi had tried to persuade her son to come with her to the Swami's ashram. Ramu had refused, quite uncharacteristically losing his temper. If the Swami was a truly religious man, Ramu argued, would he choose to live in a large, luxurious ashram in the heart of the city? Kaveri agreed inwardly, thinking of the simple surroundings in which true ascetics lived – like her family's patron saint Raghavendra Swami had in the seventeenth century.

Kaveri bit her lip, annoyed at the way she had been tricked by the promise of food. Bhargavi tugged on her arm, heading purposefully towards a long queue of women lined up to meet the Swami. Should she go with Bhargavi? She knew Ramu would back her up if she refused. But as she dithered, Bhargavi gave her a distinctly irritated look, muttering under her breath, 'Always has to be difficult, this girl.'

Kaveri tripped over her feet, feeling clumsy as she always did in environments like this, where everything she said or did was scrutinised through societal expectations. She was still adjusting to the reality of being the only daughter-in-law of a wealthy prominent family. Everything she did would reflect on her husband and her mother-in-law, whether she liked it or not. Ramu had urged her not to worry about it, but the expectations of men were so different – how could he really put himself in her shoes?

Kaveri thought of Mrs Reddy, who had urged her to try to establish a better relationship with her mother-in-law. She was prepared to bend a little to get into Bhargavi's good books. But to what extent could she reshape herself?

The problem, Kaveri admitted to herself, was that she held strong beliefs, and was not really ready to be very flexible about them, like many others seemed able to be. Perhaps that was why she was so interested in detection, which involved the pursuit of truth and justice. Those were absolute concepts, whereas societal expectations – such as being a good daughter-in-law – seemed more malleable. Just like the properties of gold described in her chemistry textbook: gold was prized in jewellery because of its lustre and malleability, but you had to mix it with a bit of copper

– muddy brown, strong, defiantly non-lustrous copper – to give the gold some strength and character.

Kaveri was deep in thought, wondering what percentage of copper was in her, as opposed to gold, when her mother-in-law came to a halt in front of the red throne.

Responding to an imperative push in the small of her back from Bhargavi, Kaveri turned towards the Swami.

Two attendants stood by his side, waving thin fans made of silk. The scent of incense was especially thick here, and Kaveri blinked her eyes to see more clearly through the smoke. The Swami's eyes bore into her through half-closed heavy eyelids, and Kaveri felt an involuntary shiver run down her spine. She tried looking away from him, but felt her feet moving instead towards him, as though she were hypnotised.

With a herculean effort, Kaveri pinched her palm with her fingernails until the sharp pain brought her back to her senses and she was able to tear her eyes away. She looked away, up at the white ceiling, gathering her wits before chancing a quick glance back at him. Swami Vaninanda was blessing a kneeling devotee – but as soon as Kaveri glanced at him, he looked up and gave her a patronising smile. His knowing smirk told her that he knew exactly what effect he had had on her, and how difficult it had been for her to regain control of herself.

Kaveri felt herself growing angry. How dare the man look at her in that way, as though she was a butterfly pinned to a board for him to scrutinise?

The smoke was still thick in the room, and she found it difficult to breathe. Behind the makeshift throne, she saw that the windows were open, and moved closer to them, hastily breathing in large gulps of fresh air. Although the back of her neck continued to prickle, she felt the cobwebs slowly clear from her brain as she focused on the sight of a bored-looking goat tethered to a large banyan tree outside.

Feeling in control of herself once more, she looked around again. Where was Bhargavi?

She could see a table against the long side of the hall, with liveried bearers standing behind it, handing out plates of crisp Maddur vada. She was eager to taste the crisp vada, a new recipe from the small railway town of Maddur which she had heard was very tasty. But her mother-in-law didn't seem to be paying attention to Kaveri, or to the food. She was standing a few feet back, looking at the long line of women who had queued up to pay their respects to the Swami.

Kaveri sighed. It looked as if she was going to go hungry that day.

Bhargavi came up to her. Hearing her sigh, she said, 'We may as well get some food to eat while waiting for the queue to shorten. Besides . . . '

Kaveri strained to hear her. 'Besides what?'

'Nothing.' But, as they picked up a plate of vadas and glasses of milky coffee, Kaveri saw Bhargavi turn and shoot a furtive glance at the window. Her mother-in-law was definitely acting very peculiarly today, Kaveri thought.

As Kaveri followed Bhargavi's gaze, she saw a flash of purple appear for a second, then disappear again behind a tree. She squinted, but was unable to see – the glare of the sunshine was too strong.

'Shall we go outside? Stand under the banyan tree for a while?' Bhargavi's voice sounded excessively hearty.

Kaveri gaped at her. Eating under a tree? The oh-so-proper mother-in-law she knew would normally have been horrified at the thought of sharing eating space with the mud-covered goat tied to the tree.

Bhargavi hastily added, 'It looks much cooler out there,' almost rushing towards a side door that led out of the building to the patch of grass at the back. She led the way as they walked down a narrow mud track, stopping below the banyan tree. Bhargavi looked at the splotches of goat droppings with distaste. Kaveri followed more slowly, focused on the plate of food and the cup of coffee. She was trying hard not to spill food on her sari. But she looked up when she saw a flash of purple. An elegantly dressed stranger stood below the tree, next to the goat. *Mrs Sharma*, the woman who had handed out the prizes at the dog show a few hours back, Kaveri realised with a start. A few feet behind her stood the plainly dressed young woman who had accompanied the Sharmas earlier.

'Shanthi and Chitra! What a surprise. Fancy seeing you here.' The note of surprise in Bhargavi's voice was so obviously false that Kaveri's lips twitched with suspicion. What was she up to? She watched as the older woman came forward, taking the plate from Bhargavi's hands and placing it on a flat rock.

'It is so good to see you, Bhargavi *akka*.' There was real affection in the elegantly dressed woman's voice as the two women embraced. Then the stranger turned to Kaveri with a big smile. 'Hello, Kaveri. I don't know if you remember me. I'm Bhargavi's cousin, Shanthi – Mrs Sharma. We met at your wedding, and then later again at your reception a few months ago.' She shook her head, correctly interpreting the look on Kaveri's face. 'But there were so many people at your reception. You probably don't remember me.'

Shanthi pointed to a group of rocks near the open window. 'Shall we sit down for a bit?' Looking at Kaveri's raised eyebrows, she continued, 'I wanted to consult you professionally. That's why I asked Bhargavi *akka* to bring you here, where we could talk without anyone overhearing us. It is a private matter. One that could be dangerous.'

3

Of Goats and Gossip

'So, you brought me here to meet Shanthi? Not the Swami?' Kaveri asked Bhargavi as they made their way to a set of flat rocks, sitting down and balancing the plates of vada and coffee at their side.

Bhargavi nodded, looking uncomfortable.

'You must be wondering why I did not just come to your house to meet you,' Shanthi said. 'But the thing is . . . ' She hesitated, then went on, 'People gossip so much. If I'd come to your house, the person we suspect might realise that I'd come to consult the famous detective and get alarmed. But here . . . ' Shanthi gave an elegant shrug. 'Here, we have all come to meet Swamiji, and our discussion can be passed off as just an accidental meeting.'

As Kaveri watched Shanthi carefully select the crispest vadas from Bhargavi's plate and share her chutney dip, she saw an affectionate smile pass between them. So they were close friends, as well as cousins. Strange that Bhargavi had never mentioned Shanthi before, she thought.

Conversation halted for a few moments as the women munched their way through the vadas. The fried circles of dough melted in Kaveri's mouth, the crisp semolina on the outside a delicious contrast with the soft filling of roasted cashew nut, crunchy slivers of coconut and fried curry leaves.

Kaveri held out her plate to Chitra, but the younger woman refused, turning her face away slightly. *Who was she?* No one had introduced her so far, and Kaveri felt it would be rude to interrupt the conversation to ask. She was trying her best to act properly around Bhargavi.

So instead, she covertly studied Shanthi, who made for a striking figure in her bright purple silk sari. She wore diamonds at her ears and throat, and her slender wrists were adorned with delicate diamond bracelets. Her dark hair was shot through with silver threads, and her face, with its high elegant cheekbones, had the faintest hint of wrinkles at the forehead and throat. *Not so young, then. Probably in her late-thirties*, Kaveri thought, as she listened to the crows cawing in the tree.

The goat lifted one rear foot in the air and let out a stream of urine. Bhargavi shrieked and moved back on the stone. Shanthi let out a bark of laughter, and nudged Bhargavi with her elbow. 'Come on, Bhargavi *akka*. Don't be such a touch-me-not. The goat is so far from you.'

Bhargavi nodded ruefully at Shanthi, tucking an unruly strand of hair behind her cousin's ear. Kaveri blinked back her shock. It was the first time she had seen her dour mother-in-law show physical affection to anyone – she had never even seen her hugging her own daughter or son.

'Now, you must be wondering why exactly I wanted to meet you,' Shanthi began. 'Actually, it is my husband who suggested it. He wanted to come too, but unfortunately, he draws attention wherever he goes. So he left to return to the office, and Chitra and I have come here with a message from him.'

'Shanthi's husband Mr Sharma is a well-known industrialist who owns Sampangi Mills,' Bhargavi broke in. Kaveri nodded. She knew the mills well – located next to Sampangi lake, it was one of Bangalore's largest and most prosperous manufacturing businesses, making woollen blankets, cotton and silk cloth, and other products.

'They were married two years ago,' Bhargavi continued. 'And this is Chitra – their daughter.'

Kaveri's start of surprise must have been obvious, for Shanthi took over the conversation again.

'I know what you must be thinking – that I look too young to be Chitra's mother.' She smiled. 'My husband had been married before – many years back. His first wife died several years ago, when their daughter – my stepdaughter, Chitra – was still very young. She is now twenty-four. A few years older than you perhaps?' Shanthi watched Kaveri closely.

'Kaveri is nineteen,' Bhargavi said tersely, giving Chitra a steady look. Kaveri knew what she was thinking. Bhargavi had got her daughter married when she was very young, only fourteen. She disapproved of young women who stayed unmarried for too long.

But Chitra said nothing, still sitting motionless on the stone, her leg placed at an odd angle. Kaveri remembered seeing her limp earlier.

'Chitra has a leg injury. A weak ankle, which she twisted some weeks back. It is taking time to heal,' Shanthi explained, having caught Kaveri's subtle glance at Chitra's leg.

But Chitra stayed silent. *Either she's painfully shy, or she wants to have nothing to do with whatever her stepmother wants to tell me*, Kaveri thought, as she shifted on the hard rock, trying to find a more comfortable position.

She noticed from the corner of her eye that Chitra had still not moved. She sat bolt upright, stiff, almost like someone had tied a ruler to her back – like Kaveri's martinet of a school teacher had often threatened to do to her students when she'd seen them fidget.

'I used to help my father, who ran a small printing press, with his accounts. After marriage, I started to help out my husband too. The Sampangi Mills has always done well, but the factory now seems to be facing financial problems, and we cannot understand why. We've tried to figure out where the money is going, but are unable to.' Shanthi looked up at Kaveri, her eyes serious under her thin, elegantly curved eyebrows. 'We suspect there is embezzlement.'

Kaveri shook her head regretfully, placing a hand on Bhargavi's arm as she opened her mouth to remonstrate. 'This is beyond my capacity. I wish I could help you, but I cannot. You have to go to the police.' She turned to Bhargavi. 'Please understand. It is not that I don't want to help. This is too large a challenge for me to take on. If I make a mistake, everyone will suffer.'

Shanthi picked up a stick and began to idly scratch a pattern into the muddy soil, her eyes all the while intent on Kaveri's face. 'I expected you might say that. But hear me out. We cannot go to the police, as it is a delicate family matter. Indeed,' she paused, and her eyes flickered towards her stepdaughter briefly, 'if we do, we fear the police may suspect our future son-in-law may be involved. Chitra's fiancé.'

Kaveri turned to Chitra, surprised. She said nothing, but Kaveri noted that she had turned slightly to the right, keeping her face in the shadow.

'Chitra got engaged six months ago, to a young man who is one of our most promising employees. It is difficult – no, impossible – for us to think he is involved. But whoever embezzled the money has to be someone with access to the safe. Besides my husband, Chitra and myself, only Kumar – Chitra's fiancé – has access to the room where the account books and the safe in which the money is stored are placed. We cannot believe it is Kumar, he is a responsible young man, but if not him . . . then who?' The police will surely pull him for questioning. Shanthi trailed off.

Kaveri couldn't understand – *why was Chitra still being so quiet?*

Bhargavi turned to Kaveri, placing a hand on her arm. 'How can they bring in the police, Kaveri? If the police interrogate Kumar, and the word spreads that he might be a thief, the gossip would spread – you know how people talk. If Kumar finds out that it was Shanthi and Mr Sharma who suspected him and called in the police, the insult would be too much for him to bear. He might break off the engagement!'

Kaveri hesitated. She knew the consequences of a broken engagement would be socially disastrous for Chitra, who might never be able to marry again. But could she take on a case as complicated as an investigation into embezzlement? This seemed like it was beyond the capabilities of an amateur detective like herself, who had only solved one major case. All the other cases she had taken on were minor ones, like the case of the man from Majjigepura.

Those cases, which had vastly increased her reputation as a detective, had been relatively quick and easy to solve. But this case seemed far more complicated.

'Please, my daughter. You have a head for mathematics and are good with accounts. Ever since you took over the household accounts, we have begun to save so much more money,' Bhargavi pleaded.

Kaveri's heart pounded. Ever since she had got married, she had ached to forge a closer relationship with her mother-in-law. Bhargavi had always been somewhat disapproving of her independent nature, expressing her distaste for Kaveri's 'detective work', which forced her to mingle with all classes of society. Now, for the first time, Bhargavi was asking for her help, and calling her 'daughter'. How could she refuse?

Kaveri wished Ramu were there so she could consult him. But Ramu was away, travelling to Mysore with a team of doctors to test out a new vaccination protocol. Confronted with two eager faces, she was only able to remonstrate, weakly, 'But . . . but managing the household accounts is so different from investigating the accounts of a large factory.'

Bhargavi stared meaningfully at Kaveri, while Shanthi said, 'I know you can do it. Please, Kaveri. You are part of the family. Whom else can we turn to at this point? We cannot speak of family matters to strangers.'

Kaveri looked between the two women and took in their hopeful faces. *How could she say no?* She let out a shaky breath, giving in. 'Tell me more.'

Before Shanthi could continue the conversation, a group of women emerged from the building and spotted them.

'Kaveri?' Mrs Reddy called out. 'Ah, there you are. What are you doing there behind the tree?'

Behind Mrs Reddy, a number of faces peered curiously at Bhargavi, Kaveri, Shanthi and Chitra.

Shanthi cursed under her breath. 'I don't want anyone to see us together for too long.'

She pushed Bhargavi towards the door. 'Go and keep the women engaged in conversation. Tell them we were feeling hot inside the room and came out to have a cup of coffee in the shade of the tree. Tell them we came to feed the goat some bananas.'

When Bhargavi looked confused, as if to say 'Which should I say?' Shanthi rolled her eyes, looking thoroughly exasperated, and gave her another push, this time a more forceful one.

'Just go! Say something, anything, to alleviate their suspicions. Go, now.'

She drew Kaveri away from direct view, towards a spot just behind the open window where no one could see them.

'Kaveri – come to the factory tonight at 9 p.m. Meet my husband, and we can explain the details of the theft, and show you the safe and the account books. Please.'

Kaveri hesitated. By now, she was used to driving the car alone. But traversing the city at night, alone? It didn't seem safe to her.

'It's too soon. My husband is away. Let's meet tomorrow evening. I can bring him with—'

'No,' Shanthi interrupted her, 'it has to be today. Have you forgotten? Today is the lunar eclipse. The night of the blood moon.'

Kaveri stared at her. Was it true? In their house, Bhargavi was the one who kept track of the *panchanga*, the Indian calendar which displayed dates and times of religious significance. An eclipse was considered to be an inauspicious event, caused by the demon god, Rahu, who swallowed the moon. Only tantrics and certain kinds of black magic practitioners were out and about at such a time, practising secret rituals that they believed would give them great power.

'Bhargavi *athe* will not allow me to go out during the eclipse,' she said, finally. 'She will want me to stay indoors and fast with her before and during the eclipse, shielding ourselves from ill fate.'

'But don't you see? That's why this is the perfect time for you to come to the factory.' Shanthi spoke in a hurried voice, looking over her shoulder at the door to the hall as though she feared that Mrs Reddy may reappear at any moment with other curious onlookers in tow. 'At any other time, the place would be bustling with people – yes, even late at night. There are guards, workers on the night shift, cooks and cleaners around. They will see you, and ask questions. We have to keep this quiet.'

Shanthi paused, looking troubled. 'Please, Kaveri. I explained to Bhargavi *akka*, and convinced her. She has agreed to let you come. Unless you believe in the idea that the eclipse brings bad luck?' She looked at Kaveri, nodding in relief when she shook her head.

'Tonight, the *grahana*, the eclipse, begins at 7 p.m. and extends until 10 p.m. Everyone in the city will be indoors, in their homes. No one will be on the streets to see you come and go. Even the thieves will be off the streets.'

Kaveri nodded. As her new friend Mala, a former prostitute, had told her, thieves were a superstitious lot. They diligently followed practices that they believed would bring them good luck and protect them from discovery.

'My husband is in his office and will be there all evening. I will leave home at 8.30 and join you at the side gate at nine. I have the key to the gate, and to the side door as well. No one will be around until at least 11 p.m., and we can examine the account books and safe together.' Shanthi reached out and held Kaveri's hand. 'Please, you must come.'

Kaveri swallowed thickly. 'I will,' she agreed, but not without hesitation.

'I must go now,' Shanthi said, but as Kaveri turned to leave, she pulled her back again.

'Ah, you have a wristwatch, that's good. We should coordinate our timepieces. The alley that leads to the side gate is isolated, and I don't want either of us to be waiting alone for the other.' Shanthi turned Kaveri's wrist and bent to peer at it carefully in the shade. Her face was close to Kaveri's, and Kaveri could smell the perfume she used, with the fragrance of roses and undertones of rich, moist earth. Just like the woman herself – strong, earthy, and confident, Kaveri thought.

Shanthi refused to go back into the tent. 'I have to go – it's getting late. I don't want anyone to wonder where I've been for so long,' she said.

She gave an imperious jerk of her head to Chitra, who was still sitting in the shadow of the rock. As Chitra got up slowly, Shanthi turned to look at Kaveri, her gaze boring into her. 'Remember. 9 p.m. sharp. Don't be late.'

And with that, she was gone, stepdaughter in tow.

4

Smoke and Ash

As Kaveri walked back inside, a number of women were leaving, moving past her in groups. Through the noise of the crowd, she could just about hear snippets of excited conversation about the Swami.

'Such an honour to meet Swamiji.'

'I shivered when he looked at me. Such burning eyes, he must be very powerful.'

Kaveri winced. Ramu was incredibly sceptical of self-styled godmen, and Kaveri could understand why. Of course, there were many religious men who truly were spiritual, but in her experience, truly spiritual men and women were not interested in public adulation or power. They were usually reclusive and lived quiet and simple lives in ashrams, absorbed in their faith and long hours of meditation. Men like this Swami, who had mass followings of worshippers who queued up to give him donations of money, jewels and land, who boasted that they had magical powers directly derived from God – rather than immersed in devotion, they seemed hungry for power.

Bhargavi, re-joining Kaveri, seemed to have no such doubts. With her eyes fixed on the Swami, she guided Kaveri to the throne-like chair and spoke in a rush.

'Come, daughter, come fast. The queue has thinned out, many people have left, and Swamiji may also leave soon. I want you to meet him and get his blessings before he leaves. If he blesses you, there's a good chance you will have a male child.'

Kaveri's mouth set in a firm line, and her spine went ramrod straight. Not this again. She knew Bhargavi was desperate for a grandchild – no, she corrected herself, a grand*son* – but Kaveri had other plans for herself. She wanted to study first. Now that she had completed her matriculation, she wanted to study further, and perhaps even teach for a while before she became pregnant. Ramu was in no hurry either, and they would both be as happy with a girl as they would with a boy.

But she bit back the sarcastic response that was at the tip of her tongue. Her own mother was even worse, she reminded herself. And, she supposed, you couldn't fault either woman for wanting to have a grandchild to shower her affection on. Kaveri had realised in the past few weeks that Bhargavi was very lonely. She had argued with Ramu that evening, after he raised his voice to his mother when she'd tried to force him to visit the Swami, saying that it was Bhargavi's loneliness that had led her to view Swami Vaninanda as a spiritual quick fix for all her emotional problems. They had to find something else to engage Bhargavi's time and attention.

Muttering mutinously under her breath, Kaveri followed Bhargavi to the Swami. The line had indeed thinned, and only two women were in front of them. Swami Vaninanda sat in a corner, near the open window, a large man who filled every inch of his massive chair. The chair was upholstered in red velvet and designed to resemble a throne – to inspire awe in his followers, Kaveri thought cynically.

He was speaking to a devotee who gazed at him raptly. Free of his disturbing gaze, Kaveri studied him closely, noting his prominent hooked nose, like the beak of an eagle. His head was shaven, except for a small tuft of hair at the base of his neck, tied into a small plait as priests habitually wore their hair.

Around his neck he wore a heavy gold medallion with a Garuda highlighted in blood-red rubies. Behind him, to the left and right, stood two attendants holding large staffs each adorned with a Garuda at the top. The menacing depiction of the Serpent Eagle God, with his hooked beak and outstretched taloned wings, sent a shiver down Kaveri's spine, and she castigated herself mentally. Kaveri had always been fascinated by the Eagle God, king of birds, who struck fear in the hearts of evildoers and protected the innocent. Her family also worshipped the Garuda, and she knew the Eagle God protected his devotees; he was fearsome only to those who had evil in their heart.

No, she was no brainless fool to get overawed by a Swami who was also clearly an expert in stage arrangements. As the queue moved, the women ahead of them stepped forward to touch his feet and seek his blessings. Next to him, an attendant stood with a bag full of bananas, which he handed to each devotee in turn after they had received the Swami's benediction.

The Swami finally turned his gaze on Kaveri. His compelling eyes moved across her face, and once again she shuddered, feeling a chill moving down her spine. What was it about this man that made her skin crawl? This time, she put on a brave face, lifted her chin, stared him straight in the eyes and refused to drop her gaze. Surprised by her reaction, he sat upright, scrutinising her closely. Gone was the slightly contemptuous smile with which he had met her efforts to look away from him previously.

Bhargavi pushed Kaveri forward, holding her by the arm. 'My daughter-in-law, Swamiji,' she said, a proud smile on her face. 'This is the clever girl I have told you about, the one who is forever gadding about and solving cases.'

Kaveri gaped at Bhargavi, her mouth falling open. Her mother-in-law had actually boasted to someone about her detective abilities?

'Please bless her, Swamiji. Bless her to be the mother of many bright and healthy boys,' Bhargavi begged, a tone of obsequiousness creeping into her voice. She reached into her purse and pulled out a gold chain.

The Swami gestured imperiously to his right. A heavy-set man emerged from behind the throne. As he held out a cloth pouch to Bhargavi, his loose shirt sleeves fell back, exposing long arms covered in wiry black hair. They reminded Kaveri of *kamblihulas*, the bristly wire-brush-like caterpillars that were so fond of drumstick trees, and which produced intense itching if you had the misfortune of encountering them. Kaveri moved a step back. The last time she had touched a *kamblihula* she had ended up covered in angry red welts that ran across her neck and stomach, their itchiness lasting for weeks.

The Swami gestured with his hand again, and Bhargavi dropped the chain into the pouch, while Kaveri's mouth fell open. Her mother-in-law, who was usually so careful with her money, was giving away an entire gold chain to this man? That could feed an entire family for six months. Of course, she knew her new marital family was wealthy enough that they could afford to give away a number of gold chains without a pinch, but she would much rather it went to a worthy cause.

Bhargavi pushed her forward, whispering urgently in her ear, 'Touch his feet. Seek his blessings.'

Kaveri wanted to step back, but she knew that if she did, she would bring shame to her mother-in-law in front of all the Swami's devotees. Unwillingly, she moved forward, and touched the area near the Swami's feet with the tips of her fingers, standing as far away from him as she could. She looked up at him. 'If you must bless me, bless me to be the mother of sons *and* daughters,' she said firmly.

Bhargavi let out an alarmed hiss at Kaveri's audacity. She was not supposed to speak to the revered man so bluntly. But the Swami waved a dismissive hand at Bhargavi. He stared at Kaveri, his eyes calculating. Again, she felt like an insect pinned to a board, being measured, weighed and assessed.

The attendant at his side, also attired in white, moved in front, holding out a banana to the Swami to hand out as *prasada*, an offering to his devotees. The Swami waved aside the bananas. He turned to the large man behind the throne, and held up two fingers. The man bowed obsequiously and darted behind the throne, returning with a small pouch. Swami Vaninanda had not spoken a single word. He took a pinch of ash from the pouch and threw it in the air.

There was a small explosion and the air filled with smoke. Even without turning, Kaveri knew that all eyes were on the Swami and her. Time seemed to stand still as the smoke slowly cleared. Kaveri's heart raced in anticipation, the monotonous rhythm of the grandfather clock the only sound in the room. After what seemed like an age, the smoke slowly dissipated as the Swami opened his cupped hands.

A scarlet red hibiscus flower, with perfect petals, lay in the centre of his joined hands, like blood spilling in a perfect pattern onto the grey sacred ash that coated his palms. The attendant handed the flower to Kaveri. Her fingers itched as she thought of the spell he had woven on her and the rest of the audience. Had he hypnotised them all?

She wanted to crumple the flower and throw it as far from herself as possible, but before she could move Bhargavi hurried forward eagerly, taking it and weaving it into Kaveri's long plait. The Swami raised a long finger smeared with sacred ash towards Kaveri's face and she felt her entire body stiffen. She closed her eyes and schooled her face into blankness as Bhargavi pushed her towards him. As he anointed her temple, some of the ash fell onto her nose and mouth, tasting gritty.

When he moved away, she took in a long breath, and felt sensation return in a rush to her body. With it, her sense of anger returned. What was it about this man that made her feel on edge? He had, after all, favoured her with his attention. But despite her scepticism, she had found it difficult to resist being influenced by his charismatic pull.

Swami Vaninanda was not a trivial charlatan. She could feel it in her bones. The man was dangerous.

'Did you see that?' the women in the room whispered to one another as Kaveri stalked past them, eager to reach the pocket of fresh air near the door. 'She's so lucky, to receive a mark of his favour like that.'

'And did you see the cloud of smoke and hear the explosion as he created the sacred ash from the air? So powerful, our Swamiji is. See the way in which he made a flower appear too. They say he does intensive *pujas* in the Himalayas that last for days, weeks, where he does not eat, drink or sleep. He even stops breathing for some time. That is the real reason behind his magical powers.'

'Have you visited his ashram? He runs a shelter for widows and women abandoned by their families. I donated my gold bangles to support the women's shelter last week.

My husband was annoyed with me, but then I convinced him. We even visited the ashram two days ago and met the women. Swamiji is a generous soul.'

Kaveri felt lost. This man was powerful, there was no doubt about it. But were his powers real, or was he an impostor? She wished she had Ramu with her, or even Mrs Reddy, to provide a voice of sanity, of balance against this incredulous wave of belief. She looked around, but Mrs Reddy was gone. She must have left with the other women when she and Bhargavi had come back inside.

Thankfully Bhargavi was ready to leave as well. The women made their way back to the parking area, getting into the car.

As Kaveri took the road back home, mother-in-law in tow, she fell into a tense silence. Her brain was churning furiously.

She jumped when Bhargavi suddenly asked, 'What did Shanthi tell you? When I left to go back into the hall?'

'She asked me to meet her at the side gate of the factory, at 9 p.m. tonight. It leads into an alley that is usually deserted and silent at this time of night. Shanthi will meet me there and take me to Mr Sharma's office. There, I can examine the books and speak to Mr Sharma without anyone else overhearing us.'

Bhargavi sounded puzzled. 'She told me she wanted you to come today. I was worried about the eclipse, but Swami Vaninanda told us at a recent meeting that it is actually a propitious time, a time of great energy in the sky, and we should not be so afraid of it. That is why I agreed. But why the side gate? Deserted at night? That doesn't sound safe. Why not meet at the main gate, where there is more light and more people are around?'

'Because we don't want anyone to take notice of us,' Kaveri explained patiently, restraining herself from rolling her eyes at her mother-in-law. Even if the eclipse meant that no one would be around when she arrived, there might be a few people at the factory by the time she left. Did she expect that Shanthi would take Kaveri by the elbow, announce to the guards and factory workers that she had brought in a detective to inspect the books, then march her through the main gate?

Kaveri deftly steered the car around a large buffalo which stood in the middle of the road, chewing cud with a blissful look on its face.

'I can't believe Shanthi left without a word to me.' Bhargavi still sounded annoyed that she had missed the end of their conversation. She started to tell Kaveri stories of their childhood. Shanthi's mother had been sickly, and so Shanthi had spent long hours in their home when she was a child, with Bhargavi looking after her. *No wonder she's so fond of her*, Kaveri thought. Bhargavi had never spoken to her so freely, or shared personal anecdotes about her life before. Kaveri was curious to know more – why was it that someone as good-looking as Shanthi had stayed unmarried for so many years? Bhargavi had said that Shanthi was thirty-five, and Mr Sharma was twenty years older than her. Shanthi did not seem to be the kind of person who would marry only for wealth – and surely Mr Sharma, if he was on the lookout for a beautiful second wife, could have selected from a number of women much younger than her. No, this seemed too much like a marriage of love to her.

But Kaveri was not yet comfortable enough with Bhargavi to ask her such personal questions. Her mother-in-law was very unlike her. She annoyed Kaveri with her insistence that she should subscribe to the social customs that confined women to the home. Kaveri could vividly recall Bhargavi's displeasure when she refused to follow the abhorrent practices of caste segregation dictated by society. But over time, Kaveri was also beginning to come to understand Bhargavi as a person. After she had lost her husband, she had become very dependent on her son, and feared losing him to his new bride. She was not a bad person at heart. She was generous with her time and attention, doing charity work in the local temple on weekends to feed the poor, and acting as an advisor to her younger relatives in times of crisis. Kaveri had seen how she had dropped everything a few months back to go and help her injured sister, taking on the entire load of domestic duties at her sister's home.

Soon after she had moved into their home, Kaveri had been feeling especially dejected after one of her mother-in-law's barbed comments. 'Leave her be, Kaveri,' Ramu had said, holding her close. 'She has been brought up conservatively, and has been trained to think a certain way. She will come around.'

And indeed, in recent times, Kaveri felt they were getting to understand each other better. She wanted to develop a closer relationship with her mother-in-law, instead of forever being at loggerheads with her. So she sat quietly in the car, enjoying this unusual chance to get to know a different, softer side of this usually abrasive woman. If helping Shanthi was what it took to bridge the gap between mother-in-law and daughter-in-law, then she would do everything she could to find out the truth behind the embezzlement.

If indeed there had been an embezzlement.

5

A Mysterious Note

Kaveri was in the bathroom washing her hands after a short afternoon nap when she heard the gate creak. *Who could it be at this time?* she thought. With the sun high in the afternoon sky, it was so hot that even the crows were taking refuge in the shade of the mango trees. No sane human being would be paying them a visit in this heat. Bhargavi was stretched out on her bed, snoring lightly.

As Kaveri hurried down the stairs, she could hear the sounds of dishes clanking in the backyard, as their maid Rajamma cleaned up after the afternoon meal. By the time she'd walked outside, there was no one to be seen – but as she looked around, her eyes landed on a large white envelope that had been placed on the wooden swing on the verandah, with a neatly printed name on top: MRS KAVERI MURTHY.

Curious. Kaveri held the envelope in her hands, turning it over. The paper was pale ivory, with a feminine scroll of flowers around the border. At the top left, a name was given – 'Sharma' – followed by an address. *This must be from Shanthi*, Kaveri thought. But why did she not come in?

Had she sent the letter through someone else? And why go to all this trouble, instead of just calling up? Someone as wealthy as Shanthi surely had a telephone in her house.

Kaveri went to the gate and peered down the road, looking left and right, but she couldn't see anyone. Wincing at the hot mud, which singed the soles of her feet, she did a quick crab-like hop back to the cool shade of the verandah. As she moved, the nape of her neck pricked, as though someone was watching her. Feeling suddenly uneasy, she looked around, but still could not see anyone. She quickly scanned the road again before closing the door and bolting it.

When she went upstairs, she saw that Bhargavi had woken up, and was peering out of her bedroom.

'What is it, Kaveri? Why were you outside at this time?'

Kaveri showed the envelope to Bhargavi, then opened it and took out a thick sheet of bond paper.

The two women read the typed note together.

CHANGE IN PLANS. COME AT 8 P.M. TO THE
FACTORY. I WILL SEE YOU THERE. SHANTHI.

Kaveri held the note close to her nose, taking a deep breath.

'Why are you doing that?' Bhargavi demanded with some astonishment, snatching the note from Kaveri's hand.

'I don't know who wrote this,' Kaveri said, inspecting it closely. 'But the "a"s are misaligned, see here? Each "a" is tilted slightly to the left, and printed a little above the line of the other letters.'

'What do you mean, "who wrote it"?' Bhargavi asked, ignoring the rest of what Kaveri had said. 'Shanthi wrote it, of course. Who else could it be?'

'If Shanthi wrote it, why would she print in capitals? It seems very strange to send someone a printed letter instead of cursive handwriting. This makes me feel that it might be someone else, trying to pass a note off as coming from Shanthi. And the perfume . . . '

Kaveri put the note to Bhargavi's nose. 'Smell it.'

Bhargavi recoiled. 'I'm not going to go around sniffing pieces of paper. You must be mad.'

'Shanthi uses a perfume that smells like roses.' Kaveri kept her voice low and patient with some effort. 'This letter has the fragrance of sandalwood.'

'So Shanthi uses two different perfumes. For all we know she has a whole cupboard filled with fragrances,' Bhargavi snapped. 'I know you are interested in detection, Kaveri. But don't take it too far and become suspicious of everything. If Shanthi has asked you to go at 8 p.m. instead of 9, there must be some reason. Perhaps Mr Sharma wanted you to come an hour earlier.'

Kaveri tried to explain to her mother-in-law. 'You don't understand. Shanthi asked me to synchronise our watches, and said that we had to meet at exactly 9 p.m. Besides, this seems like a very odd way to send me a message. Why did she not call?'

'Well, call her then and confirm,' Bhargavi said curtly, before turning to head back into her bedroom.

Kaveri was already at the phone, asking the operator to put through the call. She waited for a long while, and when the operator didn't ring back, she called again.

'There seems to be something wrong with the line. It is constantly busy,' the operator explained, almost apologetically. 'Either the line is cut, or someone has left the phone off the hook.'

Perhaps the phone is out of order. That could explain the note, Kaveri thought, as she climbed slowly up the stairs, trying to figure out what exactly was making her feel so uneasy. Something about the whole set-up seemed strange to her. She wished there was a way to call it off . . . but Bhargavi – and Shanthi – were counting on her. If only Ramu were here, so she could consult him! But her husband wouldn't be returning from Mysore until the following morning.

Despite Swami Vaninanda's message about the *grahana*, Bhargavi was unwilling to let go of all her previous beliefs. She insisted that she and Kaveri eat dinner early, before the eclipse began at 7 p.m. By 7.30, Bhargavi had escorted her to the front door. Kaveri turned back to face her mother-in-law, trying to make one last attempt to convince Bhargavi that Shanthi had asked her to come at 9 p.m., not 8.

Bhargavi shook her head dismissively. 'I don't know why you insist on dragging your feet, Kaveri. This is the only time I have ever asked you for help. Don't you want to help me?'

Kaveri could only nod, helplessly. Bhargavi continued, 'I don't want you to be late for the appointment. I hate to think of my Shanthi in trouble. I know she is a married woman with a grown stepdaughter, but to me she is still my baby cousin.'

'I will try my best to help her,' Kaveri promised, taking the Ford out onto the road. Rajamma closed the gate behind her.

As Bhargavi went back inside the house, the phone rang and she hurried in to pick it up.

'Hello? Bhargavi *akka*, is that you? I wanted to speak to Kaveri.'

'Kaveri? Oh, she just left for the factory. She will meet you there at 8.'

'Left?' Shanthi's voice seemed suddenly loud, amplified and echoing in the empty drawing room. 'What do you mean, left? I asked her to meet me at 9 p.m., not 8.'

Bhargavi closed her eyes and squeezed them tightly, suddenly afraid. 'We received a note from your house. It was on your stationery. Was that not you?'

'What did the note say?' Shanthi demanded.

'Ohhh, I have been so careless,' Bhargavi wailed. 'The note said there was a change in timing, and asked Kaveri to come at 8 p.m. to the factory instead. The note was printed, not handwritten, and Kaveri suspected it was not from you. She told me over and over again that you had asked her to come at 9 p.m. She even tried to call you to confirm but the operator said something was wrong with the phone.'

As she began to realise that she could have put Kaveri in real danger, Bhargavi burst into tears. 'Oh, if something happens to that girl, what will I do? My son is not even here. He will never forgive me.'

Shanthi's voice was brusque. 'Pull yourself together, *akka*. Weeping and wailing will not do. I did not send that note. Someone else – the same person who stole the money perhaps – must have typed it on our house stationery. The same person must have pulled out the telephone wire so that Kaveri's call could not come through. I just now saw the wire was disconnected when I came to make a call, and plugged it back in.'

There was a long pause, punctuated only by Bhargavi's wails.

'I will go now and meet Kaveri at the factory,' Shanthi said, cutting Bhargavi off. 'Don't worry. I can be there a few minutes after 8 p.m. if I hurry. I will make sure nothing happens to her.'

Bhargavi turned to Rajamma, who was standing next to her with a look of concern on her face and then fainted, falling like a sack of rice onto the Kashmir carpet.

6

Is That Gunshot?

The street lamps cast long shadows on the ground as Kaveri drove towards the factory. The furnace-like heat of the afternoon had given way to the chilly night air. She passed a small boy on the side of the road holding up a set of newspapers for sale – a local rag, sold for a couple of annas, carrying only the juiciest and scurrilous local gossip, often embroidered from thin air. Kaveri smiled to herself as she remembered how angry she had been with a similar little boy some months ago for selling a newspaper with scurrilous information about Mala, the prostitute who was now one of her closest friends. Even small boys had to make a living in a large city where poverty was everywhere, though, and it was not their fault that they traded in character-assassinating gossip for a living – no, that was the fault of the wealthy owners of the rag, along with the customers who willingly paid a few annas for some 'light' entertainment at someone else's expense.

Ayyo. Kaveri had gotten so fired up thinking about Mala and her incarceration in that horrible jail that she had forgotten to take the right turn at the crossroads towards the factory. Instead, she had driven straight on, towards the police station.

As she slowed to a stop, she noticed a light burning inside. Ismail must be working late again. The Inspector had become a close friend now, not just a work acquaintance. He and his wife were regular visitors to Kaveri's home – although Bhargavi had been scandalised the first time she'd heard of their visit, not knowing how to deal with receiving guests from another religion into their house.

'Kaveri *akka?*' A small boy dressed in a ragged pair of shorts and a torn vest, a towel slung over his shoulder, peered into the car curiously.

'Venu? What are you doing here?' Kaveri asked, surprised to see their milk boy, who usually delivered milk in the mornings, at the police station so late at night, and that too, during an eclipse.

'I am bringing tea for Ismail Sir.' Venu held up a flask of tea proudly. 'The police station is deserted as all the Hindu policemen are at home. Ismail Sir offered to do a night shift along with another young Christian policeman. But they needed something to eat. My mother and sister-in-law have started a small business from home, making tea and snacks for the people who work at night – the police, sweepers and street vendors. Our roof leaks a lot during the rains, and we are saving up for a new roof.'

'Oh Venu,' Kaveri remonstrated. 'You could just take some money from us.' Her heart sank at the thought of Venu's grandmother, mother, sister-in-law and her two infant children living in a leaky house with the cold wind blowing through at night.

Venu shook his head at her.

'No, Kaveri *akka,* we have already taken so much from you. We will manage this ourselves.' He said it so firmly that she did not want to push him further. It would only wound his pride. And Venu had a lot of pride, for someone so little.

'But why are *you* here, *akka*?' Venu asked her. 'It is so late at night. It is not safe for you to be out alone.'

Kaveri ruffled his grimy hair through the window. 'I'm on a case, Venu.'

Venu's eyes brightened. 'A new case? Shall I come with you?'

'No, I have to go alone. The person who asked me to come told me I must come alone.'

'But *where* are you going?' Venu persisted.

'To the Sampangi Mills. I was supposed to take the alley that leads to the side gate but I missed the turning.'

Venu's bushy eyebrows leapt up, almost touching the top of his untidy mop of hair. 'But that alley is really deserted at night. And today is the *grahana*, the eclipse. No one will be on the roads!' His eyes were wide with alarm. 'You can't go there alone. You must take me. Or Ismail Sir.'

Just as Kaveri was about to dismiss his concerns and tell Venu again that she must go alone, she hesitated. It was only Bhargavi's urging that had overridden her doubts about the note. Now that she had left home, her instincts had started to tingle again, signalling to her that something was rotten. *Very* rotten.

Something about the note seemed 'off' to her, like buttermilk gone rancid. What was it? Kaveri strummed her fingers on the car wheel as Venu watched her intently. One – the note smelled of sandalwood when Shanthi wore a different perfume, one with a fragrance of roses. Two – why on earth couldn't Shanthi just have called her instead of sending her a note? Three – why take the trouble to type out a note, when it was so short that it would have been much easier to just write it out? That screamed of someone trying to disguise their handwriting.

She looked towards the horizon. The dark sky that had signalled the first part of the lunar eclipse was giving way to the emerging moon. The demon Ketu had decided to release the moon from his mouth, thought Kaveri, remembering the story of the eclipse her grandmother told. The moon was a red, crescent-shaped sliver low in the sky, like a curved dagger dripping with blood. The stars shone brilliantly, like so many multi-faceted crystals, reflecting shards of brilliant blue and red at the people below. Tiny like insects, how insignificant humanity was in the planetary scheme of things! And how vulnerable. Kaveri clasped her forearms tightly, suddenly feeling very cold. Except for the small boy in front of her, she could not see a soul anywhere on the streets. Even the usually omnipresent street urchins were missing, along with the stray dogs that usually squatted on the pavements. Perhaps the blood moon had scared them also into sheltering.

The road in front of her, though empty and deserted, seemed filled with threat. Should she go in and ask if Ismail was free to accompany her? Shanthi had told her to avoid the police, but Ismail was not just any policeman. He was their friend.

Suddenly reaching a decision, Kaveri got out of the car.

'Watch the car for me, Venu. See that no one else approaches it,' she ordered, and quickly went inside the police station. The outer room was empty, and Ismail's door was closed, but a light gleamed from below it. She rapped on the door.

'Come in,' a deep voice rumbled.

When Kaveri opened the door, Ismail jumped up, pushing his chair against the wall as he unfolded his large bulky frame into a standing position. 'Mrs Murthy? What are you doing here?'

Kaveri took in the size of the man, his steady frame – and suddenly felt safe. She had made the right decision.

A few minutes later, Ismail was in the front passenger seat next to Kaveri, and they were on the road to the factory. She had brought him up to speed on the day's events, telling him about the suspected embezzlement and Mrs Sharma's request that she investigate by visiting the factory. He listened without comment to the whole story and then agreed to accompany Kaveri.

'We should reach there about five minutes before eight,' Ismail said, consulting a large wristwatch on his arm. 'You park away from the light, at a short distance from the gate, and get out. I will stay behind the car, where no one can see me. Once you enter the factory, I will follow you a few minutes later, and wait outside. No one will know I am there. But if there is any trouble and you require my help, you only have to call.'

Kaveri nodded. She knew the large policeman could be surprisingly nimble.

She turned into the dark alley that bordered the factory, parking the car in a dark spot, and got out, followed by Ismail.

Now about half its full size, the moon was higher in the sky. The road shone red, the eerie glow reflecting off the granite walls of the mills and making it seem to be bathed in blood. She took a step closer to Ismail, his stolid, large presence reassuring her. Then she took a deep breath and scolded herself. Was this any way for a detective to behave? What would her favourite heroine, Lady Molly of Scotland Yard, do at such a time? Well, Lady Molly would square her shoulders, and march straight in. She would not give in to fear.

As she turned to go, Ismail touched her wrist. 'Wait.'

He took off a whistle that was strung on a thick thread around his neck, and gave it to her. 'Put this around your neck. If you have to call me, this is louder and more effective than shouting.'

Kaveri put it on, manoeuvring it carefully around her neck to avoid getting it tangled in her chain. Then she stopped in surprise, patting her neck and looking down. The alley was dark, and she could not see anything. Noticing her frustration, Ismail looked down at her.

'What is it?' he asked in a whisper.

'My chain. The one with the magnifying glass that Ramu gave me. It's missing.'

'It must have fallen off when you were at home. You will find it later.'

Ismail's voice was reassuring. Kaveri knew he understood what the chain meant to her – a symbol of love, confidence and trust from Ramu. Ramu had given the jewellery set to Kaveri in the presence of Mr and Mrs Ismail, and they had seen the light in Kaveri's eyes when she had first seen it and put it on. She rubbed her neck again. The chain had not been off her neck since Ramu gave it to her, and the absence of it, coupled with the events of the day, made her feel even more off kilter.

'Go now, it is almost eight and you have very little time to waste.' Ismail nudged her gently, his voice soft and encouraging.

Kaveri hurried down the narrow path. The distance to the side entrance was short, but a cloud had moved over the moon, hiding the road in pools of shadow. A prickling sensation began at the nape of her neck, once again making her feel as though invisible eyes were tracking her. She stopped and looked around, but it was too dark for her to see anything.

Her foot collided with something wet and slimy. *Was that a snake?* Kaveri let out a deep breath of relief when she realised it was just a wet leaf, and told herself not to be such a ninny. Ismail was close by, and would come swiftly if she needed him.

An owl hooted in the distance, producing an unearthly screech. Without realising it, she began to move faster, almost running towards the door.

In a surprisingly short amount of time, she was at the side entrance. She looked up at the gates that barred her way, chest heaving as she fought for breath. Surprised by her shortness of breath, Kaveri made a mental note to go for a swim at the Century Club when all this was over.

When Shanthi had told her that this was a side entrance, she had expected to see a nondescript tiny wicker gate. But this was a huge side entrance, with two massive wrought iron gates. The gates were bordered with scrolls of twisted ironwork. The tall lampposts with lit lamps on the sides had been aligned to focus light on the figure in the centre of the gate.

She moved closer.

At the heart of the scrollwork was a large Garuda. This rendition of the Serpent Eagle depicted it disembowelling a large cobra, gripped tightly between its sharp talons. The black border of the scrollwork emphasised the silver paint on the Garuda, a figure meant to strike fear into all evil-doers. Kaveri took a half-step back, feeling a pulse begin to beat fast at the nape of her neck even though she knew she was on the side of the righteous, and Garuda was her ally.

No need to be so dramatic, it's only a piece of iron, she scolded herself. Yet she could not stop herself from looking around nervously. The prickling feeling at the nape of her neck had intensified and she was sure someone was watching her. But the lit lamps cast deep pools of shadow, and she could not see more than a couple of feet beyond the gate.

Shanthi was nowhere in sight. She had told Kaveri that the gate would be locked but it was now five minutes past eight. Kaveri peered at her wristwatch again to confirm the time. Should she try to go in?

She tugged at the heavy padlock, and it came apart in her hands. *Aha.* So Shanthi must have gone in then. Kaveri placed the lock at the side of the gate, then pushed it open, gesturing to Ismail. He waved back from the side of the tree where he was standing, gesturing for her to go on.

Someone must have oiled the gate recently, as it swung open noiselessly. She took one cautious step inside. All at once her senses became heightened. The wind blew the smell of a rotting carcass – perhaps a dead rat? – into her nostrils. She could not rid herself of the feeling that something was terribly wrong. She moved back towards Ismail, hesitated, then turned back again towards the gate.

The cloud had moved aside, and the red light of the moon shone down onto the entrails of the disembowelled snake, making them appear bloody and menacing. She looked up at the Garuda. His fierce eyes were focused directly on her. Her heart beat faster, tapping out an irregular rhythm in her chest – *dhad dhad dhad* – as though it might explode with the force of its pounding.

Just as she took a hesitant step into the grounds of the mills, a single, sharp explosive sound rang out, shattering the silence of the night.

7

Murder Most Foul

The reverberations rang in Kaveri's ears, mirroring the heavy thud-thud-thud sound of footsteps as she turned to see Ismail running down the path towards her, his hobnailed boots clattering on the granite. The crows scattered from the trees, cawing loudly in the night. Kaveri gulped, feeling a single drop of sweat drop from the back of her neck and slither down her spine. She was right, she thought, as she turned, as though in a dream – the big policeman could be fleet-footed in times of need.

Ismail paused in front of her, breathing heavily. She felt like screaming, but Ismail looked as calm and imperturbable as ever.

'Stand back, Mrs Murthy. I will go in ahead of you.' Even at this tense time, Kaveri marvelled at how the policeman insisted on addressing her formally, despite the fact that he was now a close friend. It was as much a part of his nature as it was for him to be protective of her. Or at least, to try to protect her, when she let him.

Ismail kicked off his shoes on the side of the stone path. Barefoot, he moved noiselessly towards the wall of the factory. Behind him, a small wooden side door lay open. The glint of a light appeared faintly at the end of the corridor. Kaveri followed him closely, removing her footwear and hitching up her sari so that her ankles were free and she could move more easily.

The sound of breaking glass shattered the silence.

They heard footsteps – someone clad in heavy boots was running fast – and then a clatter of feet and a grunt, as though someone was climbing the wall. Ismail blew his whistle hard and banged his wooden lathi on the ground. Whoever it was ignored the Inspector, and instead there was a small thump as they jumped off the wall and then the sound of running footsteps faded into the distance.

Ismail turned to Kaveri. 'That may be the killer. It will be safer for you to be here with me than outside alone. But please, Mrs Murthy, stay well behind me. And if I tell you to run, then listen.'

'No . . . ' Kaveri protested, following him up the path. 'Someone may be lying hurt in there, even bleeding to death. We must get them to a doctor!'

Ismail turned and spoke to her more forcefully than she had ever heard before.

'And what if you end up hurt and bleeding? What will I say to Dr Murthy when he asks me why I couldn't keep his wife safe?'

Without waiting for a response, Ismail moved ahead, past the doorway. They entered a musty corridor smelling of damp carpet. Kaveri scrunched up her nose, trying not to sneeze as they crept down the dark passageway towards the dim light at the end.

At the end of the corridor, the light they had glimpsed provided faint illumination that lit up the door to a large office with a brass sign above it, spelling out 'V.K. Sharma' in bold letters.

Kaveri crossed her fingers, hoping against hope that Shanthi and her husband were safe. She thought of the only dead person she had ever seen – Ponnuswamy, the pimp, killed with a sharp knife. Sometimes when she closed her eyes at night she could still see his body. When she had first seen Ponnuswamy's corpse, she had been eager, curious to learn more. But as she had got further involved with his murder investigation, she had witnessed, first hand, how a murder tore families apart, shattered once-close relationships.

Ismail tiptoed barefoot into the room. They'd only made it five steps when Kaveri heard a noise. Her eyes snapped towards the corner, and she sighed in relief when she spotted a rat, large and hairy, darting out from behind a small cupboard. Despite the false alarm, a lump of nausea formed in her throat. Was Ismail in danger? Was *she* in danger? The narrow walls of the corridor felt as though they were closing in on her.

A sharp exclamation from Ismail had her rushing inside the room to check on him.

Ismail was standing in front of a large desk, blocking her view. His face was ashen when he turned to face her. She looked without comprehension at what he held in his hands. A long gold chain swung to and fro from his thumb and index finger. The chain was delicate, made of small links joined together. At the end swung a locket, in an unusual design: a long stick with a circle at the end; a magnifying glass.

Her pendant and chain.

Before Kaveri could voice any questions, she was interrupted by more footsteps, and a hubbub of voices. Her heart pounded loudly. Was the murderer returning? Perhaps to finish them off?

Ismail moved in front of Kaveri protectively, just as a group of people burst into the room. Two men were in front, one wearing the khaki uniform of a security guard, and another wearing the white livery of a chauffeur. Behind them came Shanthi. The elegantly dressed lady of the morning was unrecognisable. Her sari was askew, and her hair had come out of its elegant chignon, flying wildly in all directions. She stopped as soon as she saw Kaveri and Ismail.

'Where is he? Where is my husband? The guard told me he heard the sound of gunshot, and then footsteps running away in the distance. Is my husband safe?'

She looked at Ismail, taking in the large man in a police uniform who stood blocking her way.

'Tell me! Where is my husband? Is he safe?' she begged. Tears ran down her cheeks.

Ismail's eyes were sorrowful as he looked at the distraught woman. 'I'm sorry,' he said simply.

As the burly policeman stepped aside and gestured behind him, Kaveri recoiled, seeing the man behind the desk for the first time. Mr Sharma – for that surely must be him? – was slumped over the desktop, a bloody wound in his chest. His arm was splayed across the desk – a mute appeal for help? His mouth was wide open, and his eyes widened as though in surprise.

The room began to spin. Kaveri held on to the door jamb with one hand, and with the other pinched the skin near her elbow until she felt more stable. This would never do. A strong detective could not afford to break down like this! She blinked rapidly to clear her eyes, refocusing on Mr Sharma.

Behind the desk where he sat she could see the outline of a large iron safe embedded in the wall. The door to the safe had swung wide open. Inside, she could see a set of large hard-bound notebooks that looked like registers. There was nothing else inside the safe. No money or valuables. Just a pile of notebooks.

Kaveri looked up at Ismail. The large policeman moved efficiently, instructing the security guard who had accompanied Shanthi to call the police station and ask two constables to come to the factory with a horse cart, and to bring the police surgeon with them. He peppered the other man, her chauffeur, with a barrage of questions. When did they hear the gunshot? How many entrances and exits did the factory have? What lay beyond the wall from which the killer had escaped?

A line of blood dripped from the wound on Mr Sharma's chest onto the desk. The puddle of blood was already beginning to widen, slowly dripping onto the blue Kashmiri carpet on the floor, staining it red. As the combination of the acrid smell of gunshot and the metallic tang of blood filled the room, Kaveri felt a trail of bile rising from her suddenly queasy stomach to her throat.

Shanthi looked at her husband. Her face paled, and she closed her eyes, her body swaying. Kaveri leapt forward, catching Shanthi in her arms as she fell to the ground.

With the help of the chauffeur, Kaveri tugged and dragged Shanthi to an upholstered couch at the side of the room. She hoisted her up onto the couch with some difficulty, then moistened her sari with a glass of water from a covered water jug that lay on the coffee table next to the couch. As she wiped Shanthi's unresponsive face and rubbed her hands, Kaveri looked around the room, trying to memorise the scene.

She saw the body of Mr Sharma sprawled on the desk, sharply illuminated from the single yellow light bulb screwed into the ceiling above. The thin stream of blood emanating from the gaping wound on his chest and beginning to congeal onto the carpet. Ismail staring at her, his face etched in lines of deep disapproval. And Shanthi, prostrate on the sofa.

The desk was covered in papers and files, all thrown askew. A few crumpled documents lay on the floor as well – as though someone had gone through them in a hurry. Had the killer been looking for a specific piece of paper?

And how had her magnifying glass chain made its way from Kaveri's neck to the dead man?

Ismail came over to Kaveri, speaking quietly in her ear. 'Tell no one about the chain,' he said and she felt his hand come close to hers and a cold metal object slide into her palm. 'Keep it safe. Put it back on your neck as soon as you can.'

Kaveri looked at him, startled. Why would he want to hide a critical piece of evidence? Ismail pressed his hand on her shoulder, and she subsided, trusting his instincts implicitly. She slid her hand towards her purse, which lay discarded on the floor a short distance from her. Surreptitiously, she slipped the chain into a side pocket of the purse.

Ismail came forward, squatting so that he was eye level with Shanthi, who was still lying face down on the sofa.

'The police doctor will be here soon, to examine the corpse.' He glanced behind him to the chauffeur. 'Can you please take Mrs Sharma home? She should not be here to witness this.'

As Kaveri moved to get up, Ismail looked at her directly. 'I would prefer it if you left too. This is not a good place for a woman to stay alone. I will ask someone to drop off your car at home later tonight.'

Kaveri tried to lift Shanthi from the sofa, but she was too heavy for her. Shanthi's chauffeur, a short young man with a pugilist build, came over. His face was still pale and tear-streaks stood out prominently on his cheeks. Very gently, he eased Shanthi off the sofa and into his arms, carrying her delicately, like he was holding a precious infant. Kaveri hurried ahead of him, carrying Shanthi's purse and shawl in her hand, easing on her slippers at the door where she had discarded them.

She looked around her, taking in the isolated road, with the moon – now white – overhead in the sky, leaving dark unlit patches of shadow ahead. It was close to 9.30 p.m., and the eclipse had almost concluded, yet it seemed such a short time since she had parked at the police station and asked Ismail to accompany her.

She sat in the back seat of the car as the stunned chauffeur drove towards the Sharma residence. As she held Shanthi's head in her lap, her head whirled with thoughts. The strong, capable woman she had met and admired just a few hours ago, whose eyes sparkled with intelligence and humour, had collapsed as though turned to jelly.

The Sharmas had been married for a little over two years, Bhargavi had said. Shanthi had found love so late in life, only to lose it so soon. Kaveri had never wanted Ramu more than she did at that moment. She scrubbed away the tears from her eyes, but they filled again and again. The road was a blur, and everything around her began to swirl. Kaveri blinked repeatedly, focusing on the road and repeating to herself like a mantra, 'It's fine, it's fine, all will be fine.'

8

A Harsh Scolding

Kaveri looked up in relief as Shanthi's car took the turn into the lane that led to her house.

Disjointed images flashed through her mind. The sight of Shanthi's face as she regained consciousness and opened her eyes, searching Kaveri's face intently. The hopeless way in which she had started to cry, looking as though she had lost all meaning in life. A long wait at the front door as Kaveri had struggled to hold Shanthi up until a sleepy maid opened the door, Chitra standing just behind her.

The awful scream that had emerged from Chitra's throat as she had realised her father was dead still rang in Kaveri's ears.

She had feared for a moment that she might need to slap Chitra to snap her out of a hysteric fit. But witnessing her distress seemed to have a powerful effect on Shanthi. The distraught woman pulled herself together, taking Chitra by the shoulder and speaking to her sharply until Chitra stopped screaming, subsiding into shuddering sobs.

Shanthi turned to the maid, curtly telling her to take Chitra to her room. She then insisted that Kaveri leave, telling her she wanted to be alone. Kaveri, who thought she should spend the night with her, was left looking at the front door as Shanthi closed it in her face. The chauffeur hurried forward, saying in a hesitant voice, 'Come, madam. Let me take you home.'

Sitting in the car, Kaveri had placed her face down on her palms, and given in to the thoughts roiling in her head, weeping till she was empty. Now, as Shanthi's car slowly approached her gate, she saw the kindly figure of Rajamma hurrying towards her.

She sighed in relief, getting out of the car as soon as it stopped. She barely noticed Shanthi's chauffeur nodding farewell before reversing the car out of the lane. Her thoughts were focused on getting into the house, where she could leave the terror, pain and confusion of the previous hours behind.

As Rajamma clasped her hands and patted them, Bhargavi's angry figure exploded into the road, glaring at Kaveri as she pulled her into the house. As soon as she was inside their compound, Bhargavi rounded on her.

'Where were you for so long? Do you not realise how late it is? What about me, and Rajamma? We have been so worried. You could have made one telephone call to let me know what you were up to.' Bhargavi kept up a continuous torrent of complaints as she pulled Kaveri into the house. Kaveri felt each word strike her with the force of bullets. She longed to respond, but the events of the evening had left her so battered that she could not speak. She felt empty, drained, without the capacity to produce words any more.

As soon as they were inside the house, Bhargavi took Kaveri by the shoulders and turned her to face her, demanding roughly, 'Well? I have been asking you so many questions. Why are you not answering?'

Rajamma finally moved to intervene.

'*Ammavere!*' she said sharply, startling Bhargavi. 'Can you not see, this poor child is on the verge of collapse?' She pointed to Kaveri. 'Look at her sari. I think those are bloodstains at the bottom of her pleats. Someone else's car dropped her back. Something has happened that is beyond her control.'

Overcome with weariness, Kaveri had begun to shake by now. Rajamma glared at Bhargavi, and took Kaveri to the sofa, taking off her slippers as though she was a very small child, and making her lie down.

'And, *Amma*, you were the one who sent her out when this child did not want to go. Is it fair to now scold her?' Rajamma added.

Bhargavi's face crumpled. She came over to the sofa and squatted on the floor in front of Kaveri, holding her hands tightly.

'Forgive me, my daughter. Rajamma is correct. I am an old, foolish woman frightened out of my wits. Shanthi called me just after you left, and told me that the note you received was not from her. I wanted to come to you, to warn you, but without a car and driver, at this time at night . . . ' She gestured helplessly with her hands. 'Shanthi said she would rush out to warn you. But after that, I heard nothing. Rajamma and I were so worried. I could not get through to Mr Ismail, Ramu or even Shanthi on the telephone.' She hugged Kaveri tightly. 'What happened to you?'

Rajamma brought Kaveri a cup of hot, sweet coffee. Sipping it slowly, she briefly described the events of the evening. Bhargavi gasped, her eyes filling with tears when she heard of Mr Sharma's death. Rajamma said nothing, but slid down to the floor, holding her head in her hands.

The three women sat silently for a while. Then Bhargavi sat upright. 'But why did you leave Shanthi and Chitra alone? You should have stayed there and sent a note to me.'

Kaveri shook her head. How could she tell her mother-in-law how uncomfortable and hostile the atmosphere in Shanthi's house had seemed to her? Finally, she said, 'I tried to, *athe*. Shanthi told me she wanted to be alone, and asked me to leave.' Bhargavi still looked unconvinced, so she added, after a moment's pause, 'Shanthi closed the door in my face. I had no choice but to return.'

Bhargavi looked very uncomfortable. 'She is too independent, that girl,' she muttered. 'Always was that way, even when she was a small child. I will go see her tomorrow. I know she needs help, but will be too proud to ask. She will not turn me away.' She looked at Kaveri, as though seeing her exhaustion for the first time. 'But why am I asking you so many questions at this hour? Go, my child. Go upstairs and sleep. Tomorrow, after a good night's sleep, you will feel much better.' She pulled Kaveri close, giving her an awkward embrace before letting go of her.

Kaveri climbed slowly up the stairs to her bedroom, holding onto the bannisters for support. Intellectually, she understood that her mother-in-law had been too frightened to know what she was saying when she had erupted at Kaveri. But it still hurt to be scolded like that when she had done nothing wrong.

She collapsed onto the bed, asleep in a minute. She did not hear Bhargavi open the door silently and tiptoe into the room, putting a cotton sheet on Kaveri and smoothing it down over her before she left, wiping tears from her eyes.

9

The Travelling Husband Returns

When Kaveri woke the next morning, the first thing she saw was a pair of large brown men's shoes – Ramu's – neatly arranged parallel to the wall on a small cotton *jamkhana*.

Ramu was back! Without waiting to arrange her sari around her properly, wash her face or comb her hair, she rushed out into the hall. Where could he be?

Kaveri ran down into the kitchen. Ramu was at the primus stove, heating up the milk. He took the milk off the stove and set it aside carefully when he saw her approach, his face lighting up. Kaveri hurled herself at him and buried her face in his shoulder.

Ramu patted her on her back, making little circular rubbing motions. The touch of warmth disarmed Kaveri's defences completely, and she felt tears fill her eyes again. Ramu pulled back in surprise when he felt the wetness on his shirt.

'Here now, what's this?' he said, wiping Kaveri's cheeks with the dishcloth, which he still held in his hand. 'What happened?'

He put his hands on her shoulders and guided her gently to the stool in the corner. As she spilled out the events of the previous day to him, he returned to the stove, preparing two glasses of steaming hot coffee, and adding a generous spoonful of extra sugar to Kaveri's glass.

'Drink,' he insisted, waiting until she had taken a couple of sips before pulling her up from the stool. 'Let's sit outside and watch the sun rise.'

Ramu pulled Kaveri along with him, keeping her hand enfolded in his warm grasp as they went out to their favourite spot on the front verandah, sitting down on the steps to watch the sun as it climbed up the horizon. The horizon turned orange, then golden, as the chill of the morning began to fade. Ramu felt his wife shiver and put his arm around her.

'Oh Kaveri. Why do you always get up to things when I am gone?'

Kaveri stiffened, and looked at him. He sighed as he saw the indignant gleam in his wife's eyes.

'What do you mean, when you are gone?' she demanded. 'Am I supposed to wait for you to come and escort me everywhere? And what if you are too busy? Do I tell the people who need my help – Oh, sorry, my husband is away, you must wait for him to return?' She bared her teeth at him in a false grimace and spoke in a sickly sweet falsetto. 'My husband doesn't allow me to take up detective cases unless he is by my side, you see.'

Ramu began to laugh, and Kaveri glared at him crossly. 'In fact, it was your mother's idea.'

Ramu tugged Kaveri to him again and patted her back. 'I know,' he soothed. 'I didn't mean to say I want you to be confined to the house when I am not there. It's just that . . . ' Ramu paused and pinched the bridge of his nose. Kaveri's entire body melted when she saw the dark shadows under his eyes. He looked so tired. After days of hectic vaccination duty, he must have travelled through most of the night to reach home from Mysore. And what had she done as soon as she'd seen him? Fallen on his chest and burst into tears, unloaded herself of her worries, then drunk his coffee – instead of making some for him, as a traditional, dutiful wife would.

'I just want you to be careful, Kaveri,' Ramu said, rubbing his thumb gently over her palm. 'I wouldn't be able to bear it if anything happened to you again.'

He gently ran his fingers along the side of her neck, where a faint scar lingered. A scar that she had received on the day an insane killer had attacked Kaveri, holding a knife to her throat and slicing into her skin till she bled.

'That day when you were attacked . . . I thought my heart was going to explode with fear.'

Kaveri placed a gentle kiss on Ramu's cheek, then blushed furiously as she realised they were sitting on the front steps, in full public view. She moved back a couple of inches as he gazed at her, heart in his eyes.

'Where is your chain?' Ramu asked suddenly, looking at her bare neck.

Kaveri raised startled eyes to him. 'I completely forgot!' She raced upstairs to their bedroom, pulling out the chain from her purse and hurriedly putting it on before running downstairs again.

'The chain was found . . . ' she began to say, then stopped as she saw a flash of movement from the corner of her eye. Bhargavi was coming downstairs. She put a finger to her lips and tapped her watch, signalling to Ramu that she would tell him later. There was no way that she could tell Ramu that her necklace had mysteriously fallen off her neck and made its way to the site of the murder, in Mr Sharma's hands – not when Bhargavi was around. She was not sure she could trust her mother-in-law with a matter as discreet as this.

A look of surprise entered Ramu's eyes, but he did not say anything further, getting up to greet his mother. Bhargavi immediately launched into telling him the story of the previous night's events, explaining everything in detail from her perspective. As she continued her voluble explanations, Kaveri slipped away to the kitchen. Ramu would be hungry from travelling all night, she thought. After bombarding him with her distressing story as soon as she saw him, she wanted to make up for it by feeding her husband well.

As soon as Ramu could manage to escape from his mother, he followed Kaveri to the kitchen, where she started to make coconut chutney, to accompany the hot dosas with ghee she planned to serve for breakfast.

'I was gone from home for three weeks, Kaveri, but it felt like three months. I missed your cooking.' As she arched her eyebrows at him, he wrinkled his nose at her. 'I missed you too, of course.' Ramu pretended to duck, grinning at Kaveri as she aimed a wet cloth at him.

An hour later, after breakfast, and a quick bath and shave, Ramu went into the bedroom, coming down the stairs with his medical bag.

'You look so tired. Why don't you take a nap, and go to the hospital in the afternoon?' Bhargavi gently scolded.

Ramu shook his head. 'Dr Roberts is waiting for our report on the vaccinations. He must be at the hospital already.'

He looked at the large cuckoo clock on the wall as it began to strike 9 a.m., waiting patiently for the wooden bird to sing out in its melodious voice nine times.

'What do you plan to do today?' Ramu asked both women.

'I will go to Shanthi's house and spend the day with her,' Bhargavi said. 'Do you want to accompany me, Kaveri?'

'I do want to, but I am not sure Shanthi *akka* is well enough to answer questions.' She also felt she wasn't emotionally ready to enter that house and its thick, troubled atmosphere so soon. Especially with the disturbing events of the previous night still raw in her memory. As Bhargavi nodded, Kaveri reached up to touch the necklace around her throat, caressing her good luck pendant. She tugged at the clasp surreptitiously, making sure it was well fastened, then dropped her hands quickly, seeing Ramu raise his eyebrows at her.

'What will you do then?' he asked her.

'I have a women's club meeting in the afternoon.' Kaveri gave her mother-in-law a sideways glance, waiting for the look of disapproval that usually accompanied any mention of the meetings that were now a regular feature in their home. But to her surprise, Bhargavi didn't say a word as she left the room to get ready, clearly in a hurry to reach Shanthi.

'Another women's club meeting? How many women have started to come in for the meetings?' Ramu asked, his eyes glinting with interest. Ever since Kaveri had begun to teach Uma aunty, their inquisitive next-door neighbour, how to read and write, the word had spread to other women, who all wanted to learn too.

'We've settled on two afternoons each week,' said Kaveri, beaming at him as she wiped the table. 'Only . . . '

'Only what?'

Kaveri hesitated. 'The women come from different castes and communities, some even from different religions, like Mrs Ismail. I think Bhargavi *athe* does not know what to make of that.'

'My mother has lived in Bangalore for decades now, but despite that, she has not picked up the tolerant habits of this city. Even my father gave up. He wanted her to socialise with his colleagues and friends, but she refused to meet with them in her home. Before you came into our lives, my mother had never invited anyone from a different community into the house.'

Kaveri gave Ramu a rueful look. 'And now, I am not just bringing them home, but also eating with them! She must be horrified that I am breaking social taboos in this way.'

'It is good for her, Kaveri. You are exposing her to different ways of thinking. As I'm sure you are doing for the other women who come home too.'

'I am so happy I can teach people like Uma aunty how to read and write,' said Kaveri. 'Uma aunty opened the Bhagavad Gita the other day and I helped her read the opening sentence. She was so proud, she looked like she would burst. I felt like a balloon, so light with happiness that I could fly away.'

'It's a good thing you didn't,' said Ramu, his eyes crinkling with amusement as he took in his wife's animated gestures. 'Then who would make me dosas?' He ducked again as Kaveri aimed the wet cloth at his neck.

10

The Women's Study Group

By mid-morning, with Ramu and Bhargavi both out of the house, it was almost too quiet for Kaveri. Rajamma had left too, done with her domestic duties for the day. The only sound Kaveri could hear was that of the bulbul, a handsome fellow with his striking black head and crest and brilliant red vent just below his tail. The bulbul let out a series of chirps, tapping at her window as she was drinking a second cup of coffee. Barely the size of her palm, the bird made a loud peremptory rat-a-tat noise against the glass, seeming to scold her with his noisy chirps. Was he thirsty? Bhargavi usually left a shallow earthen vessel filled with water outside near the mango tree for the birds to drink from. She must have forgotten today. Kaveri hurried out and filled the pot with water, as the bird hovered, keeping a safe distance from her. As she went in, she watched with pleasure as he bent down to drink.

The bird's black and red feathers shimmered in the heat, looking like jewels against the sky as it flew away. The world outside was so beautiful – and yet so ugly. Nature was beautiful, she amended. The world of man was often ugly. Not always, of course. There were generous people like Mala, who was now a close friend. Mala had escaped horrific abuse to rebuild her life and had now made it her mission to help other women who were abused or in trouble. But there were also people like the person who had killed Mr Sharma, people who shattered the lives of so many. Kaveri couldn't stop thinking about his wife and daughter, his household staff, employees, and all the others who must depend on a man like him for their livelihoods. She thought of the distinguished man, his hair shot with threads of silver at the temples, looking at her thoughtfully. She had liked him on sight. He had asked for her, depended on her to solve the mystery of who had embezzled from him. And even though the logical side of her brain said there was nothing she could have done to save Mr Sharma, she could not help but feel that she had failed him. That if she had been quicker, smarter, more resourceful, she could have stopped his murder from taking place.

Perhaps there was something in the newspaper about the murder, she thought as she walked back inside. She picked it up eagerly, unfolding and spreading it out on the dining table. But when she opened the front page, she saw only a photograph of a crumpled railway track. Her face paled in horror as she read about a train carriage that had toppled onto its side, leaving bodies scattered everywhere.

The Madras to Bangalore mail train has been wrecked, a short distance from Bangalore. The engine and front coach capsized, and the other coaches were crumpled. The authorities suspect sabotage, as the train driver appears to have been fed a paan leaf filled with cocaine paste. Investigations are in progress.

Kaveri raised a hand to her mouth. Thirteen people dead, and forty severely injured! Why would anyone want to sabotage a train – what would they achieve by killing so many innocent passengers, including children? Kaveri held back tears, knuckling a fist against her lips. She did not think she could bear to read any more about tragedies. Thankfully the next two pages had a large commemorative spread on Mr Sharma, celebrating his life as a famous industrialist and philanthropist. Kaveri scribbled notes on a piece of paper, wondering who would inherit his large home and the factory now, and who would run the factory.

At the bottom of the page, tucked away in a corner, was a short news item about the murder itself. The writer stressed that Mrs Sharma was his second wife, much younger than Mr Sharma, and came from a family that was much less wealthy than his.

Kaveri closed the paper, seething with anger. They may as well have come out and said that Shanthi was a gold-digger who had married an older, wealthier man for his money and then plotted to kill him. Was that what the police also thought? She simply could not believe that Shanthi was to blame. Bhargavi would be devastated if she read this.

Kaveri paced up and down the room, thinking furiously. What could she do to help Bhargavi and Shanthi? She badly wanted to visit the police station to find out what Ismail knew. Should she go now? She looked at her watch. No, better to wait till the next day. It was only noon, and she knew from experience that the police would take some time to gather evidence. She could ask the women's group if they knew of anything that may give her insight into the people closest to Mr Sharma – his wife, daughter and daughter's fiancé.

But the women weren't due until two. Kaveri glanced fretfully at the grandfather clock, whose minute hand was moving annoyingly slowly. At this rate, 2 p.m. would never come.

Kaveri heard the harsh call of a peacock in the distance. Her face brightened as she walked quickly into the kitchen, emerging with a round spice box filled with small containers of coloured rice flour, rangoli powder mixed with vegetable dye which she had purchased from a travelling vendor.

Every girl was familiar with the local art, deftly creating complex patterns on the floor outside their homes using white rice flour and coloured powders that lasted for a day before they were swept clean with water and a broomstick made of coconut fronds the next morning, paving the way for a fresh design to be created. Yet this was the first time Kaveri had made a rangoli in her married home. She took out the red powder and placed it away on a high shelf out of sight. It reminded her too much of Mr Sharma's bleeding gunshot wound.

Kaveri carried the rest of the colours to the yard, standing back and looking at the packed mud so she could visualise the image she wanted to create on the ground. Taking a handful of rangoli powder in a loose fist, she dribbled a carefully measured stream of white powder onto the earth, forming an intricate geometric pattern of interconnected ovals.

Kaveri filled the ovals with jewelled colours of yellow, pink, green and blue, moving outwards from the centre in a clockwise direction. As she worked, she hummed, feeling her tense body relaxing for the first time since the previous night.

When she was done, she got up, absently dusting her hands against the folds of her sari as she surveyed her design. A gorgeous peacock, radiant with colour, cocked its elegant long neck at her.

In her home town of Mysore, she was known for her

expertise in rangoli, winning every local competition. Rajamma had been in charge of the daily morning rangoli when Kaveri came in, and she had not wanted to displace her from her usual task. But oh, it felt so good to be able to do this again!

She took a long sip of water from the mud pot that they always kept filled at the side of the verandah. The sound of women talking pulled her attention towards the gate.

The afternoon was a good time for a social visit. The women had completed their household chores, the husbands were at work, and the children in school. Thrilled to be learning how to read after years of being mocked for their interest in learning, Kaveri's friends always seemed to be in such a good mood when they arrived at her home. After oohing and aahing at Kaveri's gorgeous rangoli peacock, the women stepped past it carefully, holding their sari pleats high above their ankles to avoid smudging the bird. They had just settled down in the drawing room, ensconced in chairs with pen and paper in hand, when the class was interrupted by a knock on the door. Kaveri turned from the blackboard, where she had been writing down their next lessons. Who could it be at this hour in the afternoon, when the sun blazed so fiercely overhead that even the cows and street dogs were napping?

A loud voice called out, 'Helloooo? Kaveri? Are you there?'

Kaveri stifled a smile. 'Yes, Mrs Reddy. I'm here, and the door is open. Come in.' Mrs Reddy was fascinated by Kaveri's 'detective-fying', as she called it. She must have heard the news that Mr Sharma had been killed and Kaveri had a new case, and rushed out immediately to discover more.

Mrs Reddy walked in, smiling brightly. Her smile faltered when she saw the unusual collection of people in

Kaveri's drawing room. Uma aunty, her back-house neighbour, was there of course, as she often was. She spent a large part of her day in Kaveri's home, as Kaveri did in hers. Such a woman – gently bred, from prominent local families – anyone might expect to see in a home such as Kaveri's.

Mrs Reddy blinked, visibly startled. Leaning comfortably on the divan against a pile of round cushions was Mrs Ismail, the Muslim policeman's wife, her eyes twinkling at Mrs Reddy as she gauged her discomfort. On another chair, sitting in equal comfort, was Mala – the former prostitute whom Kaveri had helped save from a baseless charge of murder. Of course, the woman was now a wealthy land owner and businesswoman, but still, one would not expect her to be sitting in a house, sharing food and exchanging stories with respectable women such as this!

Mrs Reddy was no snob, Kaveri thought gratefully, as she saw her recover quickly from her initial shock. She first went to Mala, smiling warmly and holding out her hands.

'Mala! I haven't seen you for weeks.'

She turned to Mrs Ismail next, and greeted her, before saying her hellos to the others. When she greeted Narsamma – Mala's elderly, loyal assistant, who sat in a corner, Narsamma mumbled a hello and looked away, her face darkening in embarrassment. It had only been recently, after much convincing, that Kaveri had succeeded in making Narsamma come into her home, accompanying Mala so that she could also learn.

Uma aunty pointed to the blackboard, on which Kaveri had written each of their names.

'This girl here is teaching us how to read and write.'

Mrs Reddy looked at the Kannada alphabet on the blackboard for a minute and then broke out into a broad smile.

'That's excellent! I wish everyone educated their daughters before getting them married, like my parents did. It has helped me so much – to do the household accounts, read the newspaper, help my children with their studies at home. But so many families don't. When I got married, my husband's younger sister was at home. She was ten years old but had only studied in school for a couple of years. I taught her how to read, and how to do basic sums, so she could run her household when she got married.'

'Really?' Kaveri brightened. 'Perhaps you can help me teach them then. We meet twice a week, in the afternoons.'

Kaveri and Mrs Reddy spent the next hour sitting with Uma aunty, Mala and Narsamma, teaching them the alphabet. Handing over her teaching duties to Mrs Reddy, Mrs Ismail was stretched out on the diwan taking a comfortable snooze, her belly moving up and down in sleep as the women laboured over their letters.

When they were done with writing and a short class in mathematics, the women filled their plates with snacks. Mrs Ismail had brought coconut barfi, and Uma aunty had contributed a large box of *panniyaram*, pan-fried dumplings of two kinds – savoury and sweet. Kaveri brought out cups of hot coffee, and the women settled down for the most exciting part of the day, the time when Kaveri usually read to them from the newspaper, translating from English to Kannada, so that they could broaden their awareness of current affairs.

Today was not a day to read the news, thought Kaveri, looking at the women who sat around her, their expectant faces raised to hers. She did not want to tell anyone about the derailing of the train, or the loss of so many lives. They would hear about it soon enough from others.

'Today, let us talk about what is going on around us, instead of reading the newspaper.'

'About what?' Mala leaned forward, looking intrigued.

'It could be anything interesting we heard or saw recently.' Kaveri turned to Mrs Reddy, who was positively bobbing up and down on the sofa in her eagerness to open the conversation. 'Do you want to go first?' Kaveri asked her.

11

A Beautiful Woman is Cursed

'I heard that you were at the site of a murder last night.'
Mrs Reddy cleared her throat, looking at Kaveri.

The women stopped chewing *panniyaram*, turning to look at each other. No one had heard about anything as interesting as a murder. Only Mrs Ismail appeared unperturbed, taking another sip of coffee. Of course, thought Kaveri. She must have received a complete summary of the events at the factory from her husband last night.

'I heard about it too,' Mala acknowledged, exchanging glances with Narsamma. Mala and Narsamma ran a large gambling and lending business that they had taken over after Mala's pimp had been murdered a few months ago, putting a stop to the prostitution and cleaning up the lending business and making it legitimate. Of course, they would have heard about the murder through their connections with the underworld.

Kaveri shut her eyes for a moment. Although she had planned to raise the topic with the women, she really didn't feel like talking about the murder. When she closed her eyes, she could still see Shanthi sprawled unconscious on the floor and Mr Sharma dead at his desk. But if she was going to try to solve the murder and clear Shanti's name she would need all the help she could get from these women. Men only knew the more obvious details of people's lives – their finances, investments, political leanings. It was the women who knew what really went on in a house, behind closed doors, in intimate domestic spaces.

She took a deep breath, composing herself, then told them what had transpired the previous night.

'And you are taking on the case?' Mrs Reddy pressed. All the women leaned forward, listening intently for Kaveri's response.

When she said 'Yes,' they all let out a collective 'aaahhh' of satisfaction.

'You will catch the culprit,' Uma aunty said simply. 'Just like you did last time.'

Kaveri bit her lip. 'I don't know. I wish I had as much confidence in myself as you all do. The last time may have been a fluke. I don't even know anything about Shanthi, her husband, or their family. How can I hope to help her in any way?'

'Even if the police do not think her guilty, many in society will.' Mrs Reddy frowned. 'Unless you find the true murderer, Mrs Sharma will be ostracised from society. It will also affect her in running the mills. People will shy away from investing money in the factory or entering into contracts to buy and sell from her. That is, if she inherits from her husband. Does she?'

'I don't know,' Kaveri admitted. 'I only met her yesterday. I know very little about her, most of which are things my mother-in-law has told me. And that is not much at all.'

Mrs Reddy set her plate down on the rosewood side table and cleared her throat.

'I have met Mr and Mrs Sharma before. The previous Mrs Sharma, that is. We attended their wedding reception, over twenty years ago, I think. How did the second Mrs Sharma come into his life? She seemed much younger than him, too . . . ' Mrs Reddy let her sentence trail off delicately. She looked around the room. 'I'm not implying anything, mind you. I was only thinking that it was odd for the second Mrs Sharma to marry so late in life, and to a man so much older than her. He was very wealthy. Was she from a well-off family too?'

Kaveri nodded. 'I had the same questions as you. I could have asked my mother-in-law, of course, but I didn't want to . . . '

'Of course you didn't want to.' That came from Uma aunty. 'You didn't want to offend Bhargavi by implying her cousin was a gold-digger, marrying a much older man only for his money.'

'I didn't think she was,' Kaveri continued. 'I like Shanthi. She did not seem like a woman interested only in money. On both occasions that I saw her, she was dressed elegantly but simply, in a plain silk sari without gold thread or embellishments. She wore little jewellery apart from her wedding chain and a pair of plain gold bangles. She is very beautiful, that is true. But if Mr Sharma was looking for mere beauty in his wife, he could have had his pick from a number of much younger, prettier women from poorer families, whose parents would have forced them to accept.'

'Mr Sharma did not seem to be that kind of man,' Mrs Reddy took over the conversation. 'He was devoted to his first wife. That was an arranged marriage, but when he lost her – she died in childbirth – he was devastated. He had a number of offers from other families, but he refused to marry again. Instead, he devoted himself to bringing up his daughter, Chitra, with the help of his older sister, who was a child widow and had moved into their house. She died when Chitra was a teenager. Over time, he trained Chitra to help him in the factory. When she was twenty-one, she started to accompany him to the factory, and I heard she helped him a lot. Many people used to gossip about it.' Mrs Reddy looked at Kaveri directly. 'You know how people talk when they see women taking on what they think of as men's roles.'

Indeed she did. Their pompous neighbour, the lawyer Subramaniam Swamy, was constantly complaining to anyone who might listen to him that it was most unbecoming to have a young woman who fancied herself a detective as his neighbour.

'How did Mr Sharma and Shanthi meet?' Kaveri asked.

Mrs Reddy's face fell. 'I do not know,' she admitted a bit reluctantly. 'I was away in my home town, visiting my parents for several months. When I returned, they were already married. There was a lot of gossip about it at the time. I heard various versions of the story. Some people said that Shanthi met Mr Sharma at a ribbon-cutting ceremony to open a new branch of the factory, while others said that she met him at a dog show. I heard one version that it was love at first sight. In another Shanthi set her cap at Mr Sharma.'

'What I don't understand is, how did a beautiful woman like Shanthi stay unmarried for so long?' That was Mala.

She looked at everyone and smiled – a wide-toothed smile, tinged with bitterness. 'Oh, come on! You know what I mean. A beautiful daughter is a source of much worry to her parents. They are always afraid that she will catch the eye of an unscrupulous man who will run off with her, or a powerful man who will try and seize her for his own. The prettiest girls are always married off early, to keep them safe.'

Usually quiet, Narsamma spoke up for the first time since she had entered Kaveri's home that day. 'The parents think that marriage will keep their pretty daughters safe. But a good-looking woman is rarely safe in her husband's home.' She looked around the room, baring her broken, tobacco-stained front teeth in a travesty of a grin. 'Her in-laws will confine her at home for being too pretty, or her husband will beat her, afraid that she might have an affair with someone.' She shook her head. 'A beautiful woman is cursed. Better to be ugly, like me.'

Kaveri's eyes grew moist, thinking of her schoolfriend Ambujakshi. Pretty, vivacious Ambu, married at fourteen, as soon as she started getting her menses, and forced to stop going to school. Her in-laws had sent her back to her father's home in disgrace two years later, cursing her for being 'barren' because she had not given them grandchildren. Her drunken sot of a husband had quickly re-married, and her father had sent Ambu to live with a widowed elderly aunt who had reduced her to domestic drudgery, robbing Ambu of her zest for life. Narsamma was right. The more beautiful a woman was, the harder her life often became.

'Shanthi could not get married for a long time,' Mrs Reddy explained. 'She was an only child who spent most of her childhood and adult life caring for her mother. Shanthi was free to resume her own life only three years ago, when her mother finally passed away. By then of course society termed her too old for an arranged marriage. A few months after that, she met and married Mr Sharma. Her father also passed away recently. She has no other family, except your mother-in-law, of course.' Mrs Reddy waved her hand at Kaveri.

'All this gossip doesn't really help us,' Uma aunty broke in. 'We have to find out who could have murdered Mr Sharma.'

'Why can't it be Shanthi herself? Maybe she regretted stepping into marriage, and wanted to be free again?' said Mala in her bitter drawl.

Kaveri looked at her, a little sadly. Mala had had such bad experiences with men that she seemed to believe only the worst of the entire male population.

'I don't think so, Mala,' she said. 'I saw her face when she realised her husband was dead. I held her when she fainted.'

Narsamma let out a surprisingly loud, derisive cackle. 'You are too naïve, my lovely. People like you only think the best of everyone. Listen to my mistress. Looks can be deceiving. And anyone can drop into a convincing faint.'

Stung at being called naïve, Kaveri retorted, 'Why can't it be someone else? What about her daughter, Chitra?'

'I don't know much about her,' Mrs Reddy said, tapping her fingers against the arm of the teak easy chair on which she reclined. 'But I have heard rumours. People say that she does not like her stepmother. Of course, others say it is Shanthi who does not like Chitra. It cannot be easy for a woman to get married and enter a new home where there is already a mistress. Chitra was used to running the home, and she must be only ten years or so younger than Shanthi.'

Kaveri closed her eyes, trying to recall what Shanthi had said to her below the banyan tree. Chitra did not seem like a confident woman who was used to running a large house and helping her father run a factory. She had barely spoken at all. Perhaps she was just annoyed at her stepmother for dragging her fiancé into the conversation and accusing him of embezzlement? Kaveri could not mention the missing money to these women – that had been told to her in confidence. Instead, she decided to try and fish for more gossip about Chitra.

'Chitra was engaged to be married, wasn't she? That means there is a third suspect. The prospective son-in-law. Do you know anything about him?'

Before Mrs Reddy could respond, they heard the front gate being thrust open violently. Footsteps pounded against the ground as someone ran towards the door then hit the lion's head knocker repeatedly. The loud thudding sound reverberated through the room.

'Kaveri *akka*! Open the door,' a thin voice shouted outside the door, in tune with the knocking.

'Venu?' Kaveri hurried to the door and let out a small cry.

Panting as he stood in front of her, Venu had run right through the lovely rangoli peacock which she had constructed with such painstaking effort. The bird's beautiful beak looked like it had been viciously slashed, the red mud cutting through the head and seeming to blind it.

Kaveri recoiled, holding on to the door jamb with one hand.

Uma aunty hurried forward, moving past Kaveri and holding up Venu with a supportive arm around his waist.

'What is it, Venu?'

'You have to come with me quickly,' Venu panted out. 'Ramu *anna* needs you at the hospital.'

12

Women Like Us
Are Used to Pain

'It is Anandi *akka*, she is in the hospital.'

'Who is Anandi?' Kaveri asked.

'She is Venu's neighbour.' Mala hurried up to them, turning to Venu. 'Did her husband beat her again?'

'Yes.' Venu looked at Mala, his big eyes filled with hurt. 'But this time he beat her very badly. I can tell you all this later – we have to go to the hospital immediately. The other women attendants are on leave today, and Ramu *anna* needs your help.' Venu was almost dancing with impatience now. 'And then Mala *akka* has to take her somewhere safe and hide her. If she stays in the hospital, someone might see her and tell her husband. Then he may come back again, to hurt her some more.' Venu tugged at Kaveri's sari. 'Will you come, or keep asking me questions?'

With a quick word of farewell to the ladies, they hurried towards the car. Kaveri motioned for Venu to sit in the back, as Mala sat in the passenger seat next to her. On the way,

Mala filled her in quickly, telling her that Anandi was a neighbour whose husband got drunk and beat her often.

'She is very pretty, with large black eyes, and skin that glows like a pearl. Even though her husband has beaten her black and blue so many times, and she is often covered in bruises, she still looks like a princess. I think Narsamma was thinking of Anandi today when she spoke about the curse of being born a pretty woman.'

'Just yesterday, they were fighting,' Venu said. Kaveri could see his head bobbing up and down in her rear-view mirror as he spoke. 'So loudly, the whole street could hear.'

'I told her to leave him, but she wouldn't listen to me.' Mala's face was set in grim lines. 'I warned her that he might kill her someday. He has become obsessed, thinking she has been meeting someone else. Even if she steps out of the house for a moment, to buy milk or vegetables, he accuses her of having a lover. The beatings have been getting worse every day.' She looked back at Venu. 'How bad is it, Venu?'

'Very bad, *akka*,' Venu said, sitting back quietly.

Kaveri stepped on the accelerator, narrowly missing a man on a bicycle overladen with earthen pots who was swerving all across the road, getting them to the hospital in record time.

By the time she had parked the car and entered the hospital, Lakshmikanth, one of the male attendants, was at their side. 'Ramu Sir asked you to go up. He is on the first floor, first room to the left.'

Kaveri ran in alongside Mala, as Lakshmikanth pulled Venu aside. 'Stay here, Venu. This is a woman's job now.'

As they hurried into the room, Kaveri saw Ramu bending over the crumpled form of a woman on the bed. He straightened up as he heard their footsteps resounding on the wooden steps but did not turn away from what he was doing.

'There's hot water on the stove. Lakshmikanth kept it on to boil. Can you bring it to me?'

As the women turned towards the primus stove, Ramu looked up at Kaveri briefly. There was a strain in his voice, and his eyes looked tired, as if they had seen too many horrors to stay open. His sleeves were rolled up almost to his elbows, and – surely those weren't blood stains on his hands?

The crumpled form on the bed let out a moan, and she forgot everything else, moving towards her.

'Wash your hands first,' Ramu warned, and she stepped back, moving to the sink and scouring her hands and arms with carbolic soap. When she turned back to the bed, Mala had already tipped the pan of hot water into a tin pail and brought it to Ramu.

He carefully pulled back the sheet that covered the woman. The woman was slight, a bare slip of a woman, with her ribs poking out through her blouse. Her arm looked like it had slipped out of the shoulder joint, and was hanging at an unnatural angle, and her poor face! Kaveri had never seen anything like it. Her face looked like someone had taken a hammer to it, with her lip split open and her cheek swollen with bruises. Some of the bruises looked old and yellowed.

Ramu asked in a harsh voice, filled with rage, 'Does her husband beat her often?'

Mala scrubbed her eyes with the back of her hand and said, a hoarse edge to her voice, 'Yes. I told her he would murder her someday.'

'Thankfully this time he seems to have missed,' Ramu muttered, his mouth twisting in bitterness. 'She has lost a lot of blood, but the wounds seem to be superficial. Nothing is broken. But if we don't clean her wounds well and stitch them up, gangrene may set in. I need your help,' he finished simply.

Kaveri and Mala stood on either side of Ramu, taking up positions next to Anandi. They held Anandi down as Ramu twisted her arm, which had been dislocated, back into its socket.

'I wish I could use chloroform, to make her unconscious and relieve her of her pain,' Ramu muttered, almost to himself. 'I dare not, though. She is already breathing so shallowly.'

'Women like us are used to pain.' Mala's voice took on a grim edge. 'We are hit so often. See her?' She pointed to Anandi. 'Her mind has retreated inside of itself, to its safe place. She will stay there while we treat her, separating her mind from her body. That's how she survives the violence. That's how all of us survive.'

Ramu cut away her clothes, and cleaned the worst of her wounds, closing them with delicate, neat stitches, then dousing them with alcohol. Anandi had borne the treatment with no more than an occasional whimper but she cried out then, just the once – a single sharp sound. Kaveri wiped away her tears with the corner of her sari and saw Mala doing the same.

They lost track of time. Unheeded, the sun began to move down the horizon, casting long shadows into the room as they worked late into the afternoon. By the time they were done, Anandi had relapsed into a merciful unconsciousness. Lakshmikanth brought a clean hospital robe, and Mala and Kaveri put it on her. The two women let out almost identical sighs of relief. They had done the best they could.

'Will Anandi be scarred?' Mala asked Ramu bluntly as he put away his stethoscope and began to scrub his hands.

'I don't think so,' he said, looking relieved. 'The wounds look painful, but they will heal quickly, if she does not scratch and open them.'

Mala straightened up, stretching her arms and arching her back to relieve the strain on her shoulders from crouching over Anandi. Kaveri rotated her neck from side to side and took a long sip of water from the jug on the table, swallowing gratefully, then splashing some of it onto her face and neck.

Ramu looked at his wristwatch. 'We cannot leave her here. It is almost 6 p.m. now. The hospital will open soon for out-patients, and once people arrive, someone will see her. If her husband knows where she is, he will come after her again. And this time, she may not survive.'

'Narsamma and I will take care of her,' Mala said firmly. 'We will take her home with us and hide her until she recovers.'

Ramu dried his hands on a towel, then turned towards Mala. 'She will be in pain when she wakes. You have to make sure she does not remove her bandage and scratch at the wounds, infecting them. And once every day, you must clean the area and apply a fresh dressing.'

'We will not leave her alone, even for a minute,' Mala reassured Ramu.

Lakshmikanth stood in the doorway, waiting. At a gesture from Ramu, he bent forward and picked up Anandi's crumpled body, holding her as tenderly as a child.

'I have asked a bullock cart to come around to the back gate,' he told Ramu.

'I can drive her,' Kaveri said. But Mala shook her head.

'No one should know that Anandi is in my home. If her husband knows, he will force his way into our home and take Anandi away with him. Lakshmikanth is right, it is best that he finds a bullock cart for us. The sight of a cart coming to my home will not attract attention. I can say I bought some sacks of rice from the wholesale market and took the cart into my compound. But if you bring the car . . . ' Mala looked at Kaveri, a small smile on her lips. 'You know what will happen. All the small children will come crowding in, and the young men too, to watch you drive, and touch the car. They will want to examine every inch.'

Kaveri felt a bubble of laughter emerging from her throat as she imagined the scene, then hastily turned the laughter into a cough. She felt lightheaded with the relief of knowing that their hard work had been fruitful. Anandi was safe and would eventually be well, and the day's bitter memories of seeing her bruised, battered body would fade with time.

Ramu and Kaveri stood with Mala as Lakshmikanth gently placed Anandi in the cart, shielding her from the hard sides with cushions. As the cart left, Ramu turned to Kaveri, placing a gentle arm on her shoulder. 'Did I pull you out of your meeting?'

Kaveri looked at him for a long moment, her mind blank. 'What meeting?' The sight of Anandi's bloody, wounded body had driven everything else out of her mind. Then, as the discussion of the afternoon came back to her, she shook her head. 'No, we were almost done.' She looked inside the hospital, towards the waiting room, and saw a copy of the newspaper lying on the table.

'I wonder if Shanthi has read the news,' she murmured, so softly that Ramu had to bend to catch her voice.

'What news?'

'There is an article in the paper on Mr Sharma's murder. It insinuates that the police may want to speak to Shanthi. All because she is a beautiful woman, much younger than her husband, who was wealthier than her.' Kaveri scowled.

'And knowing you, I suppose you used the discussion time with the women to find out more about Shanthi,' Ramu said.

'I hope your mother hasn't read it. She is so protective of Shanthi, she would be devastated if she knew the newspaper is focusing attention on her and her alone. Surely Chitra, and Chitra's fiancé Kumar, are also suspects. Or maybe it could be an outsider. I will go to the police station tomorrow and ask Ismail.' Kaveri's hand went up reflexively to her chain with the magnifying glass pendant as she thought of Ismail. She paused with her hand on the chain when she saw Ramu looking at her.

'What was it that you wanted to tell me earlier this morning? When I noticed the chain was missing from your neck?'

Kaveri looked around, checking that no one was in hearing distance. Pulling Ramu close, she told him the story of the missing chain in a few rapid sentences.

Ramu's eyes widened slightly. 'The chain was put in Mr Sharma's hands to frame *you*. The note was part of the plan. If you had gone there alone at 8 p.m. instead of with Ismail, what do you think would have happened?'

Kaveri looked at him, only now beginning to connect the dots. The events of the past twenty-four hours had rushed past in a blur. She was no stranger to violence. She had seen Ponnuswamy's dead body at the dinner in the Century Club only a few months back. But she had never seen a dead body up so close before yesterday, nor seen a loved one's reaction to finding someone brutally murdered. Her brain felt slow, almost comically slow, like someone had taken sawdust and put it inside her skull, gumming up the workings of her mind.

'The killer would have run away, leaving you with the body. You would have been caught there, with Mr Sharma, blood on your hands – because I know you would have leaned over to him to see if you could help him. And your chain would have been in his hands. Evidence that you were involved in the murder.' Ramu shook her shoulders gently. 'Don't you see, Kaveri? The killer is someone who knew your reputation. They wanted to implicate you in the murder. You would be caught up in trying to prove your innocence, and the killer would get away. That's what Ismail wanted to avoid. That's why he returned the chain to you, and asked you not to tell anyone. Especially my talkative mother,' Ramu added wryly.

'Thank God my instincts told me something was very wrong,' Kaveri said, looking at Ramu.

The typewritten letter, the sandalwood scent, the change in timing by an hour – that's what had triggered the insistent warning signal in her brain, prompting her to ask Ismail to come with her. But she still didn't know how the chain had gone from her neck to the dead man's hands.

As Ramu held her tightly, Kaveri closed her eyes, thinking of Shanthi, sleeping alone in her bedroom, the other side of her bed now forever empty – and of the neglected, battered body of Anandi, who had never known the comfort of a spouse's loving embrace.

She put her arms around Ramu and hugged him fiercely, burying her face in his shoulder, wanting to never let go.

13

The Rat Catchers

Bhargavi came home late that night and went straight to bed. The two women spoke briefly over breakfast the next morning, but the conversation was strained. Kaveri found it difficult to completely forget the shock she had suffered when Bhargavi had shouted at her two nights back. And for her part, Bhargavi seemed distant, preoccupied with thoughts of Shanthi and her troubles. She gulped down a simple breakfast of *uppittu* with peanut chutney, leaving so quickly that Kaveri didn't get a chance to ask her if Shanthi was in a fit condition to speak about the night of the murder. Ramu had left even earlier, well before Bhargavi was up, to deal with an outbreak of cholera – the hospital was packed with patients, he said, as he gave Kaveri a hurried peck on the cheek before leaving.

Alone in the house, worried about Anandi, fretting about whether the police suspected Shanthi, Kaveri felt at odds again. So she did what she always did when she felt troubled, going down to her shed which doubled up as her home office for detective work, and pulling out a book of calculus. Just three weeks back, she had returned from Mysore after writing her matriculation final exam. That seemed a lifetime away now, Kaveri thought as she looked at the books. The murder of Mr Sharma had driven everything from her mind. She thought she had done well in her examination and had a reasonable shot at getting a distinction. But there had been no news yet from Mysore.

Kaveri resolutely put all thoughts of murder, railroad sabotage and examination marks out of her head, opened her notebook, and began to work out a complicated integration problem in her neat, copperplate handwriting. As she wrote, the mathematics problem began to work its magic, slowly dissipating the headache that had begun to take control of her. She rolled her shoulders and stretched her arms overhead, groaning with relief as she felt the tension abating from her. The sun, which had been low in the sky when she started, climbed steadily overhead as her pen scratched across the pages.

After completing the last problem she had assigned herself, she put down her pen with a sigh. Surely Ismail would be at the police station by now. She took out the small notebook she carried in her purse, studying all the details she had written down about her first meeting with Shanthi and Chitra and the night of the murder. Then, frowning, she tapped the pencil against her teeth as she thought furiously. She turned to the next page, writing down a set of questions she wanted to ask Ismail.

Setting her notebook aside, she changed out of her crumpled sari, selecting a light pink cotton one with a delicate zari border. After carefully tracing a fresh bindi onto her forehead with a stick dipped in vermilion powder, she took her purse and the notebook and hurried towards the car, asking Rajamma to bolt the door behind her.

*

A short while later, Kaveri pulled up outside the red and white stone building where the police station was housed, and stared up at its red painted wooden arch made of long slots. Ismail had told her once that these kinds of arches were called monkey tops, so named because they were supposed to make it difficult for monkeys to climb on top of the building. They seemed to have forgotten to tell the monkeys that the arch was supposed to keep them away, Kaveri thought, looking at the troop of macaques gambolling on top of the tiled roof. A couple of young mothers held tiny infants below their bellies, one of them suckling milk as the mother held on with one paw, swinging nimbly onto the mango tree above her with the other. The muddy ground in front of the police station was littered with twigs and leaves. The constable stationed in front swung his wooden lathi, keeping a wary eye on the large male of the troop, who was baring its teeth at him in a grimace.

Kaveri skirted the twigs and the lathi-wielding constable, and started to go in. Then stopped in surprise when she saw a long line of raggedy-looking boys all between the ages of eight and twelve, clad in grimy loincloths, their ribs showing above bellies swollen with hunger. She looked at what they were holding in their hands, and took a couple of steps back. Each urchin held a number of dead rats in his hand. Flies buzzed noisily around the rats and the boys. She put her sari to her mouth, breathing through it heavily.

'What on earth?' Kaveri turned to the constable.

She saw Venu dart out from the door. 'Kaveri *akka*, what are you doing here? Come in, fast.' He hurriedly dragged Kaveri inside, taking her to Ismail's room.

'The Inspector is not here. But he said I could use his room.' Venu looked very proud of himself as he perched on the edge of a chair in the corner.

'Why are you here? And what are those boys doing outside?' Kaveri demanded.

'Didn't you see the notice in the paper, *akka*? Because of the plague, the government has offered a reward for the extermination of rats. They will pay two annas for every dead rat brought to them. No one was taking it up, though, and I know a couple of friends of mine who are leaders of local groups of boys – they are all hungry – so I fixed it up with Inspector Ismail. They will come here and hand over the rats.' Venu pointed outside. 'There is a cart parked behind the station. Once each boy drops off his rats there, he gets a chit from the constable in charge, with the number of rats marked. Then he comes to the station and gets his money.'

Kaveri winced. 'It is not safe for those children to be doing this—' she began.

Venu interrupted her, saying fiercely, 'What do you want them to do, *akka*? Just look at them. They are so hungry, they would probably eat the rats!'

Kaveri took a step back in shock.

Venu squeezed her hand, and continued in a softer tone. 'I remember how it felt to be hungry.'

Kaveri swallowed, thinking of the first time she had seen Venu, his thin ribs poking out of his shirt. She had fed him over-salted lemon rice, and he had gulped even that down with desperate hunger, asking for more.

'They need the money. Not just to feed themselves, but also to put food on the table for their mothers, sisters, younger siblings.' Venu crossed his arms and stared at her.

Kaveri could only nod mutely, as her eyes misted with tears. There must have been at least fifty boys outside. She longed to take them all home and give them a good scrub and bath followed by a large hot meal. But how could she take care of so many children? And even if she did give them one meal, how would that help? What they really needed was a way to feed themselves over the long term, and their families as well.

She thought of the gold chain that Bhargavi had taken out of her purse and placed in Swami Vaninanda's assistant's waiting hands. That was just a few days back, yet it seemed so long ago. How much gold the Swami must have collected! What did he do with it all? Like Shanthi and Bhargavi, there must be so many wealthy women in the city who were devotees of his. Why couldn't someone like him do something about all this poverty?

She looked up and saw that Venu was watching her anxiously. 'Are you angry with me, *akka*?' he asked.

Kaveri gave him a watery smile and reached out to stroke his hair. 'You did well, Venu,' she said. 'At least those children and their families will eat well tonight.'

Venu gave her a beaming smile. 'I will try and find other ways for them to earn money,' he said, bouncing slightly on the edge of the chair as he spoke. 'Inspector Ismail said he would also try to help me.'

'When will Inspector Ismail return?' Kaveri asked.

As she spoke, she heard a well-known heavy tread, and saw a pair of large black boots move and stop before her. She raised her eyes to see the Inspector's familiar face looking down at her, his eyes crinkling at the corners.

'Mrs Murthy. So late? I expected you to come earlier.'

Kaveri wasted no time in getting to the point.

'Have you found out anything new?'

Ismail looked at Venu, reaching into his pocket and pulling out a handful of coins. He dropped them into Venu's hand, giving him a rough pat on the back.

'Go and get me some food. A plate of your sister-in-law's onion pakoras would be great, along with a flask of hot tea. And close the door behind you,' he added, as the boy left in a flash, looking excited at the prospect of taking some money home.

Inspector Ismail grimaced at the smell of dead rat coming in through the window, going over and closing it tightly. He looked at Kaveri apologetically.

'I know, I understand,' she interrupted him. 'Venu told me all about it.'

Ismail looked distressed. 'I do not like it, but at least it is a way to reduce the plague *and* give these children some way of earning an honest living. Without jobs, they end up joining local gangs and becoming petty thieves.'

Ismail had a soft spot for these ragamuffin boys, looking out for them with a paternal eye. Kaveri had met a few of the urchins whom he used as errand boys for odd jobs. She knew he paid them from his own pocket, making sure they were well fed, and buying them new clothes on Id, Deepavali and other festival days.

She felt like hugging the large man, who had become so dear to her in a short span of time, like a favourite uncle, but she knew it would be unseemly, so she sat back at a respectable distance and asked him again, 'Have you found out anything?'

'A number of things, but nothing of substance.' He looked weary as he dropped down into his chair with a heavy thud. 'I have been busy with a couple of very difficult cases.'

'Related to the train derailment?' Kaveri guessed. 'I read about it in the newspaper.'

Ismail gave her a wry nod. 'That, and the cocaine trade, which was previously confined to Bombay and Calcutta, seems to be making inroads into Bangalore as well. We are at our wits' end, unable to trace the supplier. Far too many people are becoming addicted these days.' He shook his head. 'But you have not come to talk about my difficulties. What do you want to know about Mr Sharma's murder?'

'Were there any fingerprints?'

Ismail gave her a wry smile. 'Are you thinking of the fingerprints that helped solve your first case? We covered every inch of Mr Sharma's room with fingerprint powder. Even the safe. There were a lot of prints. But apart from the dead man himself, the rest were all from his family. His wife, daughter and son-in-law-to-be.

'What about the door to Mr Sharma's room? Did you find any signs that could tell you how the murderer entered?' Kaveri asked, thinking of the most recent Sherlock Holmes novel she had borrowed from the library, which was a classic locked room mystery. Of course, Mr Sharma's room had not been locked but open, but surely the same methods of investigation applied here as well.

'We inspected the door carefully, with a magnifying glass.' Ismail's eyes twinkled. He knew of Kaveri's fascination with 'The Adventure of the Empty House'. Both of them were Holmes fans, and had discussed it at length before. 'There were no signs of forced entry. It was either opened by someone who had the key, which means it was one of the family, or by Mr Sharma himself, which means it was someone he trusted enough to let them in late at night.'

'So Shanthi, Chitra and Kumar are the most likely suspects?' Kaveri asked, feeling queasy at the thought of what her mother-in-law would say when she found out.

'The family is always the most likely to be involved, Mrs Murthy. In my years of police work, that's what we usually find, time after time.'

'The fact that she called my house and spoke to my mother-in-law just after I drove out of the house, and then rushed to the factory, reaching it just after we did, means that Shanthi has an alibi. You can't consider her a suspect,' Kaveri argued.

'You know better than that, Mrs Murthy.' Ismail stared pointedly at her. 'Her home is closer to the mills than yours. She could have called from her home, quickly reached the factory, left the car with the chauffeur, run in and shot her husband, then jumped over the wall, running back again around the side of the factory to come in and "discover" his body a few minutes after we did.'

Kaveri raised a sceptical eyebrow at him.

'It seems unlikely, but we cannot rule it out,' Ismail added. 'We interviewed her chauffeur. He had parked the car a short distance away, but did not hear the shot or the sound of someone jumping from the wall and running away. The security guard heard both, but could not tell if Mrs Sharma and her chauffeur were parked outside or far away at the time. He could not tell us anything that could prove either her innocence or her guilt.'

Kaveri nodded unwillingly, and took out her notepad from her purse, looking at all the questions she needed answers to.

'Who had the keys to Mr Sharma's safe?' she asked.

'There were two keys. One was kept with Mr Sharma, and the other was with Kumar. Chitra's fiancé.'

'So Kumar should be one of your chief suspects then?' She kept her eyes focused on Ismail.

'Possibly. But when Mr Sharma wasn't at the mills, he kept the key to the safe inside his desk in his home office. The door was locked, and none of the staff was allowed to enter the office, not even the maid. But Chitra and Shanthi both had keys to his home office, as they took turns to dust the room and keep it clean. Either of them could have accessed his key, pressed a copy into a bar of soap, and taken it to the locksmith to get a set of duplicate keys made. It is not that hard.'

Ismail took a sip of water before continuing. 'My men have fanned out across the city, interviewing all the expert locksmiths. No one admits to having made copies of a key that looked like his. But they could have been handsomely paid to ensure their silence.' He shrugged, his massive shoulders moving up and down. 'And if the killer wanted to be extra careful, all they had to do was to go to a neighbouring town or city and use a locksmith there. We would never be able to find out in that case.'

Ismail leaned forward, making the chair creak ponderously again, and looked her deep in the eyes.

'Be very careful, Mrs Murthy. The murderer, whoever they are, seems to have something against you. Something personal. They wanted to frame you. They did not realise how sharp your instincts are, did not anticipate that you would come to me for help. Because I was there, you were safe. Otherwise by now . . . ' He shrugged his shoulders. 'If the news had reached a superior officer of mine, I may have been ordered to put you in a cell.'

Kaveri felt sick, remembering the women's jail from which she had rescued Mala a few months ago – the screams and pleas of the incarcerated women and the stench of fear and stale urine, which she had struggled to wash off her body, no matter how hard she scrubbed.

'You would not have been there for long, probably,' Ismail continued. 'Dr Murthy would have got you out soon. But after such an experience . . . you would have left the case well alone.'

Kaveri felt very confused. *Would* she have refused the case if she had been falsely implicated and placed in jail? She did not know. But the thought that she may have been weak enough to do so filled her with outrage.

'I will be careful. But I cannot stop. You cannot expect me to stop.'

Ismail looked affectionately at her, leaning back in his chair again.

'I do not expect you to stop detection, Mrs Murthy. It seems to be in your blood. If I did not know better, I would say you came from a long line of illustrious women detectives.'

This brought a smile to Kaveri's lips, as Ismail knew it would. She thought of her mother, grandmother and great grandmother, all of whom held strongly disapproving views of women from respectable families stepping outside their homes. They would be horrified if they heard of her foray into detection.

'I don't know what Kumar's role is in this,' Kaveri said. 'Is he a suspect, or a missing piece in the puzzle? Chitra is another unknown factor. Compared to the two of them, what little I know about Shanthi is a lot.'

'We know more about the motive, perhaps. From the fact of the embezzlement, the reason for the murder is likely to be the most sordid of them all. Money.' Ismail's face was grave.

'What happens to the factory after his death? And their property? Who inherits it?' Kaveri looked at her list again. How much more difficult this would be if Ismail couldn't answer her questions. She was thankful that the friendship she had forged with the large policeman, a friendship developed over the course of solving a previous murder, stood her in such good stead.

'I spoke to Mr Sharma's lawyer today. Half of his property goes to Shanthi straight away. The other half is meant for Chitra, but with some specifications. If she marries Kumar within the next month, she inherits the other half immediately, including the factory. If she does not marry him, she forfeits all rights to her father's property. She will only be entitled to have the use of the house as long as she lives, and a monthly payment – enough to keep her in comfort, but not in luxury.'

'That seems like such an unreasonable condition!' Kaveri gaped at Ismail. 'Mr Sharma wants to control his daughter even from the grave, forcing her to marry as he dictated if she is to have any financial independence!'

Ismail shook his head at her. 'Don't judge him so harshly, Mrs Murthy. He was a father, worried about the safety and security of his daughter if he were to die suddenly. I know how worried I was until my daughter married, and how carefully I searched to ensure we found a good man, and a kind family for her.' Seeing Kaveri looking unconvinced, he shook his head, leafing through the pages of his own notebook.

'Mr Sharma's lawyer also told me something I found very disturbing. Shanthi asked him if she could file a petition in court to overturn the will and gain sole possession of the inheritance.' Ismail cleared his throat. 'You realise what this means, Mrs Murthy. I know your mother-in-law is very close to Shanthi, but we must face the facts dispassionately. Shanthi is clearly interested in the financial benefits she gains from Mr Sharma's death. Otherwise, why would she think of trying to change the will to exclude Chitra – her husband's only child – from her rightful inheritance? If she is the murderer, and if she is unable to get her hands on all his money – then that also means that the other two members of her family – Chitra and Kumar – are both in danger.'

Ismail looked up and went to the window, peering out as the noise of a car's engine sounded close by. Kaveri peered out along with him, and saw a young man with a thick black moustache getting out of a horse cart.

'That is Kumar,' Ismail said. 'I asked him to come to the station so we could ask him a few questions.' He turned to Kaveri. 'You must leave now, through the back door. If he sees you, he will become suspicious that we are working together, and may think the police are biased in favour of Mrs Sharma. After all, he knows that you are related to her.'

Kaveri mumbled a quick goodbye to Ismail and got up, her head reeling as she walked out of the police station. She barely noticed the stench of rats, or the line of small boys that had grown even longer since the time she had walked in. She went past Venu, who had returned with a flask of tea and a steel tiffin box filled with food for Ismail, without seeing him or hearing his call of farewell.

How could she tell her mother-in-law that the woman she loved like a sister might be a cold-blooded killer?

14

Motives for Murder

Bhargavi had called to say she would be spending the night at Shanthi's home. Alone together at home for the first time in a long while, Kaveri and Ramu decided to push aside all thoughts of the case for a while over dinner. They lingered over a simple meal of lemon *saaru* with rice, accompanied by spiced fried potatoes, followed by bowls of vermicelli *payasa*, as they spoke of everything other than the murder.

Ramu traced the dark shadows under Kaveri's eyes with a gentle finger. 'You have stepped too close to the case, Kaveri. Set the murder aside for a couple of days. Take a break. You will think the better for it.' He placed a kiss on her forehead. 'You look tired, I will clean the dishes.' Ramu pressed Kaveri back on the chair.

'How is Anandi?' she called after him as he took the dishes out to the washing area in their backyard.

'She seems better. I think she may be on the road to mending and if Mala and Narsamma tend to her carefully, making sure her wounds are not infected, then I think she will heal completely, without any scars. It's what happens after she is well enough to move that I worry about. She cannot hide in Mala's home forever. And if her husband catches her again . . . ' Ramu paused and swallowed before continuing. 'I am trying to see if I can find someone in a neighbouring town who can give her a job. Unfortunately, the hospitals are reluctant to hire her as she lacks nursing experience.'

'What did she do before? Has she ever worked?' Kaveri asked him.

'Mala told me she worked as a maid in a large house before she got married,' Ramu said. 'That's where she met her husband.'

'That's it then.' Kaveri snapped her fingers. 'I'll ask Mrs Reddy if she knows of anyone in a different city who might be looking for a maid who is used to the rhythms and requirements of a wealthy home.'

Unable to focus on anything the next day, Kaveri went for an early morning swim in her favourite swimming pool at the Century Club, making use of the time when it was reserved for women only.

Miss Roberts had told her that English women swam in mixed pools in the company of men, but she did not yet feel comfortable enough to expose her body, draped in a cling-ing wet swimming costume, to the gaze of strange men. Perhaps she would never be that comfortable, she thought, as she changed out of the swimsuit into a pale yellow organza sari embroidered in light blue flowers at the edges. It was one of her favourites, especially since she had embroidered it herself. But she also loved her pretty tailored silk swimsuit in the English style, stitched by her Anglo-Indian tailor, Mrs Green.

After returning home, and feeling refreshed after her swim, Kaveri sat in the rocking chair on the verandah. She patted the lifelike porcelain statue of a dog that Ramu's father had brought from Bombay. Bhargavi had placed it on the verandah, claiming that it looked so lifelike it would deter thieves.

'Then let's get a real dog,' Ramu's father had laughed. But Bhargavi, who was so finicky about order, could not bear the idea of a noisy, smelly dog at home, chewing on their Kashmiri carpet, upsetting their tables and breaking their crockery. The porcelain substitute was ideal for her.

Kaveri liked order too, but her type of order was not as neat and sterile as Bhargavi would have liked. Thoughts swirled in her head like butterflies, and she was unable to catch them and organise them so that she could file them away. What she wanted now, most of all, was a pen and some paper, to make a list. Lists brought order to her life, adding serenity and calm, and giving her confidence.

Kaveri left the verandah and ventured to her study, sighing with pleasure as she entered. Something about that room always made her feel more grounded and in control of herself. She looked around, noting with pleasure that her book collection was in danger of overflowing her bookshelf. She took out the notebook in which she had written down questions for Ismail the previous day, studying the notes she had made for herself.

When solving a crime, always ask yourself the following questions: Who were the suspects? Which one of them had the opportunity to commit the crime? And what was their motive – did they stand to gain anything? Was it for money, or love? Or revenge?

She pursed her lips in thought. The embezzlement and murder must be connected – it was too coincidental to assume that the murder happened for an entirely different reason, but coincidentally on the same day and time that Mr Sharma had wanted to meet her. And then there was the note, the mysterious note asking her to come to meet Mr Sharma an hour earlier than she was supposed to. And the fact that he had been holding her signature magnifying glass chain in his hands. There had to be one thread that connected both crimes. If only she could find it . . .

Shanthi had said that only three people had access to the safe where the money was kept: Shanthi, Chitra and Kumar. Kaveri wrote down a heading – *Suspects* – and added the three names. All three of them had the opportunity, both to commit the embezzlement and the murder. All of them had access to the safe so they could steal the money, and none of them had an unbreakable alibi for the time of the murder.

Then she thought for a moment. What if one of the workers in the factory had somehow managed to gain access to the safe? She could not rule it out until she spoke to Shanthi further. She added a fourth name, 'Worker X', and after a pause, put a question mark after it to note her uncertainty.

Now for the motive. Money, love, or revenge? Shanthi could have committed the murder for money – if she was the embezzler and did not want to be found out. Could Shanthi have taken a lover, killing her husband so that she could be free to live with him? Mr Sharma and Shanthi looked like a well-matched, affectionate couple. Of course, Shanthi *could* be an excellent actress. Kaveri wrote down two motives next to Shanthi's name – 'money' and 'love' – with a question mark next to them.

What about Chitra? Money was a definite possibility, though Kaveri could not understand why Chitra would want to embezzle from her own factory. Perhaps Chitra did not love Kumar, and had no intention of marrying him

– could *she* have a lover? One for whom she had stolen the money? Kaveri wrote 'money' and 'love' next to Chitra's name too. She hesitated over the third motive – revenge. Was there any reason Chitra might want to take revenge on her father? By all accounts they were very close – or *had* been very close, until Shanthi had come along. Kaveri could understand why Chitra might want to kill Shanthi. But would she want to kill her father? Unlikely. No child would kill a loving parent, surely, unless there was something very dark and twisted inside their soul.

That left Kumar. He seemed the person most likely to have embezzled the money. He may well have had a lover, agreeing to marry Chitra only because he wanted ownership of the factory. But revenge? She could not see any reason why Kumar would want to take revenge on a man who had treated him most generously, raising him from the position of a regular employee to a favoured son-in-law and future owner of his factory.

And what about the possibility of a factory employee, who – despite Shanthi's statement – had found a way to access the money in the safe, then killed Mr Sharma to avoid exposure? She needed to find out more about how the factory worked, who the employees were, and whether any of them had a reason to commit the murder – either for financial gain, or for revenge. Could Mr Sharma have been a difficult employer, leaving a trail of disgruntled employees in his wake? Perhaps one of them had got rid of him because of a past grudge? Kaveri knew of many employers who exploited their workers harshly, paying them so little that they struggled to keep body and soul together, unable to feed their families and raise children.

She needed more information to solve this case. And for that, she needed to meet people. Shanthi and Chitra were in too fragile a condition for her to speak to them. Bhargavi had refused to let her meet Shanthi just yet, saying she was still too distraught and had been prescribed a heavy draught of sleeping medicine by her doctor. And Chitra, Bhargavi had reported, did not seem to want to speak to *anyone*, staying mostly in her room, and emerging only for meals, with red-rimmed eyes and a swollen face that indicated she spent all her time crying.

Kumar was also inaccessible to her. Unless Shanthi told him to speak to her, there was no reason for him to answer her questions truthfully.

Kaveri banged her pencil down on the table in frustration. While the police followed up on their leads, questioning Kumar and others about the embezzlement, she was forced to sit in her shed, scribbling into a notebook. She looked at the page again, focusing on the column reserved for an unknown worker – X – who could be a suspect.

There was something she had read in the newspaper recently. *What was it?*

Kaveri ran to the back of the house, where Rajamma stacked the old newspapers. She rummaged through them until she found the news report she was looking for, about the train derailed by sabotage. The police had investigated a possible link between the sabotage and a series of violent incidents that had taken place a couple of years back at a prominent mill in Bangalore. Could that be the Sampangi Mills?

Too eager to wait for the time it would take to drive to the police station to speak to Ismail, Kaveri hurried to the telephone. Inspector Ismail picked up, but seemed distracted. 'Mrs Murthy, I am somewhat busy right now,' he said in a formal voice, quickly disconnecting the telephone call. In the background, Kaveri heard a commanding voice with a clipped English accent shouting out instructions. Ismail's British supervisor had made one of his irregular inspection visits to the station, then. Unlikely that he would be able to help Kaveri until the man had left.

Kaveri banged the telephone down onto the receiver and paced up and down the drawing room. She could not be expected to just sit here and do *nothing*! She felt like storming into Shanthi's house and confronting Bhargavi. Her mother-in-law was the one who had dragged her into this mess when she was unwilling. Now, she expected her to sit patiently at home like a good girl, waiting to be called to see Shanthi. Well, she was sick and tired of living up to her expectations of a good girl. Kaveri crumpled the newspaper in her hand and threw it against the wall. The ball of paper knocked over a candlestick, which made a loud clattering noise as it fell from the mantelpiece.

'What was that noise, Kaveri?' Rajamma came rushing out of the bedroom above.

'It's nothing,' Kaveri assured her. Feeling a bit ashamed of her temper tantrum, she went to pick up the newspaper and started smoothing it out. As she looked at it, an idea struck her. *Newspapers.*

She took her car keys and her purse with the notes, calling to Rajamma, 'I'm going out!'

15

Old Books Smell Better Than Roses

Kaveri parked her car next to the rose garden in front of the library. The sight of the beautiful blossoms in pink, purple, white and red never failed to soothe her senses. Feeling much calmer, she walked up the steps of the massive red building, trailing her fingers on the cool granite columns. Even though she was now a regular visitor, the sheer size of the building always made her catch her breath in awe. The smell of dusty books was almost as good as the fragrance of roses – no, even better.

The senior librarian looked up from his desk with a smile. By now, the young Mrs Murthy was a regular feature at the library.

'I have something for you,' he said, his eyes almost invisible behind thick soda-bottle spectacles. 'A new book by an English woman, Agatha Christie, called *The Mysterious Affair at Styles*. It's received an excellent review in *The Sunday Times*. I've been keeping it for you.'

Kaveri eagerly took the book from him, thanking him warmly. 'Actually, I haven't come for books today. I wanted to consult your newspaper archive.'

The librarian led the way to a side room stacked with old newspapers. Kaveri went straight to the stacks that held newspapers from the previous two years. She found a newspaper that mentioned the Sharma wedding – then, after a bit of thought, picked up newspapers from a couple of months before that date, just before the time that Shanthi and Mr Sharma had first met. Flipping through the pages, she was distracted by an article on the visit of Mrs Sarojini Naidu, the well-known poetess and campaigner for women's emancipation, to Bangalore a couple of years back.

Casting an eye at the large ormolu clock on the wall, Kaveri reluctantly set those pages aside, picking up the next newspaper. Here was a report of a speech by the Dewan, describing the main industries generating employment in Bangalore. He had included the Sampangi Mills, which provided employment and housing to a large number of local workers, also educating their children. Kaveri's regard for Mr Sharma increased.

After rummaging through another stack, she found a newspaper dated approximately two years back describing the marriage of Mr Sharma. Despite being a prominent and wealthy industrialist, the writer noted, the wedding had been a simple affair, following Gandhiji's call for wealthy Indians to eschew ostentatious rituals and use the money saved for social causes. Kaveri nodded. She and Ramu had felt bad about the amount of money their parents had spent on their wedding, but they had been unable to get their parents to listen to them. Perhaps if they had had a chance to speak to each other before the wedding, they could have come up with a way to convince their parents – jointly.

But time was running out, and she needed to focus. She licked her finger and turned the pages, reading about the Sharmas' honeymoon in Ceylon. The sun's rays filtered in through the wooden slats on the window, and the room started to become uncomfortably hot. Kaveri could feel her eyelids were growing heavy, and she blinked her eyes. She had close to two years of material to get through quickly if she wanted to be back home by lunch.

Half an hour later, she had a large pile of papers on the table, and was scribbling furiously in her notebook. A couple of weeks after the Sharma wedding, there had been major changes in the Sampangi Mills. The workers had gone on strike, demanding an increase in wages. The mills had closed for a few days, opening only when the police had come in to break up the strike. Then a fire had broken out in one of the workshops, destroying their entire stock of woollen blankets, costing them several thousand rupees. The police found residues of inflammable gun cotton, indicating arson, but had been unable to find the culprits.

Kaveri closed her eyes and tried to remember what she had read about gun cotton in her chemistry textbook. A disgruntled worker could make the explosive quite easily by soaking paper, cotton or wood in a mixture of nitric and sulphuric acid, and washing out the acid with sodium bicarbonate.

All the reports she could find started around the time of Mr Sharma's marriage to Shanthi, and ceased a couple of months later. Why?

She folded up the newspapers and returned them to their stacks as the librarian came in to close up the room, then moved out towards the car. Her stomach reminded her that it was lunchtime, and she had not eaten a morsel since breakfast. She thought of the jar of *avakkai*, mango pickled in mustard and chilli paste, which Uma aunty had given them. She was eager to try it out with hot rice and ghee.

Lost in her thoughts of food, she almost missed hearing the noise behind her, a high-pitched whine.

She heard a hoarse voice raised in anger, followed by a frantic series of yips. The fear she could sense in the unknown dog's yelps made her think of Anandi. Poor abused Anandi. How she would like to get hold of her abusive husband. All thoughts of food forgotten, Kaveri tucked her sari pallu into her waist, rushing into the rose garden. Her mouth set in grim lines, she marched through the park, looking for the voices as she moved past the neatly laid path with roses on either side, ending at an untidy clump of bamboo at the back.

Kaveri stopped short when she saw the sight in front of her. A burly gardener brandished a coconut broom high in the air while a large dog cowered on the ground. A leaf plate lay on the ground, broken pieces of *idli* scattered in all directions.

'Eat my food again, will you? I'll get rid of you today, one way or another,' the gardener yelled, hitting the dog with the broom. The thin sticks made little physical impact on the dog's thick coat, but it yelped in fear.

'Stop that!' Kaveri inserted herself between the gardener and the dog, snatching the broom from his hand before the startled man had a chance to react.

The burly gardener froze for a moment. Then he looked at her, and deliberately spat a stream of blood-red saliva coloured with the betel nut onto the lawn. He bared his teeth, exposing a mouth full of rotting teeth, crimson with betel juice.

'That's just what I need,' he jeered, advancing close and stretching himself to his full height. 'Some rich woman coming to tell me what she thinks of me. Well, if you like the dog so much, why don't you take it home? It's eating my food every day, leaving me hungry.'

The dog, sensing an ally, ran out of the clump and sheltered behind Kaveri's sari, pushing its wet nose into her palm and making a piteous whine.

Sensing the dog's fear, Kaveri stiffened.

'Well, maybe I *will* take it away,' she said, resisting the urge to flee from this large man. She looked around for help, but could see no one else in the park. A welcome thought occurred to her. 'Unless you want me to report you to Inspector Ismail at the police station for animal abuse, you will get out of my way right now.'

The man deflated like a pricked balloon. 'There's no need to tell on me with the police now,' he whined, sounding like he was imitating the dog. 'I was only having a bit of fun with him.'

Kaveri's fingers itched to pick up the broom and hit him on *his* head, then ask him if that was his idea of fun. But better counsel prevailed. Even though her *kalari-payattu* teacher had taught her the basics of self defence, she knew it had been foolhardy of her to have approached this man alone. Thankfully the mention of Inspector Ismail's name seemed to have done the trick. As the gardener retreated, Kaveri turned around to get her first clear look at the dog.

'You?!' Her jaw fell open. There was no mistaking it – this was Putta, the Ugliest Dog award winner. Kaveri called out to the gardener. 'Hoy! Stop for a minute and tell me – how did the dog get here?'

The man shrugged sulkily. 'A man came by wearing white pants and shirt, tied him to that bamboo clump, and went away. I hollered after him to stop. Dogs aren't allowed here. But he picked up his pace and ran away.'

Kaveri thought back to the conversation that Palanivel had had with Miss Roberts. She had probably given him a substantial amount of money in exchange for the silver case he'd won. He should have spent that money on Putta, she fumed. Instead, he had abandoned the poor dog and run away, probably to the nearest bar.

The gardener bent down and showed Kaveri the soles of his shoes, which had come apart, giving her a sly look. 'I couldn't chase after him. See the state of my shoes? I have corns on my feet. I wish I had the money to purchase new ones.'

Kaveri hesitated. She did not want to give this man any money after seeing the way he had mistreated Putta. But neither could she leave him walking in torn shoes. She opened her purse, and placed a couple of coins on a tree stump next to her.

The man beamed, exposing his rotten teeth again. Kaveri moved away from him hastily. Putta followed, matching his pace to hers, and pushing his snout into her sari from the back, almost overbalancing her in his eagerness to make sure he was not going to be left behind.

'Oh, Putta,' Kaveri sighed as she reached the car. 'What am I going to do with you?'

The ungainly dog cocked his large head to one side, his ridiculously small tail wagging back and forth like a tiny white pendulum.

'I can't keep you at home forever.' Kaveri faced him, hands on her hips.

He moved forward and gave her right hand a delicate lick.

'Well, then.' She snorted, opening the back door. Putta jumped in eagerly. She winced as she saw the large muddy footprints he tracked into the back of the car. 'I'll have to spend all afternoon cleaning the car! Bhargavi *athe* is in

Shanthi's house for the next couple of days though. I suppose I can keep you in the garden shed where we store mangoes and coconuts. It is empty right now. But you have to find a new place to go once she comes home.'

Putta let out a small 'woof', panting with eagerness.

Kaveri got back into the front seat and took the wheel. She felt a large head slide through the gap between the seats and come to rest against her left arm, leaning on it heavily as she drove home.

After reaching home, Kaveri took Putta to the gardener's shed, calling for Rajamma. When she heard the story of his previous owner abandoning him in the Cubbon Park gardens and the menacing gardener he'd encountered there, Rajamma's kindly heart melted. She hurried to the butcher's shop and purchased two large and meaty bones of mutton.

As the dog gnawed away happily, Kaveri and Rajamma cleaned the car, scrubbing until they had removed the mud that he had tracked in. Then Rajamma brought a loose rope which they used to tie sacks of coconuts and fashioned a makeshift collar and leash from it, securing Putta to the door of the shed. He curled up on an old jute sack, looking extraordinarily content, and went to sleep.

Later that night, after hearing the story of Putta's abandonment and rescue, Ramu came to the shed to look at him. The pup was fast asleep, the folds of his ample stomach rising and falling with each breath. Kaveri looked over at Ramu, watching Putta, and noticed the lines of tension in his face from a long day's work at the hospital smoothing out, until finally he looked relaxed and happy.

Ramu turned to Kaveri. 'I don't understand how people can have an ugly dog competition in the first place. Look at Putta. He's got a unique charm. But don't get too fond of him, Kaveri. My mother has never liked pets. She did not permit me to have one when I was young. I see no reason she's going to change her mind now.' He stopped, looking as though he'd regretted saying no to Kaveri. He pulled her in front of him. 'If you badly want to keep the pup, though, tell me. I'll speak to my mother.'

Kaveri shook her head. 'I have brought enough turbulence into Bhargavi *athe*'s life. We will keep Putta only until we find him a good home. I will keep him in the shed, as much out of her way as possible. She hardly ever comes to this part of the garden anyway. Rajamma can slip out of the back door and feed him. Maybe he will be gone by the time she notices?' She looked at Ramu hopefully.

'Can you keep a dog as big as him hidden?' Ramu's eyes twinkled.

'You think he's big now? His last owner Palanivel said he's less than a year old, and will grow much bigger,' Kaveri told Ramu as they went into the main house.

'Heaven help his owners then!'

16

A Promise Under Duress

After an early morning visit to Putta, who welcomed her with an ecstatic series of barks, Kaveri returned to the main house. She heard the sound of the gate opening, and looked up to see Venu leading his cow Gauri in. Kaveri asked him to come with her to the back of the garden. Venu's eyes lit up when he saw Putta, who greeted him exuberantly – as indeed he seemed to greet everyone new that he met. Venu laughed as he squatted down to pet the dog, receiving a face-full of wet and slobbery licks.

'I didn't know you had a pet dog now, Kaveri *akka*.'

'It is only temporary, until we can find a better home for him,' Kaveri said. 'You know my mother-in-law would never allow it.' She watched the pup's antics as he pranced around the boy. 'Venu, would you be able to take him for a walk every day? Once you are done with your milk rounds? I will pay you for it.' She held up a hand as the boy started to protest that he could not take money from her. 'You have to accept the money, otherwise I will not let you walk the dog. Besides, you need money for a new roof, remember?'

Venu gave her a lopsided grin. '*Akka*, you know it is impossible to argue with you. You always win. I will go home now, and leave Gauri at home, then come back to take Putta for a walk.'

After seeing Venu and Putta to the gate, Kaveri went to her shed. She picked up her mathematics book then set it aside, feeling too restless for maths. What she needed was exercise, but the swimming pool at the Century Club was closed for cleaning, so she had been unable to go there for a morning swim.

The straw mat in the corner caught her eye, and an idea began to form. She picked it up and unrolled it on the floor. She stood for a moment and took a deep breath before launching into her *kalaripayattu* exercises. She needed to let out the excess energy surging in her body because of the forced inactivity.

When she had gone to Mysore to study for her mathematics exams, she had pressed her father to enrol her in classes to learn the ancient martial art that an elderly Malayali woman had been running a few streets away. Kaveri smiled as she thought of the acerbic seventy-year-old teacher who taught the group of young women, most of them teenagers. Her mother had objected as usual, arguing that it was not appropriate for a married woman to go to self-defence classes – what would people say? But even she could not say anything further when Kaveri had told her that Ramu approved of it. Kaveri's encounter with a murderer a few months back had alarmed Ramu so much that he had wanted Kaveri to learn some self-defence.

She moved into a series of jumps to warm up her cramped body before dipping into a crouch. As she hummed the tune her teacher had taught her to keep pace with the rhythmic movements, she launched into a set of carefully planned stretching exercises, then into a series of vigorous kicks that were meant to take an opponent down with a swift blow to the head. It felt so good to stretch her body.

As she moved around the room, Kaveri heard a slow rat-tat-tat on the door that gradually grew louder. Wrapping her sari more securely around her waist, she moved to the door, opening it and looking out cautiously.

'*Athe?* When did you get home?'

Bhargavi held a finger to her lips, beckoning Kaveri out of the study. 'Shanthi's chauffeur brought me home. But shh . . . let's not speak here.' She pointed to the gardener who was working in the gardens in the house next door, deadheading the rose bushes with a large pair of clippers. The women moved into the main house.

Kaveri rubbed the red oxide floor with a slightly grimy toe, noticing how black her feet had become as a result of her jumps and kicks on the mud floor. She earned a disapproving look from Bhargavi. 'I'll go wash my feet,' she said hastily. But Bhargavi shook her head, placing a hand on Kaveri's arm.

'Shanthi wants to speak to you now. She asked me to bring you to her home.'

Kaveri looked at her eagerly. 'Is she able to speak comfortably about the murder? There are a number of questions I must ask.'

'How long can she lie in the room and cry?' Bhargavi said, the dark shadows under her eyes betraying the strain of the past few days. 'Life must move on. There are urgent matters to attend to in the factory, and bills to be paid. It is close to pay day, and the workers must get their salaries so that their children can be fed. All of this cannot stop because of one woman's loss, no matter how severe it is.'

Before seeing Bhargavi, Kaveri had planned to tell her mother-in-law about her suspicions of Shanthi. But looking at the tired woman in front of her, she refrained. 'I cannot even imagine how difficult it would be to pull oneself out of a situation like Shanthi's,' she said instead.

Bhargavi seemed to have shrunk a little in the past few days. 'It has been a difficult time for me too,' Bhargavi said, holding onto the table beside her as if she required it for support. 'It brings back difficult memories. When my husband died . . . '

Kaveri knew from Ramu that his mother had been distraught. She had locked herself in her room when she heard her husband had died, refusing to come out for hours. Ramu had taken his father's body to the cremation grounds, and Rajamma had begged and pleaded with her outside the door to open it and eat something. And yet, Bhargavi had gone unhesitatingly to her cousin's side when she had needed her help. Kaveri had to admire her spirit.

'What can I do to help?' Kaveri moved forward, impulsively taking Bhargavi's hand in hers and gripping it tightly.

Bhargavi looked a trifle startled. Then she smiled tentatively at Kaveri, gripping her hand tightly with a calloused palm.

'Come with me. Ask questions. Speak to everyone: Shanthi, her stepdaughter Chitra, Chitra's fiancé Kumar. Someone must know something. We have to find out who the murderer was. We cannot let them get away with it.' She gripped Kaveri's hand even more tightly as she spoke.

'I will do whatever I can,' Kaveri promised.

'Not only what you can. You must go beyond it, Kaveri. Promise me you will find out who killed Mr Sharma. And avenge my cousin.'

How could she promise, Kaveri wondered? She was no magician, to be able to pull criminals out of a hat. And what if Shanthi was the murderer? She could not shield her then. All Kaveri could do was to try her best to reveal the truth, whatever that was. But as she opened her mouth to clarify her position, she caught Bhargavi's expectant gaze. This was not the right time to tell her of her suspicions about Shanthi. Perhaps it would turn out to be someone else.

She stayed silent, crossing her fingers behind her back, but Bhargavi seemed to have taken her silence as assent. Her mother-in-law leaned forward and pulled Kaveri into an impulsive embrace, whispering in her ear, 'I have complete confidence in you. Only you can find out the murderer.' Then she wrinkled her nose, looking at Kaveri more closely. 'What have you been doing to yourself? You are bathed in sweat.'

Kaveri looked down at her sweat-soaked sari and grimaced. She hurried upstairs to change, reflecting that Bhargavi certainly did not make it easy for them to build a closer relationship. She was beginning to understand her mother-in-law better, though. Under that critical, disapproving veneer, she hid a kind heart, and a keen desire to help where she could.

After cleaning up and changing into a sombre sari in elephant grey with a thin checked border in silver brocade, Kaveri rushed back downstairs, suddenly remembering Putta. She made a mental note to ask the women's club members if anyone knew someone who was willing to take in a large, friendly, exuberant puppy with a unique appearance to match his personality. Bhargavi would throw a fit if Venu returned before they left and she found out they now had a dog in their garden – however temporarily.

Thankfully, there was no sign of Venu and Putta yet.

When Kaveri returned, Bhargavi was sitting on the drawing room sofa, leaning back with her eyes closed. She started when Kaveri touched her gently. Kaveri kept a supporting arm around the older woman as she led her to the car, reflecting on their changing relationship. Despite her occasional complaints, the time of adversity seemed to have made Bhargavi less critical of Kaveri, and more dependent on her.

They kept up a desultory conversation as Kaveri drove. 'What about the death rituals, *Athe*?' Kaveri asked as she drove. 'Mr Sharma has no sons. Does he have any other male relatives who will perform these for him?'

Bhargavi gave her an astonished look. 'Did you not know? Mr Sharma was an atheist.'

'Really? The newspapers made no mention of it.'

'Didn't they? Shanthi must have kept the news from filtering outside. If people got to know, they would have pointed fingers at her, saying, 'What kind of wife is she? Could not even arrange a proper set of rituals for her husband.' But he left clear, written instructions in a letter for her. He had a weak heart, and was worried he might suffer an attack at any time, so they had also spoken about what he wanted. His body was cremated the next morning, and they took the ashes to the Cauvery River that evening. I went with her. Beyond that, he did not want any rituals to be performed. He did not believe in temples, priests or any of our Hindu customs.' Bhargavi clicked her tongue ruefully. 'I don't know how Shanthi managed to live with a man like that. But she can also be strange at times.'

Strange in what way? Kaveri glanced across at her, wanting to ask more, but they had already reached the Sharma home. They were greeted by a watchman wearing white livery edged with gold zari, a white turban on his head. He hurried towards their car, carrying a large black umbrella which he held over Bhargavi's head, shielding her from the sun overhead. As Kaveri stepped out of the driver's seat, he started, obviously fascinated to see a woman driving. Kaveri smiled inwardly. She was getting used to this now, but it still gave her a little charge of satisfaction.

The house was more like a palace than a home, Kaveri thought, blinking a little at the size of the massive wrought-iron gate as they neared it. Although she had brought Shanthi home on the night of the murder, she had not looked at the house clearly then. It had been dark, and she had been preoccupied with the task of bringing Shanthi back home safely. Now, she studied the exterior wall clearly, curious about why a private house would need such large gates. They seemed more appropriate for a fortress, lined with sharp pointed spears at the top. The walls were white, and equally forbidding, with brown glass shards from broken bottles embedded along the top. Any thief who tried to climb over *these* walls would have quite some trouble.

Kaveri sucked in her breath at the sight of a figure of Garuda at the centre of these gates. She placed her hand on the gate, studying the figure closely. This Garuda was similar in shape and appearance to the one she had seen on the gates of the Sampangi Mills on the night of the murder, though smaller. She heard a series of deep, threatening barks and moved back from the gate hastily. Guard dogs? The watchman hastily closed the umbrella and moved past her, saying in an urgent tone, 'Wait, madam, let me open the gate.'

'What are these? They don't look like any dogs I have seen before.' Kaveri looked at the tall dogs with their muscular, powerful shoulders that contrasted oddly with the flabby skin that hung in loose pouches from their face, making them looking like mournful *garadi ustaads*, local wrestlers who had lost a bout.

'Alangu mastiffs.' Kaveri looked up to see Shanthi standing at the door. 'Some say this breed of dog was a favourite of Xerxes the first, who took an army of Indian soldiers all the way to Greece in the fifth century BC. My husband went all the way to the temple town of Thanjavur to bring these two, when they were tiny pups, as a wedding gift for me. He was a big dog lover who wanted to preserve Indian breeds. That's why he sponsored the prizes for best native dog every year at the animal show.' Her voice was wistful.

Kaveri studied Shanthi closely. She was wearing a simple white cotton sari, with a small gold chain and minimal jewellery. She had lost some weight, but held herself tall and straight. She moved towards Kaveri and Bhargavi, holding out her hands.

Bhargavi flinched when the dogs got closer, and Shanthi shook her head. 'You must stop being so scared of them.' She patted Kaveri's arm and gave her a reassuring smile. 'These dogs are big babies really. They only go after you if they haven't been properly introduced.'

How do you get properly introduced to a dog? Before Kaveri had too much time to think about this, she was inside the gate looking at two of the largest dogs she had ever seen in her life. Shanthi moved towards them as they surged forward, holding out her hands and laughing as they put their paws on her shoulders and tried to lick her face. She turned to Kaveri and beckoned her forward, keeping an arm around her waist and holding her close.

'Friend!' Shanthi told the dogs, then amended it. 'Family.' She took Kaveri's palm in hers and placed it in front of the dogs.

'Let them sniff you.'

The dogs sniffed her hands and wagged their tails, licking her hands as Kaveri patted them. Then the watchman took them away, tugging on their leashes to lead them towards the back of the house.

'Come in, Kaveri.' Shanthi held open the heavy teak front door, carved with a frieze of parrots, and they entered a long corridor lined with marble and more teak. The house looked even more grand on the inside. Mr Sharma must have been a very wealthy man indeed and now Shanthi was a half-owner at least of all of this. It had taken Kaveri quite some time to feel at ease in Ramu's house, which was so much larger than anything she had ever seen. But this – it was like a small palace and made Ramu's home seem like a toy house.

Shanthi had done a good job, though. Or was it Chitra who had decorated it? After all, Chitra had run the home for years before Shanthi had come into their lives. A house this size could easily have felt like a museum – or a mausoleum – with all the marble, rosewood and teak. All cold, dark colours. But the vibrant rugs, gently glowing brass and bronze pots, richly hued paintings and soft cushions on colourful diwans made the massive living room that they entered look cosy and inviting, despite its size. Kaveri's eyes lit up as she saw the bookshelves lining the wall.

Bhargavi poked Shanthi in the shoulder. 'Didn't I tell you? The girl would have stars in her eyes when she saw the number of books you have.'

Kaveri let her eyes wander up the tallest bookshelf – then stopped. Above it, in a larger-than-life frame, was a massive portrait of Swami Vaninanda, whom Bhargavi was so enamoured of. The Swami's magnetic eyes seemed to fasten on Kaveri's face, boring into her innermost thoughts. She stepped back with a jerk, noting the garland of sandalwood flowers that hung around the portrait, and the tall pair of lit silver lamps on top of the bookshelf, paying homage to the man.

As Ramu had told his mother, such godmen were often in need of money, always on the lookout for gullible wealthy men and women to bring into their fold. Shanthi had seemed like a sensible woman to her though – how had she become a devotee? Mr Sharma was an atheist – had he not objected to having such a large portrait of Swami Vaninanda in his home? Kaveri thought of the Garuda symbol on the tall post that the Swami's hairy assistant had held up at the Dewan's hall on the morning of the animal show, and the large Garuda locket, set in rubies, that the Swami wore on a chain around his neck. *Why was it here too?*

They sat down on the large teak three-seater sofa, while Bhargavi sat opposite them in a matching two-seater upholstered in flowered green velvet. Kaveri thought again of how elegant and somehow formidable Shanthi seemed. Even in her simple cotton sari, with the lightest of jewellery, she looked like a queen. After hearing from Ismail that Shanthi benefited the most from Mr Sharma's death, Kaveri wanted to tread carefully. She needed to get information from Shanthi without alerting her to her suspicions.

Kaveri looked at Bhargavi, who was leaning forward, mouth slightly open.

'Who do you think murdered your husband?' Kaveri winced. That had come out more bluntly than she wanted.

'Kaveri!' Bhargavi all but shrieked at her, getting up in her agitation and coming to stand right in front of her. 'How can you ask her a question like that? And in that tone of voice?'

Kaveri looked sideways at Shanthi. How could she proceed on this case if her mother-in-law planned to hover nearby, checking her at every turn? But before she could say anything, Shanthi spoke up.

'Bhargavi *akka* – let the girl speak. To get the right answers, she has to ask questions.'

When Bhargavi began to protest again, Shanthi cut her short. She got up, taking the older woman by the elbow and steering her into the hall. Kaveri strained to hear their conversation. The breeze from the open window blew, and she heard snatches of their exchange.

' . . . go to your room and rest. You look quite fatigued. I will be fine . . . ' Shanthi was saying in a firm voice.

Bhargavi seemed to be arguing with her but eventually relented. She cast an anxious look over at Kaveri, calling her over.

'Take care. Shanthi looks like she is very strong, but she is very sensitive. She has just been through a big loss. Ask her questions gently, otherwise she might break down.'

Kaveri reflected that she had never seen a woman more composed or less likely to break down. Bhargavi had told her that Shanthi was very fragile on multiple occasions. To Kaveri though, Shanthi seemed in perfect control of herself, almost unnaturally so considering the horrific experience she had recently gone through. Still, she would keep Bhargavi's words in mind. If her mother-in-law would only leave soon.

When Bhargavi had left, Kaveri turned back to Shanthi. Hiding a sigh of relief, she started again.

'Who do you think murdered your husband?' The question came out softly this time. She paused when she saw Chitra come out of a side door into the living room.

Upon hearing Kaveri's question, Chitra hesitated, her hands shaking. Then she began to sway, her legs crumpling under her.

17

A Probing Conversation

Kaveri saw the watchman rush back into the room and beeline straight to Chitra, catching her just before she fell, then carry her to the diwan bed in the corner. *Was that a real faint?* Something about it seemed off to Kaveri, like milk gone sour. Perhaps it was the fact that Chitra seemed to have waited until the watchman came close enough to catch her before she had actually collapsed.

Kaveri caught a glimpse of Shanthi's face in the mirror, glaring at Chitra with a look of intense annoyance on her face. When she realised that Kaveri was looking at her, she hastily smoothed her features into an expressionless mask. The dynamic between these two women was very peculiar. She remembered how Chitra had followed Shanthi around silently at the dog show, with Shanthi appearing to control her every move. Even now, she did not appear alarmed that her stepdaughter had fainted.

'Give Chitra time. She will come around,' Shanthi said. Kaveri thought she saw Chitra's hand moving slightly. She looked at her face, but Chitra's eyes were closed, her expression slack and blank. Something about the way in which the young woman lay, her body seeming tense and alert rather than limp and flaccid, made Kaveri doubt that she was unconscious.

The relationships in this family did not add up neatly like a well-balanced equation. There were components missing on either side, and when that was the case, it was impossible to solve a problem – mathematical or otherwise. How could she track down the missing pieces?

As Kaveri got up to walk towards Chitra, she caught sight of the portrait again. Something about it reminded her of the unsettling trick that Raja Ravi Verma, the famous Indian prince well-known for his art, had used to such good effect in several paintings. The Swami's hypnotic gaze followed you, whichever part of the room you were in.

The fragrance of sandalwood filled the air as the lighted lamps below the portrait gently heated the air around the garland made with shavings of sandal bark that hung on the portrait. The scent tickled Kaveri's nose and teased her memory.

Sitting down next to Shanthi, she opened her purse to retrieve the small leather diary and gold-plated ink pen Ramu had given to her as a birthday gift a few weeks back. As she did, she breathed deeply, recovering her balance. *You are a detective*, she thought silently. *Act like one!*

'Now tell me,' she said.

'Tell you what?' Shanthi asked.

'Anything that may be important.' Kaveri looked at her expectantly. 'Tell me more about the embezzlement.' She caught Swami Vaninanda's eyes in the portrait and looked away hastily. As she glanced away from the painting, she caught a glimpse of Chitra in another mirror – was this room full of them? Chitra's body was still, but her eyes were wide open. So she had been right! Chitra's faint had been a ruse. Her eyes were watching them intently.

'I don't know what else to tell you,' Shanthi said, a desperate tinge moving into her voice. 'I told you everything I knew that day we first met. Someone has been embezzling money.'

'How do you know?' Kaveri interrupted.

'The account books. There is a master set of accounts, which my husband keeps in his office.' Shanthi closed her eyes briefly and swallowed. 'Kept, I should say.'

She continued. Kaveri sneaked a peek into the mirror and saw that Chitra was still watching them closely.

'My husband goes – I mean, he *went* – over the accounts every week, to make sure everything was on track. For the past few months he had a niggling feeling that something was wrong, but he brushed it aside. But then, last week, he received a summons from the bank. The manager wanted to meet with him.'

'And?' Kaveri prompted.

'The manager wanted to ask if he required an overdraft. My husband was startled. He had a policy of never taking a loan. He was a man who had always played it safe. As per his accounts, he expected to have a large credit balance in his account. But the manager told him that the money was down to a few hundred rupees.'

'How is that possible? Did someone else withdraw money without his knowledge?'

Shanthi shook her head. 'No. The bank has clear instructions not to give anyone else money above one hundred rupees from his account. Not even myself or Chitra.'

Kaveri raised her eyebrows at this piece of information. It made Mr Sharma seem like a very controlling man!

Shanthi seemed to read her mind, hastening to explain. 'It was not that he did not trust us, but my husband was just a careful man. He knew that thieves often tend to think of women as easy targets, so he used to go to the bank himself. But in the past few years he has not been very well and he had slowly started to hand over some of his responsibilities, first to Chitra, then later on to Kumar. Of late, he had developed a back problem, and the road to the bank is in bad condition. He wanted to reduce the time he spent in the car on that bumpy road. So, about six months ago, he stopped going to the bank, instead sending Kumar to deposit the money. As best as we can make out, it was soon after that when the thefts seem to have started.'

Kaveri reached out for a glass of water, using the cover of her movement to sneak another quick glance into the mirror. Chitra was still watching them.

'How could the money have disappeared from the bank?' she asked.

'We think it was stolen from our safe, and never reached the bank,' Shanthi said. 'The money we get from our customers is packed into metal cash boxes and stored in the safe in the factory. Only four people had access to the door to my husband's office, and to the combination lock to the safe: my husband, myself, Chitra and Kumar.'

Shanthi continued, 'The money was placed in money boxes by my husband once a week. He sealed the boxes, placing them in the safe and locking them, and writing the amount in a ledger. Kumar took the boxes and the ledger and went to the bank the next day.'

Kaveri was still puzzled. 'But didn't the bank count the money?'

'Yes. Kumar swears that the bank manager counted the money, and it matched with the amount written into the ledger. The bank manager also signed next to the ledger entry, certifying that the money was safely received and had been deposited. But when we later looked at the bank account, it did not match the amounts that my husband knew we had received and placed into the boxes.'

'So, either the bank manager was lying . . . ' Kaveri said.

'No, that is not possible. He counted it in his office, after inviting two assistant managers in with him. Kumar watched him the whole time, and verified it, also checking it against the number written in the ledger. At that time, it matched. We couldn't make any sense of it.' Shanthi threw up her hands in frustration.

'In that case . . . ' Kaveri thought furiously. One of her heroes, the famous detective Sherlock Holmes, had a saying: When all other more likely possibilities have been exhausted, then the only possibility that remains, however improbable, must be the truth. 'After Mr Sharma put the money in the boxes and placed them in the safe, the thief must have opened the safe, taken out some of the money from the cash box, then reduced the amount written in the ledger to match the reduced amount in the box. That's why no one realised that the money was missing.'

Shanthi looked at her in admiration. 'You're right. When we looked carefully at the ledger, we saw that the amount in the ledger had been altered, so cleverly that no one would notice unless they studied it with care. Kumar says he looked at the ledger and compared the amount to the money in the cash box. And since it matched, he did not realise any money was missing.'

Kaveri stood up and began to pace up and down. 'Whoever the thief was, they seized the opportunity to start to take out money as soon as your husband stopped going to the bank to make the deposits himself. But the thief did not want to take out too much at first. That would arouse suspicion. Instead, they took out only as much as they dared. I presume it was enough to put the factory in a crisis?'

'Oh yes,' Shanthi agreed. 'They only took out about a fifth of the money. But twenty percent is more than our margin of profit, you see. When we place new orders, we have to pay our suppliers. With our profit gone, we had begun to take out more money than we put in.'

'But if this theory is correct, we come back to the same question,' Kaveri said. 'No one could have taken out the money. No one except for Kumar, Chitra, you or your husband.' She paused, then pressed forward. Now was the time to ask to meet Kumar. 'I want to meet your prospective son-in-law.'

Shanthi looked uncomfortable. 'This is not a good time for you to ask him questions. I don't want him to get the wrong idea, that we suspect him. With my husband gone, we are so dependent on Kumar to run the factory.'

'Why only on him?' Kaveri could not resist asking. 'Can't you ask Chitra to help you? She used to run the factory with her father, or so I have heard. She knows the inner workings well. Surely she could take over?'

Was it Kaveri's imagination, or did a dark look of anger pass across Shanthi's face? If so, it was only for a moment. Shanthi looked over to where Chitra lay, still prone and seemingly unconscious on the sofa.

She placed a finger on her lips and looked meaningfully at Kaveri. 'Let us not disturb her,' she said, raising her voice so it carried. 'I'll call in her maid. She can sit with Chitra while we move to my room. There we can talk more comfortably.'

They waited until the maid flounced in – a sulky-looking young woman with a decided scowl on her face, who sat down on the floor next to Chitra with an audible sniff.

Shanthi smiled apologetically at Kaveri as they went out. 'It is so difficult to find good maids these days. We have gone through a series of maids in the past few months. These young women are all the same. Annoyed when you ask them to do even the most basic of things.' She sighed. 'I had to speak to this girl quite sharply yesterday. Now she has threatened to give notice. I don't know what to do sometimes. There are so many little things that require my decisions.'

Shanthi looked at the girl sitting on the floor, then led the way to her sitting room – a small, comfortable nook decorated with floral wallpaper in a pastel yellow – and closed the door.

'I don't want anyone to hear us. Especially Chitra. Don't get fooled by her innocent appearance. She did not faint. She just wanted a way to eavesdrop on our conversation.' Shanthi rolled her eyes. 'She thinks I am a fool who does not know when she is play-acting.' She leaned forward and spoke in a low voice. 'I can't trust Chitra to run the factory because I think she is being manipulated by someone else. Chitra has taken a lover.'

Kaveri gaped at her. 'What do you mean?'

'What else could I mean?' Shanthi said wryly. 'Her father used to say that she has changed in behaviour completely in the past two years. Oh, I know she has never liked me. From the moment we met, she pegged me as a gold-digger, someone who had her claws into her father only for his money. I did not let that bother me and thought she would eventually come around. But in the past few months she has become even worse. Moody, irritable, spending hours locked up in her room alone. On many nights, she goes into her room at 6 p.m. with a glass of milk, refusing to come out even for dinner. I think she might be slipping out of the house to meet someone in secret.'

'I was the one who arranged her marriage,' Shanthi continued. 'Her father – he was a lovely man, God rest his soul – but he did not have any idea that he had a grown unmarried girl at home who required his attention.'

Kaveri looked at her. 'But why? You of all people should know . . . ' Her voice trailed off. There was no way she could say this politely. 'You stayed unmarried for so long. It does not automatically ruin a woman's life if she does not have a husband.'

Shanthi shrugged her shoulders impatiently. 'I had no choice. My mother needed me. But it was not easy, being a woman alone in a man's world once she died. I did not want Chitra to go through what I had gone through.'

Her dismissive tone irked Kaveri. She tried to bite her tongue, but then burst out, 'But did Chitra *want* to get married?'

Shanthi shook her head. 'Her father gave her a lot of freedom. He took her with him to the factory, involved her in decisions about what to pay the workers, whom to promote and whom to keep at the same level. He thought she could run the place by herself. But she was immature, and made a series of wrong decisions. Her father realised that she was taking the factory down a path that would only result in further problems, but she was still his daughter, and he adored her. He was unable to be firm with her. I realised she needed a partner who made better decisions, who could guide her with a strong hand. That is when I convinced my husband to encourage her to marry Kumar. It took time, but he saw the sense of this eventually. In fact, I think he took it even more seriously than I did.'

Kaveri could feel herself getting annoyed again. She had thought Shanthi a sensible, mature woman and yet here she was, pushing Chitra into an arranged marriage because of pure pragmatism, without a thought of her emotional needs. How *could* she? With some difficulty, Kaveri tried to compose herself, refraining from arguing – this was not the time to get pulled into a long drawn out discussion of women's rights.

'How did you force . . . I mean, convince her?' When

Shanthi looked blank, Kaveri elaborated. 'Convince her to get engaged?'

'We explained to her. Kumar was her father's right-hand man. He joined the factory four years ago, and steadily worked his way up from being a floor manager to helping her father with major decisions. He comes from a modest but respectable family. His father was a school teacher in a small government school who passed away when he was young. Kumar lived in a hostel, and studied on a scholarship – he has worked hard to move up in life. He is an ideal choice for her. Marrying Kumar meant that she could continue to help in the factory, but be guided by his influence.'

'Or guide him with her influence,' Kaveri could not resist saying. But Shanthi did not appear to have heard her as she caught Kaveri by the arm with a surprisingly strong grip.

'I want you to do something for me.' She looked at Kaveri appraisingly. 'You are about the same age as Chitra, I want you to make friends with her. Get her to trust you, to confide in you. You can find out if she has a lover who has manipulated her into giving him the key to her father's office and the password to the safe. Then come back and tell me. We can go together to that large policeman who helped you in the previous case – what was his name again? Ismail? We can ask Inspector Ismail to make sure that Chitra's lover goes to jail and to keep her name out of it. Once she is married to Kumar, it will be all right. I am sure of it.'

Kaveri shook her head firmly. 'I cannot do that. It would go against my *dharma* – my principles as a detective.'

Shanthi gave her a hard look. 'This is a matter of murder. My husband's murder. What principles are you talking of? I am only asking you to spend time with Chitra. Bring her to your side.'

'Bhargavi *akka* said you are an avid reader. Do you have a membership at the Seshadri Iyer Memorial Library?' At Kaveri's reluctant nod, she said briskly, 'That's settled, then. Chitra reads a lot of books too. She goes to the library thrice a week. Tomorrow, when Chitra goes to the library, you go there too. You can meet her there as if by accident. Remember, she should not know that I sent you. If you spend some time together, you can become friends with her.'

Kaveri looked Shanthi in the eyes. 'I will speak to Chitra. But I cannot promise you that I will tell you everything she says. Only if there is something relevant to the murder.'

Shanthi looked at Kaveri with a pitying smile on her lips. 'Oh, my dear. Please remember to not be fooled by Chitra. She is an excellent actress, who can fool anyone. She certainly fooled my husband. And her fiancé, Kumar, who loves her dearly. Only I know her *true* character.'

Shanthi drained the glass of water that she still held in her hands, putting it back onto the table with a thump. 'Oh, what I do know is that Chitra loved her father and would not have tried to harm him on her own. If she was involved, it is because she has a lover, because she is being controlled by an outside influence. But me? Now, that's a very different story.' Shanthi shuddered. 'Chitra truly hates me. I fear she may even welcome my death with delight.'

18

A Good Maid Knows Her Employer's Secrets

Shanthi looked weary after her outburst, placing her hand on her forehead. 'I have a headache and I need to lie down. Can you find your way out?'

As Kaveri walked out of Shanthi's sitting room, a small figure came limping into the corridor. 'Here,' the voice said in a soft whisper, beckoning her urgently. 'Come here.'

Chitra seemed to have given up all pretence of fainting, thought Kaveri, following her as she moved swiftly through the house. Chitra did not say a word, but looked back every few feet to make sure that Kaveri was still following, favouring her right leg as she walked. Silently leading the way, she took Kaveri through a number of long corridors that turned and twisted, moving deeper into the house. Why did three people need such a large place?

They stopped outside a large wooden door near the end of a corridor, wider than the others they had been through. Chitra opened the door, and they stepped through.

'This is my set of rooms,' she announced, looking up at Kaveri. Kaveri blinked. It was not the voice she expected from the mousy, silent and subdued woman she had first seen at the function for Swami Vaninanda. Her voice was clear and musical, soft but well enunciated. Not at all submissive. Neither was the young woman before her; it was as though her whole demeanour had changed. She had extraordinary eyes – large, open, with light brown pupils. Her skin was fair, and her hair was a brownish black colour. It was the first time she had gotten a good look at Chitra, Kaveri realised. On the occasions she had seen Chitra before, the younger woman had bent her head and retreated to the shadows.

Chitra watched her calculatingly before asking her to sit down. Kaveri looked around the small sitting room, upholstered in floral wallpaper much like Shanthi's. The walls were lined with open bookcases. But Kaveri could not see what books, if any, were inside, as the cases were covered with curtains made of cloth. Curious. Was that to keep the dust out? Or to prevent people from seeing what she was reading?

'We don't have much time before my stepmother comes out and I don't want her to know we have spoken.' Chitra was still eyeing Kaveri intently. 'I hear you are a famous detective. I want to hire you.'

Kaveri could not mask a start of surprise. 'Hire me?' That had come out louder than she'd wanted. 'What do you want to hire me for?'

'Isn't that obvious? I want to hire you to find out who killed my father,' Chitra said fiercely. 'But we cannot talk here, my stepmother has spies everywhere. The watchman, the driver, the cook – everyone eavesdrops on my conversations.' She looked at the door. 'I go to the Seshadri Memorial Library in the mornings, to pick up a book or magazine. Let's meet there tomorrow, at eight. It is usually empty so early in the morning, and we can speak freely in the gardens behind the library.'

With a sudden jerk, Chitra pulled a gold bangle off her wrist, placing it in Kaveri's palm. 'Will you take this as an advance? If you find proof that my stepmother killed my father, I can appeal my father's will and inherit his entire estate. I will then give you more money. Lots of it.'

Kaveri placed the bangle back in Chitra's hand, shaking her head. 'I do not do this for money. I do it for justice. No one hires me, I work to uncover the truth. I cannot work *for* you, just as I also refused to work for your stepmother. But I will work for your father. To help bring his murderer to justice.'

Chitra opened her mouth to speak, but hearing a sound from the corridor outside, she tensed. She opened the door of her sitting room, looking out to the left and right before coming back in and grabbing Kaveri by the arm.

'You must go,' she said, almost pushing Kaveri into the corridor. 'I don't want anyone to know I was speaking to you alone. Anyone could be eavesdropping on us. Go now. Let's meet tomorrow.'

Kaveri walked down the corridor, trying to figure out the way back to the entrance. This was a peculiar pickle in which she had found herself. Even though she had told both Shanthi and Chitra that she was not working for them, she suspected each now thought of her as their own personal detective.

Her head whirling with thoughts, she stumbled out of the door, relieved to finally find the exit. She badly wanted to see Ramu. As she walked to her car, she decided to drive straight to the hospital.

Luck was on her side. As she drove into the hospital gate, she saw Ramu exiting the main door, briefcase in hand. When he caught sight of the Ford, he hurried to meet Kaveri, a smile on his face.

'I was just thinking of you!' He looked at his watch. 'It's only 6 p.m., and I've had a long day. Let's not go home just yet. How about we go to the Albert bakery?' He looked carefully at Kaveri. 'You look tired. Shall I drive?'

Kaveri handed over the keys to Ramu, her tiredness receding at the thought of spending an evening out with her husband.

They parked near a stately red building, and walked down a narrow tree-lined lane in Fraser Town to reach the bakery. The elderly proprietor, Mr Mohammad Suleman, was taking a hot tray of mutton puffs out of the oven as they arrived. They sat on one of the small benches on the footpath, chatting with him as he brought out a vegetarian selection for them. Ramu devoured two plates of potato buns and hot cross buns, while Kaveri tucked into a delicious khova naan, enjoying the taste of the soft creamy cottage cheese wrapped in crisp filo pastry.

After tea, Ramu turned the car towards Kempambudhi, their favourite lake, navigating carefully down a road packed with bullock carts, horse carts, and cars full of people returning home after a long day's work. The sun was setting, and a swarm of bats flew over their heads, hanging upside down in the hundreds on a large fig tree. Ramu parked near the lake, and Kaveri brought him up to date on her conversations with Shanthi and Chitra.

'I am afraid for Bhargavi *athe*,' Kaveri said. 'I don't like the fact that she is spending so much time at Shanthi's house. What if Shanthi or Chitra turns out to be the murderer?' As they walked around the lake, she described to Ramu how dismissively Shanthi spoke of Chitra, and told him of Chitra's fake fainting fit. 'But I especially disliked how Shanthi seemed to be pushing Chitra into a marriage that Chitra doesn't want.'

'Shanthi may have her reasons, Kaveri. Perhaps Chitra is

a very difficult young woman, and Shanthi is trying to handle the relationship the only way she can, by getting her out of her house?'

'I don't *want* it to be Shanthi. Bhargavi *athe* would be devastated if it was her.' Kaveri punched her fist lightly against a tree trunk for emphasis. 'But I do not see how *athe* can be fond of such a woman. She is so cold! You should have seen the look on her face when she said that Chitra needed a husband who can keep her in her place. Imagine the plight of that poor girl. Educated by her father to take over the factory, and then suddenly this . . . this *interloper* of a stepmother comes in and everything changes for her. Of course the poor girl hates her. I almost hate her myself!'

Ramu drew Kaveri's arm through his more tightly, patting her hand as she glared at the tree. 'Let's not jump too quickly to judgement, Kaveri. We don't know the full story, and probably never will. Let's speak of something else. Ismail came by to the hospital to meet me. He wanted to tell me that the fingerprint report from your note came back.' Ramu intercepted Kaveri's eager glance with a shake of his head. 'There were no fingerprints on the note. Whoever typed it out was careful to wear gloves. Ismail also found a typewriter in the Sharma house, stored in their garage, but the note you received was not typed on that machine. The "a" in that typewriter was perfectly aligned.'

Kaveri took out her notebook, writing this down. 'Either someone else was involved in typing that note, or it was Shanthi or Chitra, but they used a different typewriter to remove suspicion from themselves.'

'Let me play devil's advocate. If Shanthi killed her husband,' Ramu said, ignoring the curious glances that passers-by directed at them as they saw a man and woman holding hands in public, 'then why would she ask you to come at 9 p.m., then send you a typewritten note changing the time to 8 p.m.?'

'Because she wanted to trap me?' Kaveri said doubtfully.

'That is possible,' Ramu agreed. 'But the same could hold true for Chitra. What if it was her?'

Kaveri shook her head. 'Ismail and I heard the person who shot Mr Sharma fleeing. That person jumped down from the wall of the factory, which is quite high, then ran down the road. Chitra has a leg injury, remember? She walks with a limp.'

'She could be faking the limp,' Ramu said.

'I thought of that. But Shanthi told me that she had injured her ankle some weeks back, well before her father's murder. I don't think she would have planned the murder so far in advance as to create an alibi of a leg injury.'

She let out an irritated huff, smacking her forehead. 'What an idiot I am. I forgot to ask Shanthi the most important question. I wanted to ask her about the newspaper reports I read about the mill workers going on strike. That could be another angle to look at for the murder.'

'You can ask Chitra when you meet her tomorrow,' Ramu pointed out.

Kaveri let out a deep sigh. 'There's no point in talking about this any more. My mind feels like it's going around in circles. I wish I had a straightforward mathematics problem to solve instead of this complex knot of a puzzle.'

'You need a break, Kaveri. Let us talk of something else.' Ramu changed the topic, telling her about Anandi as he turned her back in the direction of the car. They stopped near a vendor who was roasting peanuts in their shells on a pan filled with hot sand and lit coals. Ramu saw a couple of children looking hungrily at the vendor. Handing the vendor some coins from his wallet, he beckoned them closer. The man twisted an old newspaper into a paper cone and filled it with roasted peanuts for the boys.

'Is Anandi better?' Kaveri turned to Ramu eagerly.

'Physically, she is healing well. She is able to move around without pain now, and her bruises have almost faded. The cut on her lip has healed. You would not be able to recognise her now. A few days of peace and cosseting by Narsamma and Mala have worked wonders on her. But her mental wounds will take longer to heal.' Ramu took Kaveri's hand in his as he continued. 'And her husband Pawan is looking for her. He vows he will kill her next time. Anandi is terrified that Pawan will find her if she stays with Mala much longer.'

'Can't the police do something?' Kaveri asked.

Ramu shook his head. 'I spoke to Ismail. They took Pawan in, and kept him for a night in lock-up, threatening to throw him in jail unless he stays away from his wife. But they had to release him the next day, since they had nothing to hold him on. They asked if Anandi would testify against him, so they could jail him for a longer duration. But she is too scared to agree. Even if he is jailed, it would only be for a short time, and then she fears he would come for her. If he kills her, he can easily hide the body by throwing it into one of the nearby lakes, or taking it to one of the forest areas.'

Kaveri thought of the pit in the Thalli forest area, south of Bangalore, where Venu told her the bodies of the rats had been taken and buried. A young woman like Anandi, who should be living the best years of her life, at the mercy of a thug like Pawan? It did not bear contemplation.

'Mala is at her wits' end, Kaveri. She will not be able to keep her hidden for long in their neighbourhood, full of small houses, where everyone knows each other's business. She was asking if you or I knew anyone in a different city who required a live-in maid. Somewhere Pawan would be unlikely to find her.'

As soon as Ramu parked the car, Kaveri ran into her shed, emerging with the pad in which she had noted down the suspects and motives.

'I have it,' she announced, brandishing the pad at him as she bounced up and down on her toes.

Ramu smiled at her, his face filled with affection. He adored the happy jig that Kaveri did whenever she felt particularly triumphant.

'What do you have?' he teased gently.

'I showed you my suspects list before, do you remember? To identify the true killer, I need to understand them better, to assess their motivations – whether by greed, love, or revenge. Neither Shanthi nor Chitra is easy to read. What we want is an insider's perspective.'

Kaveri's hands flew in the air as she gestured in excitement. 'Shanthi was complaining to me that they do not have a good maid. We can send Anandi there to ask for a job. If she is inside the house, then she can also hear what is going on, and report it to me. Their home is in Chamarajapete, far from her old home. Pawan will never find her there.' Kaveri stifled a laugh. 'A good maid knows everything about her employers. They hear it all – the fights, the friendship, nothing is private from them. The tales that Rajamma could tell about our home, if she wanted to. She knows all my secrets, even – no, especially – those I want to hide from Bhargavi *athe*. Such as when I have my period, and want to keep it from her because she will insist that I follow all those bothersome traditions of ritual purity, and stay outside of the main house, sitting in the veranda.'

'I'm not sure that it is a good idea for Anandi to get into such a dangerous situation, Kaveri. What if we are placing her at risk?' Ramu's forehead was creased with deep lines.

Kaveri shook her head. 'Anandi will be safer in Shanthi's house than she is with Mala. We will ask Venu to keep a close eye on her, and tell Anandi to visit us as often as she can so we can keep an eye on her. If we feel she is in danger at any time, we can extricate her quickly.'

Ramu looked unconvinced, but did not press her further. 'Will you take Anandi with you tomorrow and introduce her to Chitra then? Or ask my mother to introduce her to Shanthi?'

Kaveri shook her head at him. 'Of course not. We can't let Shanthi and Chitra know that I have sent Anandi to their home, they would never open up around her. Your mother will never be able to keep this matter secret either. No, we have to make sure that no one else knows there is any connection between her and me.'

'A large and wealthy house like the Sharma home won't hire a maid without a reference. She can't just turn up at their doorstep and offer her services.'

Kaveri thought for a moment, then snapped her fingers. 'I know! We'll get help from Mrs Reddy. She can drop into Shanthi's home on the pretext of paying a condolence visit. Once there, it will be a simple matter to shift the conversation around to domestic issues, and then bring up the difficulty of getting good maids these days.'

She opened the door and led the way inside their home, carrying her precious list of suspects in her hand. 'I will call Mrs Reddy now and fix it up for tomorrow.'

'And I'll send a note to Mala, asking her to tell Anandi to be ready,' Ramu agreed. They stopped on the steps, smiling to each other when they heard a series of excited barks from the garden. Putta must have heard their voices and was calling out to them. They changed direction, running down the steps and hurrying around to the back to see him. Things were looking up!

19

The Flutter of a Feather

The night was muggy and sweaty, and Kaveri kept the windows open and drew the curtains aside, hoping to cool the room down. She slipped into an uneasy slumber, snoring lightly.

In her dreams, she and Ramu were at a Yakshagana theatre performance. The artists, wearing grotesque, magnificent painted masks, began a complicated dance. Mr Sharma crouched in a corner, his hands held up in supplication as Shanthi, Chitra and Kumar circled him steadily. The rhythm of the music grew faster and faster, as the dancers whirled around him, raising pistols high in the air. When a shot rang out, Kaveri sat up with a scream. Ramu pulled her into his arms, patting her back to sleep as she lay curled in his arms.

The rain continued steadily until 8 a.m. Kaveri dressed carefully, selecting one of Ramu's favourite saris – pale yellow with a border of green parrots. Ramu poked his head into the bedroom through the open door. Seeing his wife looking at the sari blouses neatly arranged on wooden hangers, he said, 'I hope you're planning to wear one of your fetching sleeveless blouses.'

Soon after, she heard his brisk footsteps as he hurried downstairs. Bhargavi had gone to Shanthi's house again that morning, and Kaveri fretted about that as she got ready.

In one of those mercurial changes of weather that Bangalore was famous for, the sun was now out amongst the clouds, making the wet mud steam. With the sun shining steadily down on them, Kaveri navigated a number of muddy puddles dropping Ramu off at the hospital.

'Be careful.' Ramu hesitated, feeling oddly nervous about opening the door and stepping away from the car. 'I don't know why, but I am feeling very uneasy. If my mother wasn't involved, I would have asked you to drop the case.'

'Drop the case?!' Kaveri could not believe her ears. 'Why would you ask me to do that?'

Ramu touched his wife's hair gently. 'I cannot stop thinking of Mr Sharma. Married for just two years, and now – gone. Just like that. I could not bear it if something happened to you.'

'Nothing will happen to me,' Kaveri said, caressing his cheek with her hand. She looked around to check for curious eyes but no one was near, so she leaned forward and gave Ramu a small peck on his cheek. 'I will be careful. I promise.'

A crow landed on the bonnet of the Ford, shuffling its feet and cawing noisily at them for a moment before flying off.

Startled, Ramu let out a huff that was somewhere between a snort and a sob. 'Lucky I'm not a superstitious man. If I was, that black crow would have confirmed my feeling – that something bad is going to happen today.'

*

Kaveri thought of Ramu's anxious face as she drove along the road from the Bowring Hospital towards Cubbon Park, turning into the front gates and parking close to the library. Just as she reached the entrance she saw Chitra getting out of her car.

'Do you want to go inside?'

Chitra looked surprised. 'Oh, God, no. The librarian will not allow us to speak.' She cast a disconsolate glance at the rose garden. Although the sun was beating down hard on the grass, there were puddles of rain, and the benches were wet.

'Let's go inside, but head to the ladies' room. No one can overhear us there.'

They moved to the large, well-appointed women's rest area, where a pair of comfortable upholstered couches in pale chintz had been placed just inside the door, a short distance from the changing rooms.

Chitra looked around nervously and moved to the door, standing on the toes of her right leg and holding the door for support as she pulled the latch up. Kaveri studied her. *Was that leg injury real?* It seemed like it, she thought. Chitra consistently favoured her right leg and avoided putting too much weight on her left.

'Now we can talk,' Chitra said fiercely, sitting down on the sofa. 'I don't know what that witch told you—'

'Who?' Kaveri stared at her, moving back a little. Why had Chitra locked the door? Her heart began to race. Suddenly the room, which had seemed so spacious and inviting a few moments ago, seemed lonely and threatening.

'Who else? I'm talking about my step-monster.' Chitra gave a bitter laugh, chewing on her fingernail as she spoke. 'Why did she ever come into our lives? We were so happy without her, my father and I. My mother died so young, I don't remember her at all. My aunt, my mother's older sister, brought me up until I was 17, but then she took ill and passed away. It was my father whom I was closest to, though – he took on the roles of father and mother, supervising my studies, plaiting my hair, and taking me to his factory.

'When I was twenty-one, I started accompanying my father every day. He was getting tired. He had a heart condition that made it difficult for him to work longer hours, so I started to help him, taking charge of some of the operations, and supervising the men. I even introduced a number of new initiatives to save money and improve efficiency. It was all going so well, and then—' Chitra stabbed viciously at the chintz sofa with a ragged fingernail, '—two years ago, *she* came into our lives. And she ruined everything.'

As Chitra fell silent, Kaveri's breathing calmed. It didn't look like Chitra had locked the door with assault in mind, after all. She reached out to Chitra, placing her hand tentatively on her arm. 'Is she mean to you?'

Chitra clenched her hands into fists. 'She is worse than anything you could imagine. She convinced my father that his old-fashioned ways of managing the factory were better, and that I was too young to be left in charge of something so important. She convinced him that he had to train someone else as a second-in-command. He chose Kumar. Until then Kumar was just an assistant manager, but my father promoted him to his second-in-command. That was supposed to be *my* position. And then he fixed a marriage between me and him. It was all because of her!'

Chitra's voice rose higher. She stopped and panted for breath, trying to control herself. After a couple of seconds, she turned to Kaveri, gripping her hand tightly in both palms.

'I hear that you are a famous detective, that you have solved a number of murders. Can you help me? I think my stepmother killed my father. She married him for his money, separated him from me, plotted to get me married and out of the house, then killed him. Some money was missing from his bank accounts. She must have killed him to cover up the theft. I think . . . '

Chitra paused, looking at Kaveri. Her eyes glittered feverishly.

'I think she may even be having an affair with my fiancé, Kumar. The two of them must be in it together.'

How could that be? Kaveri thought. Kumar was so much younger than Shanthi.

'That is a strong accusation to make,' she said cautiously.

'They speak together frequently, deciding how the factory should be run, without taking my opinion into consideration. What was the reason she wanted Kumar and I to get married? She never does anything without a reason.' Chitra picked up her sari pallu, a wisp of blue silk delicately embroidered with forget-me-nots, and wrung it in her hands. 'No, Mrs Murthy, I know it is true. My stepmother is in cahoots with my fiancé. They have discussions without me and fall silent when I enter the room. This kind of closeness is not natural. I want you to investigate them both.'

Kaveri looked at Chitra. 'If there is proof, I will find it. But if there is no proof, I will not make something up.'

Chitra moved closer to Kaveri and threw her arms around her neck. 'Thank you.' Her face brightened. 'My father used to keep notes in a diary. I will try and find it. And I will get into my stepmother's room when she is out of it and look around – I'm sure there will be something there that can help you solve the case.'

Kaveri hesitated. 'There is one thing I have been wanting to ask. About the factory.'

'What is it? You can ask me anything,' Chitra said.

'I read in the newspapers about a previous incident of sabotage at a local mill, where an explosion destroyed a large stock of woollen blankets.'

'What does this have to do with my father's murder?' Chitra looked wary now, watching Kaveri carefully.

That seems to have hit a nerve, Kaveri thought.

'I wondered if Mr Sharma was killed by a disgruntled worker.'

'I don't think a worker could have got into my father's room,' Chitra said, her tone dismissive.

'But is there any reason for your workers to seek revenge on your father or family?'

She shook her head. 'We pay them well. Too well, in fact. We cosset them like children. Why would they have any cause to complain?'

Chitra avoided Kaveri's gaze, getting up and unlocking the door. The stiff lines of her back warned her against pushing that line of conversation further.

Why had Chitra suddenly clammed up? she wondered. Something about the questions Kaveri asked seemed to have made her uneasy.

The two women climbed down the steps of the library, Kaveri slowing her steps to match Chitra's fumbling gait as Chitra pulled out a handkerchief from her purse. The fragrance of sweet-scented sandalwood filled Kaveri's nostrils as she waved goodbye to Chitra and got into her car. A gust of wind brought with it a jet black crow's feather, landing on her windshield. Its iridescent fronds shimmered, catching the light as the feather swayed in the breeze, tapping gently on the window as if to get her attention.

'What is it? What do you want me to know?' Kaveri whispered to the feather.

The feather fluttered violently for a second against the glass, then rose up with the wind, disappearing into the dust and dirt on the side of the road.

20

Chit Chat and Coffee Pudi

Kaveri hopped out of the car and went straight across the back wall to Uma aunty's home. She hiked up her sari to her knees, climbing the neem tree that bordered the joint wall their homes shared at the back. She had done this so many times in the past few months that Uma aunty now kept a stool for her next to the wall so that she could climb down without getting her sari muddy.

'Uma aunty?' Kaveri navigated the tiny, well-kept kitchen garden, with its neat rows of chilli plants, lined with red ripening peppers, and opened the back door, calling out to her.

'Come in!'

Kaveri followed Uma's voice into the kitchen. Her grandson Raju was sitting in his usual spot, on a rug in the corner of the kitchen, banging away at a small pan with a spoon.

Uma aunty came towards Kaveri with a smile, holding out a plate of crisp mixture. The women settled down on the back steps, under the shade of the curry leaf tree, eating fried strips of curly dough mixed with peanuts as Kaveri filled her in on her discussions with Shanthi and Chitra. Raju lay curled in his grandmother's lap, sucking his thumb, slowly falling asleep.

'I can't understand this case. It is driving me mad,' Kaveri mumbled through a mouthful of spicy mixture.

'It is a dreadful thing,' Uma aunty began, as Kaveri watched her. 'To accuse a wife of murdering her husband, or a daughter of killing her father, only for money. After all, they are a wealthy family. Why would either of them want to kill Mr Sharma? They had a luxurious lifestyle even when he was around, didn't they?'

She peered shortsightedly at Kaveri, who sighed in exasperation. She had been urging Uma aunty for some weeks now to go to the eye doctor and get a prescription for glasses, but Uma aunty insisted they would pinch her nose and be too uncomfortable to wear.

Kaveri stared at a small ant climbing up the curry leaf tree, carrying a tiny piece of peanut in his mouth. She felt like the ant, picking up tiny fragments of the puzzle, unable to piece them together to make a clear picture.

'I feel like a detective in a mystery novel, searching for missing pieces of the puzzle. Right now I have more empty space than I have pieces. I must collect more fragments of the truth,' Kaveri muttered.

'You say the oddest things sometimes, Kaveri,' Uma aunty laughed, covering her mouth with her hand.

'I don't know anything about Kumar – his background, how he got the job in the factory, whether he has affection for Chitra – nothing! Kumar is a big hole in my puzzle.'

'I can help with that. I have run out of coffee. This is the perfect excuse to go visit Coffeepudi Lakamma. She knows everyone in Bangalore, and she supplies coffee to all the large industries and businesses. I have a vague memory of her telling me that she knew the Sharmas' prospective son-in-law. We can pump her discreetly for information.'

'Coffeepudi who?' Kaveri protested, following Uma aunty. 'And what do we do with Raju?'

'Yes, I can't leave him at home alone. My daughter-in-law has taken the baby and gone to her aunt's house for the day again.' Uma aunty looked annoyed. 'I love my little grandson, but if she leaves him with me all the time, how does she expect me to get any studying done?'

Uma aunty, who had recently been introduced to the joys of reading and arithmetic, was determined to graduate from high school one day. She had made a beginning by getting the primary school textbooks home and studying them with Kaveri's help. Kaveri only wished Uma aunty's son and daughter-in-law were as thrilled as she was. But while grudgingly accepting the situation, they had made it clear that they did not think that education was a priority for a middle-aged woman who should be spending her time in the kitchen or supervising her grandchildren.

'I know. Why don't we leave him with Rajamma? She can look after him and feed him if he wakes up. She has ten grandchildren of her own; she'll know what to do with him.'

'That's a good idea.' Uma aunty's face brightened. She picked up the sleeping boy and Kaveri climbed over the wall again, leaping down nimbly to her side of the compound, which Rajamma had swept clean that morning. She held out her arms to take the child from Uma, feeling her heart twist a little as she inhaled his sweet, milky scent. Bhargavi had been after her to get pregnant, but Kaveri wanted to wait for a while, until she studied further. But when she held Raju like this, and inhaled his sweet baby fragrance . . .

She moved inside briskly. She needed to focus on the case, not on distractions, however sweet and cherubic.

'Come back for me to the front gate,' Uma aunty called after her. 'You know my creaking bones will not permit me to climb over the wall like a monkey, the way you do.'

Kaveri laughed and sped into the house. A few minutes later, Uma aunty and she were on the narrow lane that led to the Basavanagudi main road, each holding a large umbrella to shield themselves from the midday sun.

'Who *is* Coffeepudi Lakamma? Such an unusual name' Kaveri asked, as they moved to the side of the road to avoid a passing goat kid. It bleated at them loudly, sticking out its tongue. On impulse, she turned and bleated back at it, sticking out her tongue so fiercely that the kid hesitated and then skipped a few steps ahead, *baaing* plaintively as it passed them.

'Always the prankster. How you can be such a good detective but such a silly girl, I will never know.' Uma aunty tweaked Kaveri's long plait affectionately as they walked.

'I love animals,' Kaveri said, looking wistfully behind her at the baby goat. 'I wish my mother-in-law was not so firmly set against pets. Ramu says she will never agree to us keeping Putta.'

'He seems to be much more comfortable in your house now. The first couple of days after you brought him, he barked so much each time you left him alone, I thought I would go mad. I gave him papayas to quiet him down. But these days, he hardly barks.'

Kaveri nodded. 'Ramu bought him some stuffed cotton dolls, childrens' toys, and he seems quite happy to play with them when we are not around. We have asked many people – some say they are interested, but when they hear about his size, they all back away.'

They continued down the road, turning right when they reached the end, into the Bull Temple road. They walked past the temple, towards the market. 'I cannot believe you have never heard of Coffeepudi Lakamma, Kaveri. She is such a well-known businesswoman. She runs a small store in Basavanagudi, not far from where we live. Her coffee is excellent. The woman is formidable too.'

'Really? A businesswoman who runs a coffee store?'

'Not just a coffee store, she also owns large plantations. She was married at 16 to a rich coffee planter, and then widowed by 18. Left alone with a small child. She has expanded the plantation and moved to Bangalore, setting up a coffee shop and processing unit. That's when she became known as Coffee Powder Lakamma.'

Uma aunty looked up at the hot sky and quickened her steps, stopping outside a small store in the market. The glass front held an attractive display, with little heaps of coffee beans in various stages of roasting. Above the small wooden door, a sign in large black letters announced that they were at 'Lakamma Coffee Works'.

'Is the coffee good?' Kaveri asked, eager to meet this interesting businesswoman .

'It's excellent – but people don't come here just to buy the coffee, they also come to chit-chat. Lakamma knows everyone in Bangalore. Writers like Masti and DV Gundappa praise her coffee in their poems and stories, the English buy coffee powder from her in bulk, and she even rubs shoulders with the Mysore Maharaja on occasion. Come, Kaveri, let's see if she can tell us anything about Kumar.'

The women took off their slippers, placing them on the steps. A silver bell chimed as they opened the door, and a woman looked up from behind the counter. Kaveri expected to see a tall, hefty, formidable Coorgi woman. But Lakamma turned out to be a surprisingly short, rotund, cheerful looking lady, with a shock of white hair. She wore a thick pair of spectacles, and her twinkling eyes peered out at them behind her glasses.

'Uma? What a delight to see you. I didn't realise you were already out of coffee, since you just bought some last week. I would have sent an order to your house.' She spoke in a torrent of words, as the two women folded their umbrellas, placing them in a copper urn that stood in the corner.

'But then how would I have had the pleasure of getting to see you?' Uma aunty smiled at Lakamma, placing a hand on Kaveri's shoulder. 'I have brought my neighbour, Mrs Kaveri Murthy. Her husband is a doctor in Bowring. She has not met you, and I told her she must purchase coffee from you now.'

Lakamma studied Kaveri carefully. 'You are the lady detective!' she announced, her face split by a smile, showing a gap between her two front teeth. 'I have heard so much about you.'

'From whom?' Uma aunty looked forlorn at the thought that Lakamma might have heard about Kaveri from someone else other than her. Kaveri realised just how starved of company Uma aunty must be, stuck in her home all day, cooking and looking after her grandson while her daughter-in-law escaped for visits to her family. Except for her outings at the women's club, Uma aunty hardly ever had any company with whom she could have adult conversation.

The store was quite empty, and they were the only customers around. Lakamma peered through a doorway covered only by a thin curtain strung on a piece of thread. She clapped her hands, calling out loudly, 'Babu! Hey, Babu! Stop unpacking those cartons, they can wait a bit. Come and attend to the store for a while for me.'

A white-haired elderly man emerged from the dark room, blinking a little as a ray of sunlight from the window fell directly onto his face. Pulling the curtain aside, Lakamma took them through a larger doorway that led to a back exit.

Kaveri looked around in wonder. Behind the tiny shop in a large open area was a massive shed made of corrugated iron sheets.

'Welcome to Lakamma Gardens,' the small, plump woman announced with a flourish, clapping her hands. 'This is where all the coffee processing takes place.' She led them inside the shed, which was packed with crates of coffee beans. Wooden partitions divided the shed into sections, and Kaveri could see a number of machines in different areas. She itched to go closer and see what each one was doing.

Lakamma smiled at her appreciatively. 'You like what you see?'

'I love machinery,' Kaveri admitted.

Uma aunty let out one of her surprisingly loud cackles, poking Kaveri in the waist with a sharp elbow. 'Such a strange one she is. Her husband gifts her all kinds of peculiar contraptions, including a machine to boil the milk, and she is as happy as if he gave her diamonds.'

Lakamma smiled at her appreciatively. 'A kindred spirit, then. Shall I give you a tour?'

'Not today.' Uma aunty took over. 'We left my grandson sleeping with Kaveri's maid, and I must return before he wakes up. Actually, we didn't come for coffee – though of course we would love to buy some too,' she added hastily.

'Well then, you must come another day, and you,' Lakamma said, turning to Kaveri, 'with your husband who loves machines – I will show you both around my factory. But for now, let us sit and drink a good cup of coffee while we talk.'

The smell of roasting coffee filled the air as Lakamma led the way to her interior office. It was spartan, with only a small table, and three folding steel chairs. She called out to one of the men in the shed to bring them some coffee, then they all sat down to talk.

'I don't know how to say this,' Kaveri hesitated.

'Don't worry, I will not reveal what you ask to anyone,' Lakamma said, looking at her shrewdly. 'You have come here to ask me about the Sharma murder, correct? Ah, you see, I know everything that goes on in Bangalore. Well, almost everything,' she amended, grinning mischievously at Kaveri. 'The Sharmas buy coffee from me in bulk, for the factory. For a long while, they used to buy the best coffee. About two years back, they moved to our cheaper version, one with 25% chicory instead of 10%. I heard rumours from a few other suppliers too . . . One told me that they used to buy four pairs of uniforms a year for their workers, but they had discontinued the order. I thought then that they might have fallen on hard times.'

'Two years ago? Are you sure?' Kaveri was puzzled. Shanthi had told her that the thefts had started only six months back, and they had only realised they were running out of money a couple of weeks ago when the bank had told them they had very little remaining in the account.

'Yes, two years back. Around the same time that Mr Sharma married his beautiful bride, and a year after they employed Kumar. Since I know him, he came personally to the shop asking to negotiate down the prices, and selected the cheapest brand of coffee.'

None of this made sense to Kaveri. Why had Mr Sharma needed to economise two years ago? Could Kumar have been doing this on his own initiative, skimming off the savings for himself instead of passing it on to the factory? Something wasn't adding up.

Kaveri pressed Lakamma. 'Do you know Kumar well? His family, his background?'

'Of course. He is one of my boys.'

'Boys? I thought you had only one son.' Uma aunty looked puzzled.

'You know I run a hostel for young men from poor families – Lakamma Bhavan – to help them move to the city and complete their higher studies?' Lakamma pointed to the framed photographs on the wall, which showed a series of young boys, smartly dressed in school uniforms and with neatly combed hair, standing proudly with trophies, certificates and medals.

'Kumar's father passed away when he was just fifteen. He is such a bright boy, but his mother was unable to pay the fees for his further education. He stayed with us, and we took care of him, enrolling him in St John's School, and then Central College, where he studied accounts and finance. He only moved out when he got the job at the Sampangi Mills.'

Kaveri hesitated, not knowing how to phrase her next question delicately. Uma aunty had no such compunctions. She asked Lakamma bluntly, 'Do you trust Kumar? The police consider him a potential suspect. We want to know if he was involved in the murder.'

Lakamma glared at her. 'The boy is like my son. I would trust him not only with my life but that of a stranger.'

The wrinkles on her face had congealed into grim lines, and the conversation petered out into uncomfortable silence. Kaveri looked up gratefully when Babu came in carrying an ornate silver tray with three silver tumblers of coffee. They had been honoured guests, but Kaveri suspected they were no longer so honoured. Lakamma's stiff spine looked like the bristled back of the cat that Rajamma had chased away from their kitchen with a broom the previous day. She only opened her mouth once to say, curtly, that this was one of their special coffees, a single bean from the high hills of the Anamalai ranges. After looking at Lakamma's scowling face, Kaveri thought it may as well have tasted of sawdust.

After they had drained their tumblers and stood to leave, Kaveri decided to make one last attempt to explain herself to Lakamma.

'Please do not mistake me, aunty,' she said, standing directly in front of her. 'A man has been murdered – an innocent man, with a wife and daughter who may have loved him dearly. We know the killer was most likely an insider who had a key to Mr Sharma's office.'

Kaveri hesitated for a moment before deciding to not mention the embezzlement. That was not public knowledge yet and could harm the future of the factory if it became more widely known.

'That is why we had to find out more about Kumar,' she said. She reached out a tentative finger to touch Lakamma's shoulder.

The older woman suddenly stood up, her hands twisting at her sides. 'No one trusts orphans,' she said through clenched teeth. 'They have no family, people say. Who knows who their parents were? They must have come from bad blood.' Her eyes were fierce on Kaveri and Uma aunty. 'Kumar was so surprised when Mr Sharma offered his daughter's hand to him in marriage, because he was an orphan. My boy worried that people might gossip, calling him a gold-digger. Mr Sharma reassured him, saying he did not care about Kumar's past – he was only concerned about his future. He extracted a promise from Kumar that he would take care of his family and factory as though they were his own.'

Kaveri could feel a knot of guilt squirming in her backbone, like an annoying worm. She thought of Venu, whom they all loved so dearly. What if he had been orphaned, as could so easily have happened when his brother Manju had been arrested for murder, and his sister-in-law Muniamma put in a coma. Would he have been considered untrustworthy by everyone? People distrusted the poor, the homeless, those without parents to take care of them. She thought again of the boys lined up outside the police station, rats in their hands. What a contrast with that neatly dressed thin man she had seen coming to be interviewed at the police station. Could Kumar have ended up like those boys if it had not been for Lakamma?

'I am sorry, aunty,' Kaveri said quietly.

Lakamma shook her head. 'I should not have snapped at you. You had to ask, it is your *dharma* as a detective.'

Lakamma wiped her eyes with a corner of her sari, then moved ahead of them into the processing area like a small, efficient hurricane, once again the formidable proprietress.

'Did you like the coffee? It is our best variety. I will pack some for you.' She waved Kaveri's money away. 'It is a gift for this first time,' she added. 'Once you taste this coffee, you will not be able to drink anything else.' She flashed Kaveri a mischievous smile. 'That's why I reserve it only for my wealthy clients. When you finish this and come back for more, *then* I will charge you.' Too short to touch Kaveri's shoulders, Lakamma reached up to put an arm around her waist. 'But for you, from now on, the family discount.'

Kaveri touched the older woman's feet in a traditional sign of respect. Lakamma looked down at her, blessing her with a hand on her head. 'You are a true seeker. May justice prevail.'

'Aunty, you know as well as I do that Kumar is a suspect,' Kaveri said. 'Even if the police never find a murderer, people will always look at Kumar with suspicion, hesitating to invite him home for a meal, or to give him a business contract, always wondering if he might cheat them.'

She saw Lakamma's eyes grow thoughtful as she studied Kaveri. 'What can I do to help?'

'Take me to Kumar, introduce me to him. Convince him to speak to me freely. There are many things that do not add up here. I have to understand the circumstances of the theft better, and to learn more about the workers' strike and the incident of sabotage. Perhaps there is someone else involved, one of the workers maybe, someone who is trying to place suspicion on the family. I have already spoken to Shanthi and Chitra, but I need Kumar's help to understand many things that puzzle me.'

'I do not know if Kumar will be willing to meet you,' Lakamma said bluntly. 'That boy is so focused on his work that he has not noticed that his head is in a noose, with these two women pulling on the rope.'

21

The Most Important Fellow in Bangalore

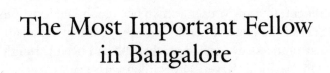

Kaveri's stomach rumbled loudly as she trudged in through the gate after dropping Uma aunty at her house. She smiled as she heard an excited squeal and saw Rajamma handing Uma aunty's grandson over the back wall to his grandmother. She was so hungry she could eat an elephant! Well, maybe not an elephant but a nice plate of rice and sambhar, with some thick curd on the side and a generous serving of the sweet mango pickle that her mother had sent over from Mysore last week.

As Kaveri hurried into the verandah, a small figure unfolded itself from the long passageway, making her jump with a startled shriek.

'Kaveri *akka*?'

'Who is it?' Kaveri squinted in the dim light.

'It's me, Anandi.'

'Anandi! How have you been? I have been thinking about you.' She ushered her into the house and opened the shutters so she could see the young woman's face more clearly.

Anandi gave her a lopsided smile, and Kaveri noticed that her swelling and scars had gone. She looked completely different from the battered woman who had had to be held down that day in the hospital while Ramu rotated her dislocated joint back into place. She looked happier, more confident, like any young woman her age should look. Only the cut at the edge of her lips and the remnants of a fading bruise on her arm gave away what she had been through.

'Oh, Anandi!' Kaveri's eyes filled with tears. 'You – you look so different. I would not have recognised you if I saw you on the road.'

Her stomach rumbled loudly again. Anandi giggled, then covered her mouth in embarrassment.

'Have you eaten?' Kaveri asked. When Anandi hesitated, Kaveri dragged her to the dining table, where Rajamma, knowing Kaveri's ways well, had already laid out two plates.

Anandi's bottom lip trembled. 'Akka, I cannot sit with you at the table,' she protested. 'Just give me a plate of food and I will sit outside and eat, on the verandah. Or on the floor here.' She gestured to the door.

Rajamma shook her head at Anandi. 'There is no point in protesting,' she advised her kindly. 'Our Kaveri will not rest until you share a meal with her at the table.'

Without further ado they tucked into a quick meal of *annada pudi*, spiced lentil powder with hot rice and ghee, and curd rice accompanied by mango pickle. Knowing that Anandi was feeling uncomfortable, Kaveri kept up an inconsequential flow of chatter as they ate.

Once they had finished, she took Anandi out to the front steps again. Rajamma let Putta out to play in the front yard, and the two women took turns throwing him a stick, watching him retrieve it as they chatted.

'There is so much I have to tell you, Kaveri *akka*!' Anandi said. 'I have joined Mrs Sharma's house as a maid.'

'That soon?' The sun was still high in the sky. Mrs Reddy must have gone to see Shanthi quite early that morning.

'Yes, the girl they had employed wanted to leave. I believe they have been having a lot of trouble with maids lately. And no wonder – there is so much tension in that house! The two women barely speak to each other, and they constantly bark out contradictory orders to me.' Anandi shrugged her shoulders. 'But cross words are nothing to me, I have endured much worse than this. I will stay. But I said I would be back in an hour after completing some shopping for the house. I must be quick.' She looked around fearfully.

Kaveri had seen her do this a number of times. 'Your husband?' she guessed. When Anandi winced, Kaveri placed a comforting hand on her shoulder.

'He lives in another part of the city. How will he even guess that you are here? You are safe now.'

'Yes, he probably would not expect to see me in such an expensive part of the city,' Anandi agreed, her voice edged with bitterness. 'I lived well before I met him, I worked in a grand house. But he – he was the driver there – he forced himself on me one evening, got me pregnant, and then forcibly married me. What choice did I have? My parents threw me out of the house. Even when he beat me, and I lost the child from the kicks he gave me on my belly, they refused to take me back. I had to stay with him, in that hovel where he beat me every day. And I had barely any food.' She hunched her shoulders, tucking her sari around herself tightly as though she were wrapping herself in a protective cocoon.

Kaveri's gut roiled in sorrow. She was reminded of Mala's tales of abuse, first at the hand of her brother, then her pimp.

Anandi looked at Kaveri uncertainly, then looked down again, tracing a pattern with her finger on the dusty floor 'I have food in my stomach now, and don't have to tiptoe around the house, fearful that anything I say might set off a cycle of beating again. But I don't feel relaxed. There is something wrong in the atmosphere of that house.'

'Be very careful, Anandi. It seems like the murder was an inside job,' Kaveri said, leaning forward to speak closer to her ear. The wind sometimes carried, and she did not want any passers-by to overhear.

Rather than afraid, Anandi looked excited, even eager. 'So, it may be one of the two women, then?'

'Or Kumar, the fiancé,' Kaveri said.

'He was there this morning, speaking to Mrs Sharma,' Anandi said. 'They sat together for quite a while in Mr Sharma's room, with the door closed.'

Kaveri thought of Chitra's assertion that Shanthi and Kumar were having an affair. She had not provided any proof when Kaveri pressed her, but could it be true?

'What about Chitra? Did they spend any time together?' she asked Anandi.

'Very little, they mostly ignored each other. Or rather, she ignored him, responding only in the shortest possible sentences when he spoke to her.' Anandi shrugged. 'I told you, there is something very disturbing about the atmosphere of that house. The tension is thick. I can feel it pressing down on me.'

'Maybe you should leave, Anandi,' Kaveri suggested, thinking of Ramu's statement that she was sending Anandi into danger. 'I can find you another place to work. It is not worth the risk.'

'No, I will stay.' Anandi looked firm. 'I want to build up my savings so that I can move to another city where my husband will never be able to find me. You know, I am getting paid twice here.' She smiled at Kaveri's look of puzzlement. 'Mrs Sharma pulled me into her room, closed the door, and gave me five rupees, asking me to keep a close watch on Chitra, and to report back to her on where Chitra went, and whom she spoke to. Then Chitra took me into *her* room, and gave me another five rupees, telling me that she would give me more money if I quit my job the next day.'

'What did you tell them?' Kaveri asked, bile rising in her throat at the thought that Shanthi was paying people in her employ to spy on her own stepdaughter. So Chitra had been right when she told her that Shanthi had people following her around, reporting back to her on everything Chitra did. How unbearable it must be for her to live in such a house! She almost wished Shanthi *was* the murderer, if only because that would then free Chitra to take control of her own life again. But if that turned out to be true, how the news would devastate Bhargavi.

Kaveri looked at the series of tight knots she had made in her sari pallu, shaking her head. She needed to concentrate on what Anandi was telling her, and not let her anger derail her judgement. She started to remove the knots, turning and giving Anandi her full attention.

'I did not dare say anything to Mrs Sharma. She is the mistress of the household, and I thought she might dismiss me if I refused. But I told Chitra that I could not leave the job, that I needed the money to send home for my sick mother's treatment.' Anandi shrugged again. 'She went dark in the face with anger and stormed out, slamming the door.'

'Try to spend more time with both women, separately, to get to know them better.'

Anandi looked doubtful. 'I don't think Chitra will speak to me. Shanthi *ammavare* might. I can offer to give her a massage. I used to press my earlier mistress' feet with warm sesame oil heated with a couple of peppercorns every week. And I can give her a good oil massage for her head also.'

'That sounds like a great way to get her talking, while she is relaxed and in a private setting.'

'I won't have to try too hard – women always talk to their personal maids.' Anandi grinned mischievously as she moved towards the gate. 'In my previous house, my mistress had developed a fascination for one of her husband's friends. For a full week before he came she would almost starve herself, asking me to prepare vegetable juices for her so that she could drape a clinging sari tightly around herself, accentuating her slim figure. So I ate her lunches, and made juice for her in the early mornings and afternoons when the kitchen was empty so that no one would suspect. I gained so much weight. It was fun.'

'This is not a game, Anandi,' Kaveri warned, feeling terrible as she did for spoiling the lighthearted atmosphere of their conversation. Anandi had had few opportunities for fun in the past few months. But she had to make sure Anandi did not take foolish risks. 'You are poking around the edges of a murder. If you feel something is dangerous, leave immediately.'

Anandi shook her head. 'The only thing I am scared of is meeting my husband again. As long as I am safe from him, inside the four walls of that house, I have no fear.'

Kaveri watched Anandi as she looked up and down the road for her husband, then wrapped her sari around her head and shoulders, swathing herself so completely that very little of her face was visible.

The sun's rays filtered through the leaves of the large rain tree, falling upon her like a benediction.

*

When Ramu returned home that evening, he found the house in turmoil.

'We are doomed.' Kaveri moved through the house towards him, wringing her hands. 'Shanthi called to let me know your mother is going to be returning home in a couple of hours. Now that Shanthi has recovered somewhat, she feels she does not need to keep Bhargavi *athe* from her home any longer. But now as soon as *athe* returns, she will hear Putta, and go to find out what's going on. And then what will we do?'

Ramu put an arm around his wife and led her to the sofa, where she perched nervously on the edge.

'I wish we could have found another home for him,' Kaveri wailed. 'I tried in so many places. Mrs Reddy's house is too large and filled with too many breakable items. Mrs Ismail's house is too small and cramped. Mala and Narsamma said they could not because her brother's friends, the petty criminals whom they now employ in their business, would be terrified of a dog so large.'

Ramu took her hands in his. 'And you know I asked Mr Roberts and all the doctors and attendants in the hospital. They all refused. No one is ready to take such a large dog, who will grow even bigger. Most people are scared of his size.'

'Perhaps Rajamma can take him home for a few days?' Kaveri looked at him hopefully. 'Only until we find a way to break the news to Bhargavi *athe*. Her home is small too, but their cowshed is empty right now.'

Ramu started to shake his head. 'They have purchased a new cow. I don't think this will work,' he began, then stopped as he heard a series of unmistakeable yips that announced that Putta had a visitor.

Kaveri and Ramu hurried into the garden, stopping suddenly when they saw Bhargavi standing next to the shed, her back ramrod stiff with disapproval as she glared at Putta. Tied to the corner of the shed with a long piece of rope, Putta came to stand two feet from Bhargavi, his massive tongue hanging out as he panted at her happily.

'What is the meaning of this?' Bhargavi demanded, facing them.

'Amma? We did not hear you come in,' Ramu began.

She cut him off. 'Don't try to change the subject. Shanthi's car dropped me off at the corner.' She gestured to the papaya in her hand. 'I walked home from the fruit stall, and heard the sound of barking as I opened the gate.' She crossed her arms. 'You know I do not approve of dogs at home.'

Ramu cleared his throat. 'Amma . . . the dog was abandoned, hungry, starving. What would you have us do? Leave him to die?'

'Don't be so dramatic, Ramu. Surely there were other people who could have taken him in.'

Was it Kaveri's imagination, or had Bhargavi's tone softened slightly when Ramu told her that Putta had been abandoned?

'We did try, *athe*,' Kaveri said. 'We've asked everyone we know.'

'You are so clever at these sorts of things, Amma,' Ramu coaxed, moving forward to put an arm around his mother's shoulders. 'We were waiting for you to come back home and find a solution. As you always do.'

'Humph. Don't think you can bring me around with your flattery.' Bhargavi sailed out of the shed, her back still stiff. 'I will find a new place for him, within a week. Now I am going upstairs to take a nap. We will talk more about this in the evening.'

Kaveri reached out with her sari pallu to wipe her perspiring face. 'That was not as bad as I thought it would be. I thought she would scold us much more.' She cast a wistful glance at Ramu. 'I hope *athe* finds a good home for Putta. I'm going to miss him more than I thought.'

'I will too,' Ramu said, looking rueful. 'He is so happy to see me every time, and greets me with such ecstasy, I feel like the most important fellow in Bangalore. The house will seem empty when he leaves.'

22

The Home for
Destitute Women

The next morning, Bhargavi got up much later than she usually did, joining Kaveri at the breakfast table as she was finishing her meal. 'It is good to be home, Kaveri,' she said as she piled her plate high with *avalakki*, flat rice spiced with peanuts and coriander leaves. 'Shanthi's home is luxurious, and I had an entire suite of rooms to myself there, but I missed the simple comforts of my own house. And I missed the two of you.' She leant across and patted Kaveri's hand. The simple gesture took Kaveri by surprise, and she blinked, surprised to find her eyes filling with tears.

Bhargavi continued speaking, but Kaveri's mind wandered to Putta. She and Ramu had begun to spend increasing amounts of time in the gardener's shed playing with him, but the dog whined so plaintively when they left. Kaveri had asked Ramu if they dared smuggle him into their bedroom at night, but Ramu had ruled it out. He told

Kaveri that he and his sister had tried many times to get their mother to let them adopt a pet when they were in school, but she had been adamant. Since Bhargavi seemed to be in a better mood today, did she dare ask her mother-in-law what her plans were for the dog?

Lost in thought, Kaveri only looked up when she saw Bhargavi push her plate aside, looking satisfied. 'Good, then that's settled,' she said briskly. 'Go up and change, Kaveri. We will leave in ten minutes.'

What was settled? Kaveri opened her mouth to ask where they were going, but closed it again quickly. Bhargavi would only scold her if she asked her to repeat herself. Hoping to get a clue, she said instead, 'What kind of sari should I wear?'

'A Kanjeevaram silk. All the women at the ashram will be very well dressed. Take off that plain cotton sari you have on now.'

I hope it's not the Swami's ashram, Kaveri thought, her eyebrows creased in worry as she hurried upstairs. She opened her steel almirah, selecting a mustard yellow sari shot through with thin maroon stripes, and an elegant design of maroon and yellow checks on the pallu. It had been a wedding gift from Ramu's married sister, and one of Bhargavi's favourites. Indeed, she looked quite approvingly at Kaveri, her eyes resting on her face.

'You look beautiful, Kaveri,' Bhargavi said to her, holding out her hands as Kaveri walked down the stairs. 'But you have dark circles under your eyes. Have you been sleeping enough?'

Kaveri stifled a sigh as they walked towards the car. However hard she tried, Bhargavi always seemed to find at least one flaw in her appearance.

She focused on driving, noting the route as Bhargavi guided her towards the ashram. Near a busy intersection, the building was tucked away from sight behind a grove of coconut trees, well protected by a large compound surrounded by high walls embedded with sharpened metal spears. The pair of massive wooden gates that marked the entrance had the same Garuda motif at the centre that she had seen on the Swami's wooden staff. It seemed strikingly similar in appearance to the motif on the gates of the mills as well.

Kaveri thought of the Vishnu temple in Mysore that she had often visited with her parents. Built centuries ago, during the time of the Hoysala kings, the walls were also lined with representations of the Garuda in various forms. The ashram Garuda was depicted in a more ferocious style, and she saw Bhargavi wrap her sari pallu protectively around herself, shrinking from it as she hurried past.

Kaveri looked at the iron padlock that held the gates closed. 'How will we get in?'

'The ashram itself is not open to visitors, Kaveri. I told you the Swami runs a women's home for widows and destitute women inside. For their safety and security, he keeps the gates locked.'

Were the gates and the high walls meant to keep outsiders from getting in, or the women from getting out? Kaveri wondered. But her mother-in-law was already shepherding her into the next compound, where a smaller enclosure housed a simple hall, its plain whitewashed walls contrasting oddly with the ornate ashram gates just outside. The Swami sat at one end, on the same red throne-like chair in which Kaveri had last seen him. She could see the hairy armed attendant standing behind, fanning him with peacock feathers to keep away the flies and gnats.

'He is giving a *pravachana*, a discourse,' Bhargavi whispered in her ear, pulling her close. 'Come, let us sit.' She pointed to the heavy jamkhanas, red and blue striped cotton rugs, lining the floor. A large group of women sat on the rugs, dressed in expensive silks with large gold zari borders, their arms laden with bangles and their necks heavy with large chains. Many of them were also wearing thick arm and waist bands of gold, decorated with rubies and diamonds. *There must be several pounds of gold and gems in this room*, Kaveri thought to herself.

Bhargavi and Kaveri sat at the back of the room. Kaveri was curious to hear the Swami speak. She had thought his voice would be deep and guttural, but it was soft, musical, almost hypnotic. Involuntarily, she found herself leaning forward to hear, looking around to see that all the women in the room were doing the same.

Dressed in white robes, a group of attendants moved forward with lamps and placed aromatic sambrani resin and sandalwood powder on pans of hot coals. The heady smell of sandalwood incense filled the air. The cadence of the Swami's voice rose and fell, moving her into a dream-like state. Her throat felt dry, but her body seemed weightless, as though she was soaring above the ground.

Later, when Ramu asked, Kaveri could not remember what she had heard the Swami say, only the way it had made her feel – every hair tingling on edge, every nerve fibre quivering with awareness. She had never felt more alive.

On hearing the audience erupt into loud applause as Swami Vaninanda completed his speech, Kaveri was jerked out of her daze. She blinked slowly, looking around to see the woman in front of her rubbing her eyes, while another woman was crying quietly. Bhargavi seemed to be waking up from a trance as well, wiping her face with a kerchief. The attendants hurried to the windows, flinging them open. The cool air blew in, slowly dispelling the haze in the room.

The women then formed a queue to meet the Swami. The assistant stood at the end of the line, pointing to the large iron box, the *hundi* for collecting donations. People gave generously, opening their purses to drop quantities of coins and notes into the box. She saw the jewellery-laden women take off their chains, bangles, armbands and waistbands, even their earrings, dropping them into the collection bags that the attendants passed around. If the ashram collected this much at every meeting, then Swami Vaninanda must be a very rich man indeed, Kaveri thought. This much gold would feed hundreds of people. How many women did his shelter accommodate?

Kaveri thought of the chain Bhargavi had previously donated to the ashram at the dog show. She looked sharply at Bhargavi, seeing her mother-in-law's hand move to her bangles.

'Let us ask if we can enter the ashram and meet the women. I would like to volunteer my time. We can also make a donation there,' Kaveri said.

'That is a good idea,' Bhargavi agreed. 'Surely Swamiji will allow a young woman like you to interact with the women. You could even teach them how to read and write.'

The Swami's hooded eyes surveyed them with faint distaste as they approached, lingering once again on Kaveri. Kaveri looked away, unwilling to meet his hypnotic eyes. She could still feel the after-effects of the trance-like state she had been in, and refrained from speaking. Bhargavi rushed into headlong conversation, gushing as she brought Kaveri forward, asking if she could visit the ashram and bring her teaching material with her.

Swami Vaninanda's response was distant and curt. 'The ashram is not open to visits from every curious do-gooder,' he said in a hard voice. 'These women have gone through significant hardship. They do not like to be disturbed.'

He looked over their heads towards the few people remaining in the queue. 'I cannot stand here chatting to every devotee. Please move along.'

The attendant chivvied them along, seeming to rejoice in Bhargavi's discomfiture.

'Well, I never . . . ' Bhargavi's voice shook as they hurried out of the building. 'Did we annoy Swamiji with our request? I have never heard him speak so sharply to any of his devotees before.'

Kaveri grimaced. 'I don't think he wants anyone to see the women he has in there. Doesn't that seem suspicious to you?'

'You see suspicious activity wherever you look, Kaveri,' Bhargavi said automatically. But her heart was clearly not in the rebuke. She followed up with, 'Do you really think so? Swamiji had his photograph in the newspaper last week with one of the Mysore royal family members.'

Kaveri turned to her. '*Athe*, think of the number of people the King and Yuvaraja must meet. Taking a photograph with someone does not mean they support everything he does. They may not even know the man personally.'

Bhargavi looked troubled, but did not say anything as they walked out towards the car. When they reached it, Kaveri stopped Bhargavi with a hand on her arm. 'I want to see the ashram. Let us walk around it. How many women are in the shelter home?'

Bhargavi shot her a worried glance. 'I'm not sure. Perhaps thirty? Fifty? Why is the shelter home so important to you?'

'I don't know. But if they are being so careful to hide it from us, there must be something they want to keep secret. Let's see if we can find out more.' Kaveri pulled her along, finding a narrow path in between the coconut plantation that allowed them to make a circuit of the ashram.

Bhargavi looked uncertain, but followed Kaveri slowly. 'I don't like the way Swamiji spoke to me. I have been very generous,' she complained again. 'And it was only an innocent request.'

Despite her annoyance, Kaveri smiled to herself. Calling her a curious do-gooder had clearly offended Bhargavi. Could this incident make her mother-in-law re-think her devotion to the Swami?

The women walked around the forbidding high walls, arriving at the back of the ashram, where a small door revealed the presence of a back entrance. 'This must be what the maids and attendants use,' Kaveri murmured. The pointed spears embedded in the walls protected them from visitors. But Kaveri's sharp eyes spotted a small gap between the spears and the back door. A small child could squeeze through such a gap. Or a small-sized woman, she thought to herself, turning the door knob.

'*Kaveri!*' she heard Bhargavi's scandalised whisper. 'What do you think you are doing?' But the door was locked, and Kaveri stepped back. She placed a hand to shield her eyes from the sun's rays, and squinted up at the roof.

Two women in old patched saris stood on top of the roof. Their hair uncombed, their dress unkempt, they looked wild, uncared for. As Kaveri stepped back to take a clearer look at them, motioning to Bhargavi, she suddenly found the attendant in her path. He had stepped through the small door, which was slightly ajar.

'Did you want anything, madam?' he enquired, standing in front of them with a scowl on his face.

'We were just taking a stroll,' Bhargavi said hastily.

'This is private property, and visitors are not allowed in this part. Let me escort you back to your car.'

He followed them all the way. As they got in, the man leaned into the window on the passenger side, his face unpleasantly close to Bhargavi, who flinched, moving back as far as she could.

'I suggest you do not visit us again,' he said, dragging out each word in an unpleasant tone as he leaned further towards the two women. 'This is not a place for inquisitive women to wander around as they please.'

Bhargavi gave Kaveri a horrified look. Furious with the man, Kaveri stepped on her accelerator without giving warning, and he stepped back hastily as the car zoomed away.

As Kaveri drove, she looked in the rear-view mirror. The man stood still, arms crossed, frowning at them. The nape of her neck pricked with unease. She glanced at Bhargavi, but she was deep in thought.

'No one has ever spoken to me like this before, Kaveri,' her mother-in-law said slowly. 'And to think how much I've donated to the ashram . . . Surely it is not rude to ask to see the women to whom I am donating funds?'

Kaveri remained silent, not knowing what to say.

'And to call me nosy, and a do-gooder . . . ' Bhargavi now sounded indignant. 'I have never been so humiliated in all my life! That too, when I have helped the ashram so much, in addition to introducing them to so many wealthy donors.'

Kaveri was just about to reach out and pat Bhargavi's hand when she heard a small chuckle. Surprised, she looked over at her.

'You should have seen the look on that hairy man's face when you suddenly sped the car away, Kaveri! He was terrified you would run over him. Serves him right.' Bhargavi sat back in the car, a satisfied expression on her face.

23

An Unexpected Visitor

The next morning, as Kaveri was clearing up at the dining table, she was surprised to hear a loud, peremptory
knock on the door.

Kaveri opened the door, falling back in surprise.

'Lakamma aunty?'

The tiny woman came in like a whirlwind, talking
nineteen to the dozen.

'I have never been to your lane before, isn't it strange?
Well, maybe it's time I did so I can get to know you better.
Did you like the coffee? Is this your husband?'

She stood in front of Ramu, who was in the midst of
pulling on his socks. He stood up hastily, folding his hands
in a *namaste* as proper when faced with an elderly lady, even
if she was a complete stranger.

'Well? Did you like the coffee?' Lakamma demanded.

'Erm . . . ' Ramu looked to Kaveri for help. There had
been so much going on in the past couple of days that while
Kaveri had managed to tell him about Anandi, she had not

got around to telling him about their visit to the ashram, or to Lakamma's coffee works.

'He had the coffee, aunty, and liked it – so did I – but I have not yet been able to tell him anything about my visit to your factory. He came home so late last night.'

'Humph.' Lakamma let out an exasperated sigh, and settled herself on the sofa, spreading her pleats a little to make herself more comfortable. 'Young people today – you're slower than my generation was. I hope you're ready to go.'

'Go where?' Kaveri could not remember making any plans with Lakamma the previous day.

'Go to visit Kumar. I told him we would be coming to see him.'

Ramu, who had picked up his briefcase and was just leaving for the door, stopped. 'Kumar?' He came back and sat down on the opposite sofa. 'Can one of you please tell me what is going on?'

Kaveri gave him a quick update as Lakamma looked at her with bird-like expectancy. 'You told me yesterday that you had some questions to ask Kumar. I know he will not answer, not if you are the one to ask. He is a reticent boy, and does not trust others easily. He told me that he had advised Mr and Mrs Sharma against seeking your help. He feels that there is no point in bringing in outsiders. They should be able to solve their problems themselves.'

Kaveri exchanged glances with Ramu. That seemed like a suspicious stance to her.

Lakkamma continued, 'Don't worry. That is why I am coming with you. I sent him a note this morning, and asked him to expect us at the factory at 9 a.m. The workers come in at 10, so we will have an hour to talk to him in privacy. But if we sit lolling around on the sofa like this we are not going to get there in time.'

Ramu pulled Kaveri aside. 'Are you sure this is safe?' He cast a glance at Lakamma, who had picked up the newspaper and started to solve a crossword puzzle. 'We don't know her at all. I have a morning surgery, otherwise I would have come with you. Shall we ask Uma aunty if she can accompany you?'

Kaveri cut him off, reaching up to straighten his tie, which had come askew and was hanging crookedly.

'Your patients need you, and Uma aunty is going out with her daughter-in-law today. I will be fine. What can happen to us in a factory full of people? Even if the workers have not yet come in by the time we arrive, the guards will be there and it is broad daylight.'

Lakamma looked up from her crossword, pointedly clearing her throat.

'I hope you know what you're doing, Kaveri. I have an uneasy feeling about this,' Ramu whispered into her ear as he left.

Lakamma kept up a non-stop flow of conversation as the two women drove down to the mills. Kaveri had a moment of apprehension just before she drove through the gates, thinking that the sight of the massive wrought iron scrollwork would bring back nightmarish memories of the night of the blood moon. She had forgotten, however, that they were not going through the back gates this time. Her dread melted away as soon as she drove through the front entrance. These gates, though large, looked inviting, welcoming even, with motifs of cheery-looking flowers and twisting vines with leaves that gleamed in the sunlight. Such a stark contrast to the forbidding exterior of the black wrought-iron gates at the side entrance, thought Kaveri, her interest piqued. How come there was no Garuda figure on these gates?

Kumar was standing at the door to welcome them when they arrived, and dutifully bent to touch Lakamma's feet. Kaveri studied the lanky man with interest. Plainly dressed in an ill-fitting loose black jacket that clashed with his brown shirt and blue tie, he looked like a man who had no interest in fashion or fripperies. Kaveri nodded back as Kumar folded his hands in a quick *namaste* to Kaveri. His face was aloof and distant, and his body language hinted strongly that he had no interest in speaking to Kaveri, but at least he seemed to be making the effort to be polite.

'So plain, these walls,' Lakamma scolded him fondly while looking at the limestone-finished walls of his office. 'You should have photographs on your table at the very least. There isn't even one of your beautiful bride-to-be! Have you set a date for the marriage yet?'

Kumar looked ill at ease as he took off his glasses, polished them with a kerchief, then put them back on his nose.

'We have to do it soon. The will, you know . . . ' He broke off, casting a quick side-eye glance at Kaveri before looking back down at the table.

'You can trust her, Kumar. She only wants to find out the truth,' Lakamma said.

Kumar spoke to Lakamma in a clipped voice. 'Amma, you always believe the best of people, but life is not so straightforward.' His body seemed to stiffen as he turned his gaze back to Kaveri, who was sitting quietly in the corner. 'Forgive me, madam, but it is difficult to trust anyone that easily. I am sure you can understand.'

'I do,' said Kaveri instantly. That seemed to surprise Kumar, who dropped his glasses onto the table. 'After all, what do you know about me? I could be a thief, a murderer, someone out to trick Shanthi – Mrs Sharma – and Chitra – out of their money.'

'Exactly!' Kumar leaned back in his chair.

'And equally, you could be a saviour, come to help these two women in their times of need – or a charlatan, or even worse, a potential murderer.' Kaveri gave him one of her most dazzling smiles.

Kumar jerked upright, looking affronted. 'Madam. If you think . . . '

'That's just it,' Lakamma interrupted. 'She doesn't know what to think. Just like you can't trust her on first sight, she can't trust you. More to the point, the police have no reason to trust you.' She paused, then continued in a softer voice. 'My son, I don't want to see you accused of murder and thrown into jail. If it is a choice between you and one of those women, we all know that a judge is more likely to find you – an orphan – guilty, and throw you in jail to rot – or worse, hang from the end of a rope.'

Kumar stiffened. 'I have shown the police everything. I have nothing to hide from them.'

'But the police are not mind readers. They have only asked for evidence. They do not ask you how you think or feel, do they? They cannot know what goes on in your mind, how you met Mr Sharma, what Chitra said to you, why you do what you do, what your dreams and hopes are for the future.' Lakamma patted Kumar's hands, covering them with her smaller ones. 'I did my research on this young woman yesterday. I met people – a number of people whom I trust, who have helped me so much when I came to this unfamiliar city – and everyone had only good things to say about her. She only wants to seek the truth, and you have to help her, because if you don't, you may have no way to prove your innocence.'

They sat still in the small, airless room, the only sound coming from a large purple-coloured bumblebee buzzing outside the window. Just as Kaveri thought she could bear the silence no longer, a strangled sob came from the man sitting in front of the two women, who had buried his head in his hands.

Kaveri stood and went to the window, opening it to get some fresh air. She fussed for a few moments with the catch, giving Kumar some time to settle down. She could hear the rustle of Lakamma's sari, and a muffled exchange of words between them. When she judged that enough time had passed, she came back to the chair and sat down. Kumar's eyes were faintly moist, but he sat straight in his hard chair and looked directly at her.

'Tell me what you want to know.'

Kaveri took her notebook out of her purse, looking at the list of questions. 'Let's start with the will. What are the exact terms?'

Kumar hesitated. 'It is not public knowledge. But I suppose there is no harm in telling you. The police know, and so do Mrs Sharma and Chitra – either of them could tell you. The house goes to his wife, although Chitra has the right to live in it as long as she is unmarried, with a monthly allowance of a hundred rupees. Most of Mr Sharma's wealth was tied up in the factory. That is equally divided between Chitra and Mrs Sharma, with one condition. It is an odd condition – I do not know what Mr Sharma had in mind. The will says that until Chitra is married, Mrs Sharma is the full owner. Once Chitra and I marry, she becomes a 50% owner of the factory. However, Chitra has only a month to marry after her father's death. If she does not get married to me within that time, she forfeits all rights to the factory.'

'What?' Lakamma looked horrified. Kaveri had heard this before, from Ismail, but even she felt disgusted.

'Why would a man who educated his daughter to be independent do something like this? Write a will to rob her of her inheritance if she did not marry?'

Kumar looked uncomfortable. 'Sometimes I wonder whether Chitra would have married me if it had been her own choice. Or if she only agreed because she had no choice.'

Lakamma bit her lip. 'I was so excited when I heard that your marriage was fixed with Chitra that I never thought to stop and ask you if this was something you wanted.'

Kumar cleared his throat. 'I admire and respect both Mrs Sharma and Chitra very much.' His eyes were filled with affection as he looked at Lakamma. 'They remind me of you, *Amma*. They are both strong, independent women. I recognise that the family are paying me an honour by selecting someone like me – from a nondescript humble family – to join theirs. But I did not agree to the marriage because I wanted to become rich quickly.' He stared fiercely at Lakamma. 'You have to know that.'

'I do know,' Lakamma reassured him. 'But why *did* you agree?'

'Mr Sharma had a weak heart, for some years now. He was unable to put in the long hours of work he used to previously. Mrs Sharma and Chitra both have very different views on how the factory should be run. Left alone, they had started to rub each other the wrong way, and the factory suffered. Mr Sharma asked me to take over so that I could work with him more closely.'

'But you could continue to do that even if you did not marry Chitra,' Lakamma argued.

'Mr Sharma seemed to have got it into his head that Chitra needed to be married, required a man to settle her down. He had his sights fixed on me. I think . . . ' He paused. 'I think she may have had a lover, someone she wanted to marry before Mr Sharma brought me into the picture. Someone undesirable. They did not tell me anything, but I could gather from all the things they did not say.'

He put his glasses back on. 'I know what you must be thinking. Why would I want to marry a woman who is not in love with me, and who may be thinking of an old lover? But if I did not agree to marry Chitra, her father was clear that he would disinherit her. That did not seem fair to me. And I . . . I have become fond of her.' He cleared his throat briskly again. 'I assured Chitra that we could have a marriage of convenience if she wanted. At home, I would stay at a distance from her, but in the office, we could share the responsibilities, and work as partners. But she was distraught at what her father had done, the two of them were so close – and she holds her stepmother responsible.'

Kaveri looked at him. Could she believe this story? Kumar seemed reliable and straightforward. But then she thought of Chitra's suspicion that Kumar and Shanthi were having an affair. Anandi had also said that the two of them seemed very close. Why would Mr Sharma, who had previously been so close to his daughter, suddenly begin to control her just after he got married? Shanthi claimed that her stepdaughter would dance with delight to see her dead. Yet Chitra seemed to be the exploited one who had most to lose. It was Shanthi whose role reeked of manipulation.

24

Down With Corrupt Management

'I also heard that you have been facing some problems with disgruntled workers,' Kaveri said, thinking of her visit to the library, and the unproductive conversation with Chitra. 'I read about the worker strike, and the incident of fire and sabotage.'

Kumar looked at her with new respect. 'Yes, the press covered it extensively.'

He got up and moved to a window, pulling back the curtains and showing them the compound wall, with torn posters tacked to it.

'Down with corrupt management,' one poster read. 'Our managers feast on mutton and we subsist on old gruel.' 'Help us keep our children in school.'

Kaveri read the signs with growing horror. 'How can this be?' She thought of the large, elegant Sharma mansion with its massive bronzes, collection of marbles, and silver tea trays.

Lakamma's face had turned maroon with anger. 'You never told me this, Kumar. How could you sit back and watch this unfold? You were once in the situation of these workers. And besides all of that, it makes no business sense,' she added, turning to Kaveri. 'If you don't pay your workers well, they will resent you – rightfully so. And resentful workers spell death for any good business. I pay my workers 20% more than the going rate, and take care of their children's education.'

'Wait a minute,' Kaveri said, turning to Kumar. '"Don't stop our bonuses" – that means you used to pay bonuses? And then stopped?'

Kumar pushed his heavy spectacles back onto his nose.

'When I joined the Sampangi Mills, four years ago, it was a well-run place. The workers were paid well, and satisfied with their work. There was no workers' union. But about a couple of years after I joined, around the same time . . . ' He hesitated.

'The same time as?' Lakamma prodded.

'It was around the time Mr Sharma met madam. Shortly after that, he started to implement a number of new changes, saying that we had to improve our profitability. We cut worker bonuses that year for the first time in twenty years! And within a month, we also started to implement other cash-saving mechanisms. The workers used to eat for free in the canteen, but we started to charge them at market rates. And . . . ' He cleared his throat, 'We bought grain from the cheapest wholesale merchants on Avenue Road – the ones who mix *ragi* with stones, and the rice . . . it crawls with worms.

'The workers suddenly found their salaries reduced by about a third, cut to cover the costs of food. The factory used to give loans to workers at the beginning of the school year so that they could pay their children's fees – we used to pay for their children to go to school, and cover the medical bills for the workers *and* their families. We stopped all of that, to cut costs.

'I was only an assistant manager then. When the workers protested, I tried to speak to Mr Sharma, to get him to reconsider the changes. But he was spending a lot of time with madam, and he never seemed to have the time to listen to my concerns. That was when things became ugly. The workers formed a union, and all of them went on strike. The master and madam had gone on honeymoon for a month, to Ceylon, after they got married.' Kumar looked uncomfortable.

'Honeymoon to Ceylon?' Kaveri thought of Shanthi and her husband sailing away on an expensive ship, staying in the best hotels while their workers were striking. How could she have misjudged the woman so? To think she had actually liked her when they first met.

'I tried to send messages to him, but they were moving around from place to place, and the messages didn't reach them. By the time they returned, the factory was in chaos and we had lost a month of production. The fire destroyed much of our valuable stock as well. Mr Sharma was furious, bringing in the police and threatening to throw the ringleaders in jail. I spoke to him, and I think Chitra and maybe Mrs Sharma did too. We had no evidence that the workers had committed arson. After all, many of them had been with the mill for decades and nothing like this had ever happened before. Eventually, he relented. We reinstated the worker salaries and bonuses, and all the perquisites that we had previously put in place. He and I began to work more closely, and I took over much more of the day-to-day decision making. But ever since, the relationship between the workers and the management has been very tense.'

'I tried asking Chitra about this,' Kaveri said. 'But Chitra clammed up, refusing to tell me anything. She asked me why the workers would be dissatisfied, telling me you treat your staff so much better than many other ventures.'

Kumar looked uncomfortable. 'People who have been wealthy sometimes do not understand what it is to live on the edge with very little money as a buffer between you and penury,' he said.

Kumar seemed very cooperative, but he was also very careful in what he was willing to say directly, Kaveri realised. He was not going to say anything that might implicate Chitra or Mrs Sharma.

She changed the subject. 'Can I see the ledgers? To know more about the embezzlement?'

Kumar pushed a large hardbound accounts ledger book towards her.

'I have a feeling that a disgruntled worker may be at the root of the embezzlement,' he said. 'After all, why would either Mrs Sharma or Chitra want to steal money from their own mills? It doesn't make sense. It must be one of the workers who also murdered Mr Sharma in a showdown at his office.'

'How would they gain access to the ledger or the safe?' Kaveri asked. 'Can we see the safe again?'

Kumar pulled the curtain back in place and ushered them out of his room. They followed him down the corridor to Mr Sharma's room. Kaveri swallowed in relief when she saw that the room had been cleaned thoroughly, removing all traces of the murder. The bloodstained Kashmiri carpet had been removed, and replaced by a plain maroon rug.

Kumar opened the safe using a large, old-fashioned key, taken out of his pocket. 'Only Mr Sharma and I had access to the key that opens this locker,' he said.

'Mrs Sharma told me what must have happened,' Kaveri added, turning to Lakamma. 'Someone opened the locker, took out some of the money in the box, and cleverly altered the numbers written in the ledger to match the reduced amount. Mr Sharma has one key, but Shanthi told me that no one else in their house, apart from her and Chitra, had access to that. What about your key? Could anyone else have taken it, even briefly, to make a copy?' Kaveri asked.

'No. When I am in the office, I keep it with me all the time.' Kumar took it out of his pocket to show her again – a large key on an old-fashioned heavy iron keyring. 'And I live alone at home. I cook and clean for myself. Any time I leave my home, I take the keys with me. I knew what a big responsibility Mr Sharma had placed on my shoulders. I can assure you, I guarded this most carefully.'

'You are not making it easy for yourself, Kumar,' Lakkamma said in an exasperated tone. 'If you eliminate Shanthi and Chitra, because they would not steal from themselves, and the workers, because they had no way to access the safe or keys – that leaves only you.'

Kumar ran his finger around his collar, trying to loosen it. A sheen of perspiration had appeared on his forehead, but he still looked steadily at them – at Lakamma, his foster mother.

'I did not do it,' he said.

Kaveri gazed at him. Either he was a very straightforward man, determined to tell the truth even at cost to himself, or a very accomplished actor.

'No one else will believe me though.' Kumar gave her a small smile. 'I know that very soon the police will come to arrest me for the theft, and possibly the murder. They have already come to the office several times and called me to the police station for detailed questioning.'

'What does Mrs Sharma say?'

'She says she has every confidence in me, like you do.' His smile was tired. 'Chitra says the same. But deep in their hearts, perhaps they suspect me too.'

'Do you think it was one of them?' Kaveri asked, thinking of Chitra, to whom he was engaged, and Mrs Sharma, with whom Chitra claimed he was having an affair.

'I cannot believe a woman would commit a crime of this kind. Women are kind, gentle. Nurturing. This kind of crime requires sharp brains and strategy. It bears the clear hallmarks of a man.'

Kaveri knew of murderers who had been women, and she certainly knew of many who were clever enough to pull off something like this admittedly complicated theft. She decided to hold her tongue though, especially when she saw Kumar glance at the clock again, and Lakamma shake her head slightly at her.

Kumar thrust the accounts book at Kaveri, along with the small notepad in which he had written down the details of the two different sets of transactions.

'You must go now. The workers will be here in fifteen minutes and I don't want them to see you. They will gossip. There are already rumours spreading like wildfire that we don't have money to pay their salaries. Mrs Sharma has already made arrangements with her lawyer to sell their second home in Mysore so that they can keep the factory running for another few months. Business will be back on track soon, and the factory will turn a profit again if we are careful. But rumours – they could destroy the factory completely. And Mr Sharma would have hated that. The factory was his life,' Kumar finished fiercely. 'This was my first job. He took me in, an orphan whom no one could vouch for – except *Amma* here – no family to speak of. Not only did he promote me to become his trusted assistant, he offered me his daughter's hand in marriage. I cannot let the factory fail.'

Lakamma looked at the tall, thin man, whose shoulders were shaking.

'Kaveri,' she said calmly. 'Will you take the books and go back home? I think I will stay with Kumar for a while. He can send someone to drop me back home.'

'Of course.' Kumar was probably five or six years older than Kaveri, but she felt like comforting him herself just like she was used to doing for Venu. 'But please be careful with them,' he said. 'They are the only ones I have. We do not keep copies. All our records for the past year are here, and I cannot afford to lose them.'

'I will be very careful,' Kaveri promised, taking the account books and holding them in her arms. After saying goodbye to Lakamma and Kumar, she walked outside and got into her car.

As she started the engine, she frowned. The bonnet was loose and making a rattling sound. Strange. She could have sworn that sound had not been there when she'd driven in with Lakamma that morning. She got out and inspected the front of the car. Sure enough, the front flap was loose. She opened it and peered in. A twig was lying on its side, caught between the bonnet hood and the engine.

How had that happened? Kaveri removed the twig and banged the lid of the bonnet shut, taking a quick sniff as she smelt the unfamiliar fragrance of sandalwood. What did that remind her of? A memory twitched at the corner of her mind, but she could not grasp it. Should she drive to the garage? Something really didn't feel right about the car, but her fingers were itching to open the account books and examine them more closely. Numbers always spoke to her. Perhaps they would give her a clue about what was happening.

As she got into the car again, Kaveri felt eyes on her. This seemed to be happening all the time these days, that feeling of being constantly watched, she thought, looking around but seeing no one.

As she started the car and moved forward, the dry twig caught under the wheel and snapped in two, causing Kaveri to let out a tiny yelp. The sound was loud in the stillness of the morning and reminded her of the gunshot she had heard the night that Mr Sharma had been killed.

As her thoughts rolled back to the blood-stained carpet, the car jolted violently, stalling in position and making a grinding noise. Feeling a little foolish, Kaveri waited for her heart to stop thumping so violently.

Once she had calmed down, she scolded herself for overreacting, then she started the car again, driving out of the gate.

On the side of the road, below a large banyan tree, a coconut seller caught her eye in the distance. He sat with a large pile of coconuts and a machete, deftly lopping off the tops of the nuts and then handing them to a teacher standing with a gaggle of students.

Still feeling on edge, the idea of fresh coconut water made her turn the wheel towards the banyan tree. But as Kaveri pushed down on the brake and turned the wheel, the car continued on its steady course, taking her closer to the vendor and the group of children without the slightest sign of slowing.

With mounting panic, she tugged the hand brake, only to find it come off into her hand. A bus crossed her on the other side, the driver honking hard on his horn as he swerved to move out of her path. He shook his fist as he passed, shouting out abuses in a loud voice. She stepped hard on the brake, pressing on it again and again, her heart thumping violently.

The children were coming even closer. Unaware of her struggles to keep the car under control, they laughed as they monkeyed around with the coconuts, darting in and out of each other's reach as the teacher opened a knot tied in his *dhoti* and counted out coins to the coconut vendor. Kaveri spun the wheel without hope, watching horrified as the car, refusing to slow down or be turned from its path, moved towards a direct collision course with the children. She pressed down on the horn, but the children, who were now just a few yards away, were laughing and shouting so loudly that they could not hear the blaring of the horn, or her cries to them to move.

What could she do?

She took a quick decision and spun the wheel hard, directing the car at the large tree and hoping it would halt the movement of the vehicle. She rolled down the window, pressing furiously on the horn and shouting 'Move! Danger!' at the top of her voice. The car moved closer and closer to the tree, and – thank *heavens* – away from the chattering bunch of students. She caught a glimpse of the horrified face of a young boy who finally heard the horn blaring next to him just before the car smashed into the large tree trunk.

She heard the reverberations of a loud scream, realising dimly that it came from her own throat.

Then everything was darkness.

25

An Enforced Rest

Thirst. Her throat was so dry, it ached abominably. She needed water. But she could not open her eyes to look for the glass. She groped around in panic. *Why couldn't she see?* Her flailing fingers caught the hold of an edge of cloth. Someone had tied a bandage around her head and eyes. She felt around with her hands, looking for the bedside table, but stopped in confusion when she felt the outlines of a metal bed. But her bed was made of wood! And where was the jug that usually stood there? She tried calling for help but only a whisper came out.

Nevertheless, someone came running. She could hear their footsteps. Whoever it was held her by the shoulders and lifted her up from the bed a few inches. Kaveri groaned in pain.

'Shh,' the voice said. 'Drink this.' A few spoons of cool liquid dribbled into her throat. Then she fell asleep again, sinking gratefully into blessed unconsciousness.

*

The next time she woke, she could open her eyes. It was dark. She was in her room, in her own bed. She patted the outlines of the wooden bed with relief, seeing the bedside table next to her, with a jug of water. She squinted, trying to see clearly in the dim moonlight that filtered through her bedroom window. Why was Ramu in the easy chair instead of lying in bed next to her?

She reached out for the water, trying not to make a sound, but as soon as he heard the steel tumbler moving on the wood of the table, Ramu sat up with a start. When he saw that she was awake he came swiftly to the bed, dropped to his knees and took her hands in his.

'You woke up!' He buried his face in her hands, his shoulders shaking. 'Finally, Kaveri. You woke up.'

Kaveri blinked, smoothing her hand over his hair with tenderness. 'What happened? Why are you crying?' Then she stopped, hearing the soreness in her own voice. 'Water,' she whispered.

Ramu raised her up, propping her upright against a pile of pillows, and helped her to drink. 'Rest now,' he said when she'd finished drinking. 'No more conversation tonight. Tomorrow, we will speak.'

'But sleep with me,' Kaveri pleaded. Ramu got into bed, holding her carefully as she relaxed again, comforted by his presence, listening to his steady breathing as it lulled her to sleep.

'And so someone sabotaged your car!'

Kaveri was sitting up in her bedroom, propped against a soft pile of pillows. Uma aunty, sitting near her feet, was giving her an update.

'How long has it been?' she asked. She had only the faintest memory of the accident, though she could remember the angry fist of the driver of the bus, and the horrified face of the schoolboy who had jerked his friend to safety just before she shot past them. Ramu said it was selective memory loss – that her brain, not wanting to process the trauma of the accident all at once, had tucked most of the incident away somewhere deep in her brain, keeping it for a later time when she was calmer.

'Three days – you were unconscious for three days, because your head hit the steering wheel so hard when you collided with the tree.' Uma aunty clucked her tongue. 'That poor husband of yours, he has not slept a wink during that entire time. He spent night and day watching over you in the hospital, and has been at your bedside ever since you were brought home.'

'My car! What happened to the car?' Kaveri tried to get up but sank back into the pillows with a cry of pain.

'It is in the garage.' Uma aunty patted her hand. 'The bonnet was dented, but the garage has assured your husband that they can repair it and make it look like new in a couple of days.'

'Thank goodness,' Kaveri said fervently.

'You know, you're a heroine in the eyes of those schoolchildren.' Uma aunty pointed to the greeting cards tacked on the wall, childish drawings of a stick figure driving a car or propped up in a hospital bed. 'The way you decided to steer around and avoid them . . . that almost cost you your life. If you had kept your course, they would have been in danger, but you would have been better protected.'

Kaveri bit her lip. 'I'm no heroine. I was terrified.'

Rajamma came in with a glass of pomegranate juice, shaking her head at Kaveri as she began to refuse. Ramu had made a roster of food and drink for her, and Rajamma came in every hour to give her something restorative.

'You lost a lot of blood, Kaveri. You have to drink this.'

Kaveri made a face but drank it obediently. 'She gave me beetroot soup in the morning,' she complained, scowling at Uma aunty as she burst out laughing. Then a thought occurred to her.

'What about Putta? Is he still here, or has *athe* sent him away?' She made as if to get up, but Rajamma hushed her. 'We are taking good care of him. Don't worry. You lie down. The doctor has said you need a lot of rest after the way in which you hit your head.'

'Where are the account books?' she demanded, thinking of the books that Kumar had handed to her. 'They were in the car . . . '

'What books? There were no books!' Uma aunty said, looking puzzled.

'Then what? Who . . . ?' Kaveri suddenly felt exhausted. Rajamma exchanged a look with Uma aunty, who got up, swiftly drawing the curtains back to block out the sun.

'Sleep now. We will talk later.'

'All I do is sleep,' Kaveri grumbled, but she *was* tired, and her head was aching again. Uma aunty placed a cool wet cloth on her forehead, and she moaned with gratitude, closing her eyes.

A couple of days later, after a long debate with Ramu, who seemed to be hovering around her like a brooding hen with an especially fragile chick, Kaveri was finally allowed to get up and leave the bedroom and go to the drawing room. She leafed through a pile of her favourite magazine, *Women's World*, which Miss Roberts had sent over. Mrs Reddy had borrowed a Sherlock Holmes book from the library for her, and Mrs Ismail had dropped off a book of mathematics puzzles that her daughter had given her for Kaveri to look at. But nothing could hold her interest for long.

Kaveri went out through the back door to look for Putta. She missed the large dog, and wanted badly to bring him into the house, but she knew Bhargavi would never settle for it. But when she reached the back garden, she stopped. Her mother-in-law was standing in the shed, petting the large dog on his head, feeding him bits of *jolada rotti*, a chappati made from millet, as he jumped around her.

Kaveri craned her neck to hear what she was saying.

'You sweet boy,' Bhargavi laughed, as Putta came closer to her, panting in his eagerness to get at the *rotti*. 'You remind me of my son when he was young. He also loved eating from my hands.' She looked wistful, speaking to Putta in a baby voice. 'What a *bangaari* you are, such a darling. Eat, *kanna*, my little one. Then we can go for a walk together.'

Kaveri backed away slowly, trying not to make any sound. The last thing she wanted to do is to interrupt this tender scene, possibly making Bhargavi defensive. For the past two days, Bhargavi had hovered around her quite like Ramu did, driving her insane with her constant reminders to stay in bed and her offers of help. Perhaps looking after Putta would give her mother-in-law something to do, and get her off Kaveri's back.

Kaveri went in and sat on the sofa again, restlessly leafing through the pages of her notepad, which she had asked Rajamma to retrieve from her shed earlier that morning. She so badly wanted to know what was happening with the case. But no one told her anything. Each time she asked, everyone deflected her, saying that she would know soon enough, and she should not worry herself.

She heard the gate open and Bhargavi speaking tenderly to Putta as she led him out. After a short while, she heard the gate open again. Were they back again so soon? But no, the footsteps were light, and quick. That must be Venu.

'It is so good to see you sitting up, Kaveri *akka*,' Venu beamed, dragging a footstool over to sit next to her, taking her hand and squeezing it lightly. 'You looked scary, in the hospital. All drained of blood, covered with white bandages. Like a ghost, a *pisachi*,' he said as he gave her an impish grin. 'I came every morning to see you, but you were sleeping. I have some news for you. I have been trying to find someone – anyone – who was near the car that day.'

'Someone who can tell us what happened to my car?' Kaveri sucked in a deep breath, regretting it instantly as a wave of pain washed over her.

'Yes. The police asked around, but of course no one will talk to them. I thought there may have been a child who saw something, though. Ramu *anna* gave me some money to pay for the information.'

'And?'

'I found a boy. He had climbed a *honge* tree in the compound to collect its seeds, which he sells to the oil maker for a few annas. A man opened the bonnet of the car, fiddling inside. He'd seen you and the old *ajji* drive in, so he knew the car did not belong to the man. He wanted to ask him what he was doing, but was afraid, because the man looked scary.'

'Did he describe him, Venu?' Kaveri pressed him.

Venu shrugged. 'He could not see his face. The man was of average height – not too tall or too short. Slightly plump, with a small paunch. He wore a pair of khaki pants and a dirty white *banian* with an unbuttoned khaki shirt. And a cap over his head.'

Kaveri's face fell. That could describe any one of hundreds of people.

'Is he sure it was a man? Not a woman in a man's clothes?' she pressed.

'Yes, the man smoked a *beedi*, and cursed under his breath in a rough, guttural voice.'

'What's that?' Ramu stepped in through the door, breaking into a smile when he saw Venu.

Kaveri listened with half an ear as Venu excitedly filled Ramu in on his conversation with the boy. As Venu concluded his conversation with Ramu and ran out, Kaveri drooped, suddenly feeling drained of all energy. Ramu moved to sit next to her, pulling her down to lie with her head in his lap. He showed her a report that had just arrived from the garage, but Kaveri handed it back to him, too weary to open it.

'What does it say? Why did the car crash?' Kaveri asked.

'Someone seems to have done a thorough job on your car – probably the same man that the little boy saw fiddling with your bonnet. The wires that connected the clutch, brake and handbrake had been neatly severed with a sharp knife.'

'I wish I had not lost the account books when I had the car accident. Maybe I could have found some clues to the identity of the embezzler if I was able to look at them carefully enough.' Kaveri looked up at Ramu.

'That must be what the person who caused the accident wanted to avoid, by sabotaging your car and stealing the notebooks before you could take a look at them.' Ramu wound a coil of Kaveri's dark hair around his fingers.

Kaveri got up from Ramu's lap, reaching for her notepad. 'That means we should cross out Kumar. He would have no reason to give me the account books himself, then stage an accident to take them away.'

'That could be exactly what he wants you to think,' Ramu pointed out.

'What do we do now? It's all so confusing.' Kaveri let out a sigh of frustration. 'I don't seem to be crossing out any suspects. I'm only adding new ones. Shanthi, Chitra, Kumar, and now the possibility of an unknown mill worker. How will I ever solve this case?'

'First, eat. Then you take a nap.' Ramu put a finger to her lips, gently hushing her as she attempted to argue. 'Another couple of days of rest and you will be as good as new. But if you strain yourself overly and have a relapse, you will not be able to leave the bedroom for a week.'

As she grumbled indignantly at him, he picked her up and carried her to the dining table. 'If you are good, and rest all of today, I have some news that will make you happy. I have arranged a women's club meeting at home for you tomorrow. You can do some more sleuthing from the safety of your drawing room.'

26

A Feminist Manifesto

'You should read the latest edition of *Saraswati*,' Mrs Reddy said, passing around a few slim copies of cyclostyled paper, neatly bound together, to the women who were gathered in Kaveri's drawing room the next morning. 'It's a new women's magazine, started just a couple of weeks back, by a woman editor, Kalyanamma.'

'Saraswati, the Hindu goddess of learning – a perfect name for such a magazine,' Mrs Ismail said, leafing through the pages with avid interest. 'Your mother-in-law may like it too, Kaveri. Where is she?'

'Visiting Shanthi again,' Kaveri said, flipping through the pages, her interest piqued. She had never read an Indian magazine for women before. The British and American women's weeklies that she read seemed to think women were empty-headed creatures, only covering topics such as how to decorate your home, cook meals for your family, and dress to keep your man's interest.

But this magazine was very different. Kalyanamma did not consider women to be empty-headed creatures, curious only about fashion and fripperies. This magazine was full of interesting material – politics, children's welfare, and the place of women in society.

When she heard excited affirmations of '*houdu, houdu*' – 'yes, yes' and '*thumba* correct' 'very correct', Kaveri looked up, smiling when she saw that the women had formed themselves into smaller groups, readers assisting non-readers. Uma aunty was sitting shoulder to shoulder with Mrs Reddy, while Mrs Ismail had moved to the corner where Mala, Narsamma and Anandi were sitting in a tight cluster. '"The Women's Suffrage Movement in Bangalore – A Personal Story",' she read, turning to Kaveri. 'I admire the suffragists in London, and the innovative protest in which they shackle themselves to public places to ask for the right to vote.'

'I do too.' Kaveri moved to read over her shoulder, then stopped.

'Look at the by-line!' She underlined the name with her finger.

'Mrs Shanthi Sharma?' The conversation faded as the women looked at the magazine.

'I don't believe it,' Kaveri said flatly. 'Shanthi, a suffragist who fought for women's rights? Why, she was the one who told me she urged her husband to get Chitra married to Kumar so she could be guided by a man. What a hypocrite the woman is.'

She tossed the magazine onto the sofa. 'I have no idea how my mother-in-law can be friends with such a woman. It doesn't make sense. But then, nothing about this case makes much sense.'

Kaveri stopped herself from ranting further, seeing Anandi casting sideways glances at her. 'But we have to discuss the case too, and quickly. Anandi has to get back home in . . . ' Kaveri paused, looking at the young woman.

'An hour,' Anandi said. 'I asked for two hours to visit my "sister" who I said works in a home in Basavanagudi. They said I had to be home by 11 a.m. That's just half an hour away. I have a lot to tell you.'

'How is the atmosphere in the house? Do the two of them talk to each other at all?' Kaveri asked.

'Both women keep to themselves. They even eat their meals separately. They have contempt for each other – and, I think, a touch of fear as well. They bolt themselves into their bedrooms at night,' Anandi said.

Kaveri made a face. 'How must it feel, I wonder, to feel so unsafe that you lock yourself into your own room at night?'

Mala looked at her with some amusement, and a flicker of – something. Was it regret? Envy?

'Only women like you would say such a thing,' she told Kaveri bluntly. 'Our kind of women' – she swept her hand in a wide arc that covered Narsamma, Anandi and herself, pointedly leaving out Mrs Ismail, Uma aunty and Mrs Reddy – 'we don't live like you, in houses that have front doors with locks, and bedroom doors with bolts. We live in huts and hovels, where we may at best hang a piece of cloth on some string for some privacy. But if we did have a way to bolt our doors at night . . . ' She paused, looking around the room at the faces intent on her. 'Believe me, we would all lock our doors. To keep us safe from the assaults of men. The night is a dangerous time for women like us.'

A dog with a litter of pups swarming around her gave a mournful howl from outside the window. Anandi jumped.

Narsamma cackled. 'The old bitch agrees with us! It was a male who got her into this mess.'

Everyone laughed, but uncertainly. Not for the first time since meeting Mala, Kaveri felt a deep sense of discomfort with herself. She tried hard, but feared she found she could not understand how different the lives of these women were from her own, relatively well-ordered ways of living, with societal structures that kept women like her safe. She had never had to fear going hungry or thirsty or worry about the ever-present danger to her body or mind posed by strangers, which women like Mala had experienced from an early age. Kaveri wished with all her heart that she could find a safe shelter for women like them, a place where they could be free to live and breathe with comfort, and just be themselves.

Mrs Ismail passed a plate of *Mysore paak* to Anandi, who continued her story, looking around at the women as she spoke. 'I sleep in the maid's room, which is at the end of the corridor near the drawing room. The very first night, I was half asleep when I heard a noise. It took me a while to realise what it was. Someone had opened the windows in the drawing room.'

Anandi looked around the room, holding everyone's eyes. 'I opened the door and tiptoed down the corridor, peering into the room. I saw a dim figure, only faintly visible in the light from the street lamp outside, wearing a large, loose shirt, pants and cap – all black.'

'And then?' Narsamma's eyes were large and rounded.

'The person turned around, and I felt scared, so I ran back on my tiptoes to my room and closed the door,' Anandi continued. 'I was lucky, for I managed to reach my room without making any noise, and I don't think the person realised I saw him. The branches of the tree outside the window rustled, followed by a heavy thump, as though someone had jumped onto the road wearing heavy boots. After a short while, I came out of the room and found the window ajar and swinging in the wind, but there was nobody there. I waited for a while, but then worried that I would be seen, and returned to my room. Then . . . ' Anandi paused dramatically before she continued, 'Then I felt thirsty, and drank a glass of water. Immediately after that I felt very sleepy. I closed my eyes, only planning to sleep for a short while. When I woke up, it was morning, and the window was closed.'

'Somebody drugged the water?' Mrs Ismail looked at Anandi.

'My mother-in-law told me that Shanthi and Chitra had been given sleeping draughts by their doctor. Perhaps they slipped one of those in your water,' Kaveri said.

'Maybe. I made a very stupid mistake. The next morning, I raised the issue with both my mistresses. I told them that I'd had a really bad dream the previous night, that I'd heard someone's footsteps in the night in my dreams and thought there was a thief – and I was very relieved to wake up in the morning to see that the house was safe, and no robber, no *dacoit*, had entered.'

'And?'

'Neither of them said anything. They looked at me with impassive faces, and I could not read their expressions. But ever since I told them this, I find that I am also bolted into my bedroom at night. Someone comes and unbolts it early in the morning, but I am too scared to open the door and see who it is.'

Mrs Ismail looked across the room at Anandi. 'Be very careful, Anandi. Don't drink the water again, if you think they may be putting something in it to make you sleepy. You might find yourself addicted. My husband says that that there are a number of addicts in Bangalore, addicted to all kinds of stimulants.'

'After that night, I haven't drunk the water,' Anandi reassured her. 'I pour the water out onto a tree before I go to bed, and pretend to be fast asleep. Every night, I hear the sound of someone stopping outside my door, and their heavy breathing as they listen for sounds in my room. I stay still and pretend to be asleep. The person then bolts me in, and I hear them moving around in the drawing room. After a while, I hear the window being opened, and someone jumping down onto the street below. I have been too scared to mention it again to either of my two mistresses. I can tomorrow, if you want me to.'

'No, Anandi, you must be careful,' Kaveri warned her. 'There is a ruthless killer who has already committed one murder. We do not know whether they would hesitate to commit a second, if it comes to that.'

'Perhaps I should ask my husband to station a policeman outside the house,' Mrs Ismail suggested.

'No,' Kaveri said immediately. 'The constables are too conspicuous. Someone will see them and talk – the beggars on the street, the vendors . . . someone, and then word will spread, and the person who is sneaking out will know we are onto them.'

She turned to Anandi, remembering something. 'But Anandi, how did the person you saw jump from the tree to the wall? When I went to the Sharma home, I saw that the wall was protected by sharp glass pieces embedded along its length.'

Anandi nodded. 'I checked that spot the next day, pretending to be dusting the window as I looked out. There is a tiny spot to the left of the window, just below the tree. There, three of the glass shards have been neatly removed from the concrete where they were embedded, and placed back onto the wall. You can see that they are loose, and can be removed – but only if you look carefully.'

The clock chimed, and Anandi jumped. 'Eleven already! I must leave.'

'What do you plan to do, Kaveri?' Uma aunty asked.

'I will think of something,' Kaveri told her. She was sick of resting in bed, and was itching to get back to the case.

She planned to stand watch herself that night, outside the window, disguised in a man's clothes. There was no point telling the women, who would only attempt to dissuade her. They would not understand how suffocated she was beginning to feel, with Venu and Mala checking in on her hourly, and Ramu, Bhargavi and Rajamma fussing over her as though she was an invalid. So she sat quietly, listening to the women exchange farewells as they left, plotting what she would wear that night.

27

A Midnight Escapade

'Absolutely not!' Ramu's voice was forceful as she explained her plan to him over lunch.

Kaveri looked at him. 'I will dress up as a man, you will be with me and we will hide in the shadows. What is there to fear?'

Ramu groaned, pinching the bridge of his nose. 'It is not safe, Kaveri. You almost got killed a few days ago because someone tried to sabotage your car, and now you want to risk your life again?'

'We have to solve this murder fast,' Kaveri said, looking into his eyes. 'Don't you see? The next time, and I'm sure there will *be* a next time, I may not be so lucky as to escape unscathed. We need to find out who is behind all this – the embezzlement, the murder of Mr Sharma, the attack on me – and put them in jail.'

'Why don't you just ask Ismail to pull the lot of them in for questioning again? Kumar, Mrs Sharma and Chitra. A few days in the lock-up and they'll be falling over themselves to tell him who planned the attack on you.'

'They're too well connected, and we have no evidence against them,' Kaveri argued. 'You know as well as I do that even if Inspector Ismail does manage to put them in jail, Shanthi and Chitra will be out in less than an hour. Soon after, the Inspector will be out of a job. The only one left in jail will be poor Kumar, and he may or may not be the real innocent here. All we will achieve is to drive their activities further into the shadows and then we'll keep living in danger, always wondering where the next threat may be coming from.' She gave Ramu a pleading look. 'I cannot live like this.'

'Why can't you stay at home while I stand watch with Venu?' Ramu started to say, then stopped himself, looking at Kaveri. 'That won't work, will it? What am I to do with you, Kaveri? You are a stubborn woman, and a curse and a plague on my life.' But he said it softly, placing his hands on hers.

She gave a little squeal of delight. 'Then you will come with me?'

Ramu gave her fingers a little shake, still holding them tightly. 'What choice do I have? If I say no, I am sure you will do it anyway as soon as my back is turned. This way, at least, I can keep an eye on you. But what will we do about my mother? She will want to know where we are going at night, and may tell Shanthi.'

'I have an idea.' Kaveri looked at Ramu a trifle hesitantly. 'I have already organised it in fact. Unless you object.'

'What is it?'

'I asked Uma aunty to stay back after the women's meeting, and told her of my predicament, asking if she could think of some way to keep Bhargavi *athe* preoccupied. It turns out that she knows just the thing! Her sister-in-law's daughter is getting married, and she had been asking Uma aunty to come over for a couple of days and help her with the shopping, writing of invitations, and the other last minute details that need to be done. Uma aunty asked Bhargavi *athe* if she would be willing to go along with her and help. *Athe* jumped at the idea. You know, I think she is really looking for things to do. We need to give her an occupation, something she can do where she feels useful.'

Seeing Ramu sit silently, Kaveri paused, giving him a look of appeal. 'Are you annoyed with me, for plotting to send your mother away?'

Ramu got up, pacing up and down. 'Ever since my father died, my mother has been withdrawn, anxious, on edge. I scolded her for going to the ashram, but what else did I offer as an alternative? Perhaps that made her feel valued, a part of a community, where she introduced other wealthy women to the Swami and thought she was contributing to a larger cause. Now that my sister and I are both married, and don't need her as we used to, she must feel there is a void in her life.'

He sat down next to her again, putting an arm around her. 'No, Kaveri, how can I be annoyed with you? I should have thought of this myself. And it will be good to have the house to ourselves for a couple of days.' He smiled, a boyish grin that lit up his face, caressing her shoulder as she blushed.

'You know,' Kaveri dropped her voice to a whisper, moving closer to him, even though she knew Bhargavi was not in hearing range, 'I saw Bhargavi *athe* playing with Putta, and taking him for a walk. Putta has some new toys this week, including a small wooden horse that has become his new favourite chewing toy. I suspect she has been secretly buying him things to play with, though she will never admit it.'

'So, Putta has worked his magic on her! My mother, who I thought was anti-dogs for life, seems to be re-thinking her attitude towards pets.' Ramu rubbed his hands in glee.

Kaveri looked at him, lounging in his elegantly cut suit against the sofa, and jumped up. 'We need to organise men's clothes – not just for me, but for both of us. Your clothes are too well cut – if you walk around at night dressed like this, you will attract the wrong kind of attention, from thieves and scoundrels.'

She hurried through the kitchen to the courtyard behind, calling out, 'Rajamma! Rajamma, can you rush home and bring us two pairs of your husband's oldest clothes?'

'*Cheee*!' Later that night, Kaveri wrinkled her nose in disgust, trying to hold the soiled shirt she wore as far away from her nose as possible.

She could see a flash of white teeth in the dark as Ramu grinned at her, pulling her close and whispering, 'Rajamma's husband must have gone on a drinking spree.'

'How can you bear the stench?' Kaveri whispered.

Ramu shrugged, pulling her away from a stray dog sleeping on the pavement. 'I am used to this, Kaveri. I see drunks all the time in the hospital.'

They stopped at a safe distance outside the Sharma house, near the large Garuda motif gates. A man stood next to a small cart piled high with crumpled clothes at the side of the gate. He was opening a large *istri*, an ironing box, and placing lit coals inside.

Kaveri looked up and down the street. No one else was there. They weaved to and fro like two drunk men as they passed the man with the *istri*, who paid them no attention.

They settled down near a tree, where the *istri* man could not see them. The light of the moon filtered out faintly.

'That's the spot where the tree reaches the window.' Kaveri pointed. 'That must be the section of the wall where the person climbs down.'

The *istri* man ironed five saris, yawning loudly, before he pushed the cart away, done for the night. Kaveri's eyes felt heavy, and she closed them for a second.

Ramu pressed her head onto his shoulder.

'Sleep. I'll keep watch and wake you.'

But just as she made herself comfortable, they heard a rustle of branches. Kaveri squinted, unable to see clearly in the dark. Was that an indistinct figure climbing down the tree?

The figure carefully levered itself onto the wall, removing a set of glass pieces and keeping them to the side, then looking around onto the road. Ramu and Kaveri shrank back into the shadows.

The figure squatted, then jumped onto the road, landing on their feet. The light of a street lamp fell on the person, silhouetting their figure.

'That's not a man,' Kaveri whispered, leaning close to Ramu and speaking directly into his ear. 'It's a woman. But is it Chitra, or Shanthi?'

They looked at the figure closely, but at that distance, and in the low light from the street lamp, it was impossible to make out. The figure moved closer to them, and Ramu pulled Kaveri up from the pavement, whispering, 'Let's move ahead of her, otherwise she'll suspect we are following her.'

He broke into a drunken warble, singing an old Kannada song tunelessly in a high falsetto, as he pulled Kaveri along with him, casting a quick glance at the road behind as he sang. The person was moving in their direction, staying in the shadows and keeping behind.

Ramu stopped suddenly, letting out a violent series of oaths. 'My shoe,' he said loudly, dropping to the ground. 'It's broken.'

He squatted on the side of the road, pretending to squint at his shoes, pulling Kaveri down with him. The figure hesitated, then moved forward past them, breaking into a run.

Ramu waited for a second, slipping off his shoes. Kaveri did the same.

'Quick, let's follow.' The two of them ran, noiseless in bare feet, keeping a few yards behind the figure. But when they reached the corner of the road, they stopped, looking around in confusion.

The narrow, unlit section of the road opened into a larger intersection of four roads. They could not see the person anywhere.

Kaveri went in one direction, while Ramu sped down another. In a second they were both back gasping for breath. They looked at each other, then in unspoken accord, reached for each other's hands, running down the last road together.

Nobody was in sight. Only the dark streets, illuminated in spots by patches of light from the street lamps, and an occasional street dog. In the distance, a large bandicoot darted across the road, dragging a piece of meat in its mouth. Kaveri shivered.

Ramu took her by the elbow. 'Let's go home,' he said. 'We can come back tomorrow and find out what buildings lie in this area.'

'We need to talk to Inspector Ismail,' Kaveri said. 'We can go straight to the police station tomorrow. There we can speak to him in private.'

Ramu shook his head. 'Too many people can overhear our conversation there. You have already got the murderer agitated because of your investigations, and there has been one attempt on your life. I'll go to the police station tomorrow morning and ask Ismail to come home, to speak to you in private so we can ensure no one else overhears.'

'You can't always protect me like this,' Kaveri argued.

'Don't fight me on this, Kaveri. You are too precious to me to lose.' Ramu's voice was hoarse with fear.

28

Through the Coconut Grove

'Shanthi and Chitra are about the same height. It could be either of them,' Ramu said, looking at Ismail as they sat on the sofa the following morning. Ismail had come to their house as soon as he'd received Ramu's note. 'We thought a man was sneaking *into* the house to meet one of the two women. Instead, one of them seems to be sneaking *out* to meet someone.'

Mala and Venu looked at them from across the room, having come in as they did every morning since the accident, to check on Kaveri. Even though she had tried to reassure them that she was now fine, they had refused to stay away.

'But I still think it is Shanthi,' Kaveri insisted. 'Chitra has a bad leg, remember?' She looked at the two men, and held up her hand. 'I know, I know, you are going to tell me that she may be faking it. But I don't think so.'

'The fact that Shanthi is forcing Chitra to marry Kumar is really bothering you, isn't it?' Ramu said gently. 'But that doesn't automatically mean that Shanthi is the murderer, or the one sneaking out.'

Kaveri swallowed a lump in her throat. Ramu usually agreed with her. Why was he being so difficult all of a sudden?

'You forget what Inspector Ismail said,' she retorted, pointing to the large policeman. 'Shanthi even asked her lawyer if there was any way in which she could overturn her husband's will to gain control of the entire factory and its operations. She is a scheming sort of woman. Chitra told me she suspects that Shanthi and Kumar are having an affair. Is Shanthi sneaking out to meet Kumar?'

'*If* it is Shanthi who is sneaking out, Kaveri,' Ramu remonstrated.

Kaveri sat up a bit straighter, and gave him a small glare.

Ismail looked from one to the other, and cleared his throat, before stating diplomatically, 'Where did the woman go when she disappeared? That may tell us something.' He reached into his capacious pocket, pulling out a folded map, creased and wrinkled from use.

Ramu and Kaveri pulled their chairs closer, opening the map and laying it flat on the table in front of them. Ramu patted Kaveri's hand pacifically, watching her closely. She swallowed the little lump in her throat again, and gave him a small reluctant smile. Perhaps he did have a point. She should keep an open mind, as a detective's *dharma* dictated.

'The Sharma residence is on this side road.' Ismail reached out with his pencil and made an X mark on the map.

'The place she went, wherever it was, was very close to the junction where we lost sight of her. We were only a few seconds behind her, but she disappeared from sight,' Ramu said.

Mala, who had been listening to the conversation with fascination, got up unnoticed to come closer to the table and peer at the map. Now she cleared her throat.

'What is it, Mala?'

Mala pointed her finger at a patch of land without buildings, near the intersection where they had lost sight of the woman.

'Isn't that the coconut grove that is at the back of the new Swami's ashram?' she asked.

'Of course!' Kaveri smacked her forehead with the back of her palm. She should have remembered this herself, but the car crash seemed to have driven many memories out of her head. Ramu had reassured her that they would return in time, as her brain healed from the impact. 'Swami Vaninanda's ashram is right there. I went with Bhargavi *athe* just before my car accident. The coconut grove belongs to him. The buildings are on the other side. There is a small mud path here.' She picked up the pencil that lay on the table, growing more confident as she spoke. 'The path goes through the grove and ends at a back gate into the ashram.'

Mala nodded. 'My neighbour Ratna works in the ashram, and I walked with her to the grove once on my way to the market. It is a shortcut taken by the workers.'

Ismail gave Mala a sharp glance of interest, as Kaveri mentally castigated herself. Why had she not thought of asking Mala before? Mala had connections with the underworld, as well as with so many people who worked in a variety of odd jobs across the city. She should have been the first person Kaveri asked. But in her excitement at being introduced to Lakamma and meeting Kumar, she had forgotten to follow up on the ashram. And then the accident had happened, and driven everything else out of her head.

'Has your neighbour seen the destitute women in the shelter?' Kaveri asked her eagerly. 'The Swami and his assistant refused to allow me in when I visited with my mother-in-law. I only caught a glimpse of the women, but what I saw disturbed me. I don't know what goes on in that place in the name of charity, but they do not seem well taken care of at all.'

Mala frowned slowly. 'Ratna's job is to take care of them. There are about thirty women in the shelter. Ratna is a simple, trusting woman who has a limited knowledge of the world. She is not worldly wise. She is a hard worker, but had struggled to find a job until the ashram finally took her on a year back. From what she says, I think the ashram is a very dangerous place. The women are largely kept confined to their rooms, and only allowed to step out occasionally, onto the roof. There are many things going on there that I cannot understand. I have asked her many times to leave the job, but she refuses, worried that no one else will employ her. I think she is also afraid of them.'

'Does Ratna stay there at night? Can she help us sneak in during the evening to lie in wait for the woman, to see if it is Chitra or Shanthi?' Kaveri asked in excitement, ignoring Ramu as he frowned at her.

'No, she and all the other part-timers leave at 6 p.m., just before it gets dark. After that, apart from Swami Vaninanda and Murali, who live there, only the women live there.'

'Who is Murali?' Kaveri asked.

'The Swami's assistant,' Mala replied.

Finally, she was able to associate the hairy armed man with a name! Murali. Kaveri turned it over in her head. What *was* that thought tickling the corner of her mind?

'Wait . . . ' Kaveri closed her eyes, as pieces of the puzzle finally started snapping into place. 'The ashram. They light incense sticks perfumed with the sticky sweet smell of sandalwood. The note that I received on the night of the murder, asking me to go to Sampangi Mills at 8 p.m. instead of 9 – that note had the same fragrance. And I got a whiff of the same scent the day I visited Kumar, when I closed the open bonnet of my car, just before the accident. Someone from the ashram must be involved.'

She turned to Venu.

'The little boy you found who saw a man tamper with my car – he couldn't see the man's face, you said. But could he see his arms?'

'Yes, Kaveri *akka*, I forgot to tell you. He said the man had very hairy forearms, which glistened in the sunlight as he straightened up to light his *beedi*.' Venu looked worried. 'Was it very important, *akka*?'

'It is a very useful piece of information, Venu,' Kaveri said, patting his back. 'Murali has very hairy arms. He lights the *oodo kaddi*, the incense sticks. His hands must be soaked in that perfume. He has to be the man who sent me the fake note, and who sabotaged my car.'

She fingered her pendant as another piece of the puzzle fell into place.

She turned to face Ramu. 'Remember my chain? How it was found in Mr Sharma's hands?'

'How could I forget, Kaveri?' Ramu gave her a wry grimace.

'Well . . . it was on my neck before I left the house to go to the dog show. I know I had it on because I looked in the mirror. Later that morning, Bhargavi *athe* made me touch the Swami's feet to take his blessings. He then did some "magic" hocus pocus,' she waved her hands dismissively, 'generating a flash of bright light and some smoke. I smelt a trace of gunpowder. I'm sure he has a lot of chemicals stored in his bag, and knows how to use them . . . Anyway, the point is, for a moment, I was blinded by the light and smoke, and the noise of people exclaiming all around me. I'm sure he must have taken my chain then. That was the perfect moment for an expert theft, when I was bent down in front of him, my neck exposed.'

Kaveri paced up and down. 'But what I don't understand is, why would he want to remove my chain, and why would Murali try to sabotage my car? Is there a connection between the ashram and the murder of Mr Sharma?'

'Do you think it could be a coincidence, Mrs Murthy?' Ismail asked.

Kaveri let out a frustrated huff. 'That man seems to be everywhere. He is too powerful and omnipresent for this to be a coincidence. My mother-in-law and half the women in town seem to be his followers. He exploits their true devotion to Garuda for his own manipulative purposes.'

Ramu patted the back of her neck, calming her down. Kaveri took a deep breath and continued, 'The same depiction of the Garuda is everywhere in Mr Sharma's properties, on the gates at the mills as well as in his home. The Swami's photo hangs prominently in Mr Sharma's living room, which means Shanthi must also be a follower. Both Kumar and Shanthi said Chitra may have a secret lover. Chitra said she suspected Kumar and Shanthi were having an affair, but perhaps it is Shanthi and the Swami who are having an affair? And that is why the Swami decided to kill Mr Sharma?'

Mala spoke up. 'There is something about the ashram that I must tell you. It is about the women. They are all in a very bad condition, after having been abandoned by their own families. My neighbour says they sleep all day and all night. It is very peculiar, the way she describes them, almost as though they are drugged.'

'Drugged?' Ismail looked at her intently. 'Are their eyes dilated? Could it be opium?'

'Their eyes seem normal,' Mala said, fixing Ismail with a direct gaze. 'But their tongues are black and swollen, she says. The women are given *paan* twice a day, to which apart from betel nut and spices, Murali adds a foul-smelling paste. He has warned Ratna never to touch the *paan* herself.'

'Cocaine,' Ramu said instantly. 'We have had a steady trickle of addicts coming to the hospital in recent months. The tongue is a dead giveaway.'

Mala nodded. 'One of my former clients, who came from Calcutta, was addicted to the drug and I have seen his tongue. I had not heard of cocaine being used in Bangalore before, but I have suspected these women are being drugged, ever since Ratna spoke to me about this a few weeks back.'

Ismail frowned at Mala. 'Why did you not tell me this as soon as you heard it? I have been on the track of a cocaine smuggling ring in Bangalore for some months now.'

'You did not ask me,' Mala responded. 'These are dangerous people, and I don't want to get dragged into this mess unless I have to.'

'Why tell me now, then?' He threw up his hands in exasperation.

'Because, after the car accident, now my friend Kaveri is in danger. For her, who saved me from the gallows, I am willing to risk everything.'

Kaveri's eyes filled with tears, and she gave Mala a swift hug.

'For the past few months, we have heard rumours that the cocaine trade, which is already widespread in Bombay and Calcutta, is also spreading in south India,' Ismail said, looking around the room. 'It is locally distributed by a network of *paan* vendors, but comes in from Japan, via the seaports. Large quantities are then smuggled into Bangalore by an overland route. But we have not been able to find the mastermind who coordinates the cocaine trade, or trace the route by which it comes in.

'On two occasions, we managed to acquire details of a small paan vendor involved in petty drug trade from a consumer, and arrested him. But the vendors were small fry in a big net. They were given messages to drop off the money and pick up the drugs at specific locations, and were unable to tell us anything further that could help us track down their suppliers.'

He let out a frustrated sigh. 'I never thought of the ashram as being a possible conduit until now. The Swami is so prominent and well connected. But that also makes him the perfect person to arrange something as complex as this. It will be very hard for me to get permission from my superiors to investigate him. He has very powerful supporters in high places.' Ismail fell silent for a moment, then turned to Mala. 'Is there anything else that your neighbour says is strange about the ashram?'

'In the morning, she told me, she sometimes sees large and muddy tracks of bullock carts. She is asked to sweep them clean as soon as she comes in, and then she doesn't see them again for several days, but eventually the tracks reappear. But she has never seen any carts. Only the tracks made by the wheels.'

Ismail banged his fist on the table, making the tumbler of coffee in front of him rattle. 'Then the cocaine must be brought in at night, on bullock carts.'

'The women could be kept as props to show donors that they are running a legitimate institution. But then they drug them, so that they don't prove to be a nuisance.' Kaveri's eyes narrowed, as she remembered the two unkempt and dishevelled women she had seen on the roof of the ashram. 'Those poor women! We have to get into that ashram and rescue them.'

'*We* may have to, but that does not include *you*,' Ismail said, staring at her very pointedly. Kaveri shifted in her seat, as Ramu placed a comforting hand on her arm. 'Mrs Murthy, you are still in danger. Please, stay home, and let us take care of this.'

'What do you plan to do?' Kaveri demanded.

'I will speak to my superiors and ask them if they know or have heard anything about Swami Vaninanda. Where he came from, what he was doing before, and what the source of his money is. And then I will ask for permission to raid the ashram.' Ismail looked worried. 'But it won't be easy. He has a lot of influential supporters. All it will take is for one informant to leak this news back to him and he will clear out the entire ashram, removing the drugs and destroying any way we have of catching him red handed.'

'I have a better idea,' Ramu said, looking at Ismail.

'What is it?' Ismail pulled his chair closer.

'We are currently doing a vaccination drive at the hospital. I will take some vaccination kits with me and go to the *ashram* with a letter from the Bowring Hospital, saying I have been sent by the government on a vaccination campaign. Dr Roberts will give me permission, I'm sure. The ashram will then have to let me in. We can examine the women and get proof of something suspicious going on, proof that enables you to get permission to raid the ashram.'

Ramu gave Ismail a grim nod. 'Swami Vaninanda and Murali tried to trap Kaveri into being arrested for murder. When that failed, they tried to kill her by sabotaging her car. They will not get away with this.'

'We will make sure they do not,' Mala chimed in.

29

Infiltrating the Enemy Camp

'You're right. It is not fair,' Anandi said, accepting a coconut *barfi* from the plate that Kaveri passed around. At the women's group meeting that afternoon, she seemed in her element. 'Women don't get to do anything interesting. All our lives, we are supposed to be good women. From when I was six, I was helping my mother cook, my young hands covered in scars from the hot coal. I always carried at least one of my younger brothers around, bathing and feeding them, washing their clothes, and cleaning up after them. Then my rotter of a husband expected me to do the same for him.' Anandi bit down on the barfi as though she were chewing her husband to pieces. 'I was so glad to hear today that my husband was arrested.'

'Arrested?' Mrs Reddy asked.

'It seems he was stealing from his employer and had given all the money to a woman.' Anandi's eyes flashed. 'All this time, he had a mistress, a second wife whom he had set up in a second house. And while I struggled to get a handful of rice to feed myself, he bought her fancy saris and jewellery!' She slammed the plate down on the table. 'I hope the bastard rots in jail.'

Kaveri looked around, expecting to see frowns of disapproval. But every woman was nodding along.

'How long is he going to be in jail?' Mrs Ismail asked. 'My husband often says that we need stricter laws. If it's theft, he will be out in a few months, and back to bothering you, Anandi.'

'That's the best part,' Mala took over the story, her eyes shining with delight. 'He handed over the stolen jewellery to some accomplices in Bangalore, whom I know well through my old contacts. When the police brought him in, he broke under their questioning like a rotten breadfruit, and revealed the names of his fences. I made sure that his erstwhile accomplices knew that it was Pawan who turned them in.' She gave them a wicked smile. 'Now they are furious and Bangalore is no longer a safe place for him. They will kill him if they find him. As soon as he is released from jail, he will have to flee the city.'

'And these people have long memories.' Anandi pursed her lips and let out a long, low whistle. 'He will never be able to return to Bangalore. I am finally safe.'

No wonder she looked so happy and relaxed, Kaveri thought.

'How are things at the Sharma home?' she asked.

'I have started giving Mrs Sharma a daily massage, and we have become quite close now. She gave me several nice saris she was no longer wearing and some jewellery.' Anandi touched the delicate silver chain around her neck, looking pleased. 'They feed me well too. I only have to remember not to drink the water in my jug at night . . . ' She glanced at Kaveri. 'Don't worry, I have taken your advice and am staying in my room. I haven't tried to find out who is stepping out at night. Except, I don't think it is Mrs Sharma, she cannot do it with her bad back.'

'Bad back?' Kaveri asked. She had not seen any signs of a bad back.

'Yes, Mrs Sharma has a weak back. She can't bend or stretch easily.'

'And Chitra has a bad leg,' Kaveri said. 'One of them must be faking it.'

'But who is the woman going to visit? A secret lover?' Uma aunty asked, looking avid.

Anandi hushed her. 'So what if she is? Women have such little control over their lives anyway. If it is Chitra, you know she is getting married soon, an arranged marriage to someone who is not of her choice. Maybe she wants to have a brief time of pleasure before she has to do her duty. If it is Shanthi, well, she was married to a man much older than her. Who can blame her for seeking pleasure outside the marriage bed?'

'Whoever the woman is, she seems to be going to the ashram,' Kaveri said. The women looked up, their coffee and snacks forgotten. They moved their chairs together to discuss this new piece of information.

Some time later, Kaveri heard the familiar sound of running footsteps, halting outside the door.

'Venu?'

Venu rushed in, thrusting a note into Kaveri's hands.

'What does the note say, Kaveri?' Uma aunty's eyes gleamed with excitement.

Kaveri unfolded the note and groaned aloud.

'They refused to let him in!'

'How can they refuse? He is a government vaccinator, and they are supposed to be allowed everywhere. My son grumbled about it last week at dinner after a team came to his office. He did not want to get vaccinated against cholera but they insisted. They said they would bring the police if he refused – he could choose to go to jail or get poked with a needle.' Uma aunty's eyes sparkled with laughter.

'The person who opened the door was the cook,' Kaveri said. 'He said that the Swami was away, and so was his assistant. The women are in *purdah* and because they are all widows they cannot see strange men. He closed the gate on them.' Kaveri looked up. 'Ramu sent the note instead of calling, because he fears that the Swami may have spies listening in on the telephone. Now that they have turned him away, they must suspect we are up to something. The Swami has gone to Mangalore for a *puja*, but he will be back tonight. As soon as he comes, he will probably clear up whatever evidence they have of wrongdoing. We must find a way to act before it is too late.'

Kaveri stopped. 'Wait, there's more.' She turned the note to read the postscript Ramu had scribbled on the side: '*I hope the women's group has not yet left. I hate to involve them, but now there is no alternative. Can you ask Narsamma to get in, posing as a destitute widow who needs help?*'

When Kaveri read the note out to the women, Narsamma looked excited, but Mala protested. 'Narsamma is old . . . if there is something going on, and she has to escape, she won't be able to run fast, or climb over the wall. I couldn't bear it if anything happened to her. I'll do it.'

The two women began to argue heatedly, their voices raised.

Anandi moved between the two of them, grabbing their hands. 'Stop! Narsamma, you really can't do this. You are too old, and Mala *akka* is right. You will not be able to run around and spy for us or escape quickly if you must.' Narsamma looked disappointed as Anandi continued, 'And Mala *akka*, you are too well known in this city. When you were in jail a few months back, your face was splashed all over the newspaper . . . everyone knows you now.'

'What do you suggest then?' Mala demanded, hands on her hips as she turned to face Anandi. 'Look at these women here.' She pointed to Kaveri, Mrs Reddy, Mrs Ismail, and Uma aunty. 'Do you think any of them can pass off as a woman abandoned by her family and on the streets? They are women of privilege, they have grown up in wealth and comfort. Even if we place them in rags, they will stand tall and proud. No one will believe it of them.'

'I will go,' Anandi said, coolly taking the last piece of coconut barfi from the plate and biting into it. Only the slightest shake of her hand, and the way her eyes darted around the room, betrayed her nervousness.

'You? But what about your job?' Mala asked.

Anandi shrugged. 'The job was for me to find out what was going on, correct? Now the need is somewhere else. Besides, I can always return tomorrow. I will send a note through one of the boys to my mistress, telling her I was taken ill with a bad stomach, and am resting in the hospital for a night.'

The room was suddenly filled with noise, as Mala and Narsamma attempted to shoot down Anandi's plan, making her dig her heels in and insist that she would go.

Feeling like a school teacher, Kaveri raised her hands and clapped loudly, motioning the women to silence.

'That might work,' Kaveri said, looking at Anandi. Mala and Narsamma stared accusingly at her.

'We have to solve the case,' Kaveri continued. 'Someone needs to infiltrate the ashram to find out what's going on, and we need to do this quickly. Mala, we can ask your neighbour Ratna to take Anandi to the ashram, introducing her as an abandoned woman searching for refuge.'

'But we may be putting Anandi in danger!' Narsamma wailed.

'Don't worry. We will ask Venu to loiter in the coconut grove near the ashram at night. Anandi, if you need help,

234

send him a signal. He will come to us, and we will be with you in a few minutes.'

Anandi's face was set in resolute lines. She held up her right wrist. 'See this red sacred thread I have tied here? If I need help, I will untie it from my wrist and tie it to a stone, tossing it over the high walls into the coconut grove. That will be the signal that I need help.' She raised a hand to silence Narsamma and Mala, who were still protesting, though more quietly now. 'When you saved me, I felt as though I received a new life. I want to thank you best, by using that life to protect other women in danger. If there are women being held captive and drugged in the ashram, we have to free them.'

Mala reluctantly agreed, placing a hand on Narsamma's arm to silence her. Narsamma looked mutinous, and grumbled under her breath, but did not say anything aloud.

'She is in your hands. We trust you, Kaveri, otherwise we would never have permitted this.'

'I don't want to disrespect you or your help,' Anandi said to them. 'But I don't need anyone's permission to do this. When I left my husband, I vowed to myself that I would never put myself in a position again where I allowed some-one else to determine my life. To permit or disallow me to do anything. I am the only person who can decide that. And I have decided. I am going to do this.'

30

The Plot Thickens

Anandi left the house with Mala, wearing an old and dirty sari and rubbing dust into her hair and hands. They were headed to Mala's neighbour Ratna's house. Kaveri and Mala had devised a story that was close to the truth, planning to tell Ratna that Anandi was a young woman whose husband was abusing her, and was in urgent need of shelter and protection in a place where he could not find her. They could not explain the intricacies of the plot to Ratna, and it was better for them all around if the woman believed the story, anyway. Less likelihood of being caught.

Mrs Ismail headed to the police station, where she would bring Ismail up to speed on their plan. Venu was sent to the hospital with a note to let Ramu know of the plans, after which he would go to the coconut grove that night. He had also asked one of his friends, another small boy, to keep watch at the Sharma mansion to see if anyone climbed out through the window. If they did, he was to follow them and report back to him.

That should cover it, Kaveri thought, but she still fretted as she worked in the kitchen, wondering if they had forgotten anything or anyone important. She tried to prepare a simple meal of *pongal*, boiled dal and rice with a few spices, for her and Ramu to eat tonight. With her mind on the complex cascade of events they had set in motion, she was clumsier than usual, overturning a ladleful of ghee onto the floor. Large black ants hurried up to the puddle of food and Kaveri watched as they struggled to crawl through the viscous fluid, feeling as though they matched the infinitely slow crawl of time. She watched the minute hand on the grandfather clock, counting time through every jerk forward of the minute hand. 7.01 p.m., 7.02 p.m., 7.03 p.m.

She looked up eagerly as Mala came in. 'Is everything all right?'

'I think so,' Mala said. 'I sent Ratna off with Anandi. Kind soul that she is, she was very distressed by Anandi's story, and immediately took her to the ashram.'

Kaveri breathed a sigh of relief, pacing up and down on the porch as she waited for Ramu to return. As soon as she saw him appear, she hurried to the gate.

'Anandi got in, Kaveri,' he told her as soon as he saw her. 'Venu came running to let me know, but he said that she was only admitted after a long discussion – almost an argument – at the gates. Venu could not hear what was being said very clearly, but it seemed like the guard was saying that today was not a good day for them to admit new people. Mala's neighbour stood her ground and refused to go in unless she was allowed to take Anandi in with her. Venu said he could also hear some sounds of large boxes being dragged to and fro, and of raised voices inside.'

'Are they preparing to move out the drugs then?' Kaveri said, giving Ramu a worried look.

'It seems like it. I hope Ismail gets permission for a raid so they can break open the ashram doors soon. I think tonight is a critical one for us.'

Would the night ever come?

After a quick dinner, Kaveri and Ramu sat on the steps of the verandah, looking out onto the road. Kaveri leaned against one of the large teak pillars and took in a deep breath of the night air, inhaling the sticky scent of the night queen blossoms. Ramu leaned back in his wicker chair and looked at the pattern the stars made in the sky above.

'What are you thinking about, Kaveri?'

'How people can view the same thing so differently,' Kaveri said. 'I was thinking of the night I saw the blood moon in the sky, the day Mr Sharma died. Your mother and so many others believe that the eclipse takes place when the demon Rahu swallows the moon. And yet our own mathematicians like Aryabhata showed how eclipses occur using principles of geometry 1500 years ago. We all see the same eclipse, but deduce different stories to explain how it happens. What are the truths we miss when we see a murder, and try to judge who is responsible?' Kaveri looked at Ramu.

Ramu looked down at their joined hands. 'Soon, we will know the truth. I know Ismail has kept a large set of policemen ready. He is just waiting for a message from Anandi before we go in so that they can find the evidence they need to arrest the Swami. If they go in there now, the Swami will barricade the gates against them, and in the time it takes for them to break open the gate and enter, he will hide the evidence.'

'But what will happen to those women once they are freed?' Kaveri demanded. 'They will be sent back to their families. There must have been some problem they were running away from in the first place. Otherwise, the Swami would not have been able to convince them to leave the comfort of their homes and come to him. We will be sending them back, perhaps from the proverbial frying pan into the fire.'

She brooded, looking at the dark sky. After a while, Ramu stirred. 'I know you will be able to find an alternative if you think about it long enough,' he said. 'Speak to the women's club too. And to women like Lakkamma and Kalyanamma. They will be able to suggest something, I'm sure.'

They turned their head as a slim figure came running in through the side garden that led from Uma aunty's house.

'I think Anandi sent us a message asking for help,' Venu panted as he rushed up to them holding a stone with a red thread wrapped around it.

Just then another small boy skidded around the corner, his small frame looking incongruous in a clean blue shirt that was at least two sizes too large for him. He held up his too-loose knickers with one hand as he ran.

'You're here too? What happened? This is my friend Chandan,' Venu explained to Kaveri and Ramu. 'He works for Inspector Ismail. The Inspector asked him to stand outside the Sharma house.'

'A woman came out of the window, wearing men's clothing and a cap,' the skinny boy told them, still trying to catch his breath. 'As she climbed down the tree branch outside the window to reach the wall, her plait came loose and swung down. That's how I knew it wasn't a man.' He grinned cheekily. He couldn't be more than ten years old, Kaveri thought. She called for Rajamma, asking her to bring him a plate of food.

'And then?' she asked.

'I followed her at a distance and she didn't see me.' He grinned again. 'I kept behind the trees. At some point, just before the road ends in a junction, she broke into a run. I ran too, keeping behind the trees. He pointed to his knee, which had a raw red patch where the skin had been scraped. 'I hit my leg against the tree as I ran. But I didn't stop.' Chandan looked very proud of himself, puffing his chest out. 'I kept her in my sights the entire way. She went to the back gate of the ashram and knocked sharply. She knocked in a pattern – three times. It seemed to be a signal. I ran away to tell Inspector Ismail, who asked me to come and tell you as well.'

Rajamma came out with a steaming plate piled high with rice and *saaru*. The boy took it and sat down with a quick thank you to her, shovelling large handfuls into his mouth.

'I almost forgot,' he mumbled, spraying bits of rice everywhere. 'As I ran away, I saw the gates opening to let a large bullock cart in, pulled by two massive bullocks.'

'So, Shanthi went into the ashram,' Kaveri said, turning a worried face to Ramu. 'Almost immediately afterwards, Anandi sent the stone with the red thread over the wall, as an SOS call.'

'It could be Chitra, not Shanthi, Kaveri,' Ramu reminded her. 'Whoever it was, do you think she has spotted Anandi? And that's why Anandi is in trouble?' Ramu moved towards the car as he spoke. 'Let's go to the police station and pick up Ismail first.'

'No need,' Venu spoke up. 'I ran past the station to tell him about Anandi *akka*'s signal before I came here. He was going to round up all his men first, as he may need to break down the gates. It will take him a while to do that, I think.'

'That will be too late for Anandi. She needs help now!' Kaveri rushed to open the gates, as Ramu jumped into the driver's seat of the car, motioning Venu to the back seat.

Fortunately, the ashram was very close, and the roads were empty this late at night, Kaveri thought, as she watched Ramu pressing hard on the accelerator.

Once they'd arrived, Ramu, Kaveri and Venu hurried to the back wall of the ashram, towards the gate where Murali had previously rebuffed Kaveri's entry. Though narrow in width, it was solid and tall, impossible to scale easily. There was no sound from inside except the steady scrape of heavy objects – *crates?* thought Kaveri, mouthing the word to Ramu, who nodded.

'They must be packing boxes, probably containing cocaine, into the cart – which means they will move them out later tonight,' Ramu whispered in her ear.

The sound of hammer started up, then ceased abruptly, and they heard the hoarse voice of a man say, 'That's the last one. Now, we need to get them loaded onto the cart.'

The other man with him grunted, sounding cross. 'We need a lever for that, Murali. These are too heavy for the two of us to lift by ourselves. You should have let me get some people to load.'

'Idiot! How can we let strangers in here to see what we're loading?' Murali responded, an edge to his voice.

'No one can see anything,' the first man muttered sulkily. 'You've wrapped it up in oilskins, and tied it in cloth. Even if it were a pile of diamonds, they wouldn't know.'

'Even if they won't be able to see what we are loading, they will be able to smell it, you fool. Come, let's go down to the basement to look for the lever,' Murali said tersely. 'I hope the women are still asleep.'

'I gave them a double dose. They won't wake up for a while – if they ever do.' The first man gave a coarse laugh as Ramu and Kaveri turned horrified eyes on each other.

The voices of the two men grew faint, and finally faded away.

Kaveri pointed to the small gap between the sharp spear-like protrusions at the top of the gate that she had observed on her last visit with Bhargavi. 'See that? There is just enough space for me to squeeze through.'

'No.' Ramu's refusal was immediate. 'We will wait for Ismail.'

'We can't! It will be too late by the time he gets here.' Kaveri shook Ramu's arm. 'You heard the men. They won't be back for twenty minutes. We don't have much time, but I can quickly slip in and look for Anandi. She isn't safe there. Whether it is Shanthi or Chitra, a woman who is capable of murdering her own husband or father will not hesitate to get rid of a maid with whom she has no connection.'

'Don't worry, I will also go with Kaveri *akka*,' Venu said, wriggling in between them. 'I can keep her safe, Ramu *anna*. You will be right outside, and you will be able to hear us.'

'No!' both of them said at the same time. Venu was far too young to send into such a dangerous situation. Spying on people from a safe distance was one thing, but if they sent him into danger, and something happened to him . . .

'We need you to run to Ismail. Tell him that Kaveri has gone inside, and he should come as soon as he can with whatever men he can gather. Ask him to bring a long ladder with him.' Ramu clapped Venu on the shoulder and gave him a gentle push, turning him towards the road.

They watched him speed away, then Ramu turned to Kaveri. 'I don't like it, but I suppose you are right. I wish there was another way,' he muttered, pulling her into a hard embrace. She hugged him back tightly, suddenly feeling afraid. What if this were the last time she was to see Ramu?

No, she couldn't think like that.

Ramu had already hoisted her up onto his shoulders. He supported her as she held onto the sharp spears set in the wall, making her way carefully up to the small gap on the top of the gate.

'Don't worry,' she mouthed at Ramu, blowing him a kiss and squeezing through the gap, then jumping down from the gate. The ground seemed a long way off. She braced herself before crouching and landing with a wince as her feet hit the hard-packed earth. Ouch!

She had removed her slippers before climbing onto Ramu's shoulders so she made no noise, but she still looked around nervously. The walls stood high and tall, closing in on her and making her feel trapped.

She saw she was in a large open area, with a single temple building in the centre with a small *mantapa* and a low ornate dome. In one corner, she saw a two-storey set of rooms. *Those must be where the destitute women stay*, she thought, squinting at the roof. That looked like the place she had seen the two dishevelled women that day, with Bhargavi.

Near the large gates at the front entrance, three wooden crates stood on the ground next to a large cart. Tethered to the cart, two massive bullocks stood placidly chewing hay from a pile stacked in front of them, their humped necks and shoulders testifying to their strength.

Kaveri stood for a second, debating whether to enter the temple or move towards the rooms where the drugged women were probably sleeping. Where would she find Anandi?

She looked at the tall pillars of stone that marked the entrance to the temple *mantapa*, lit up by torches on both sides. The flames from the lit torches shone on the terrifying face of the *dwarapalakas*, carved stone demons who guarded the entrance. Kaveri gazed in horrified fascination at their long curls, which fell like poisonous snakes from their heads, and their teeth protruding like fangs, coloured blood red with vermilion. A necklace of grinning skulls adorned their necks, and in their stout arms they held large clubs studded with nails, holding them menacingly over the heads of anyone who might enter the temple.

A cricket started a loud *chik-chik-chik* noise that reverberated through the still night air, in time with the thudding of Kaveri's heart. She pulled herself together with effort, swallowing past the lump in her throat. It would not do for her to break down now. Anandi needed her.

When Kaveri heard the sound of footsteps, she darted into a pool of shadow cast by the torches, and held her breath. Were the two men returning with the lever already? They had said it would take twenty minutes. From the corner of her eye she saw a flash of saffron cloth in the doorway of the temple. That must be the Swami. Who was he speaking to – was it Shanthi?

She strained to hear what he was saying. The men in the basement must have found the lever now, and were bringing it upstairs. The grating noise they made was deafening and Kaveri couldn't hear anything above the din. She darted towards the entrance of the temple, hiding behind one of the *dwarapalakas* and trying to listen.

'Let's kill this meddlesome woman, and leave her body here for the police to find.'

That was the Swami's voice!

31

Saved by a Mouse

Kaveri dared not step any closer to the entrance of the temple for fear she would be seen. She cast a worried glance towards the low row of rooms at the other end of the compound, from which the grating sound seemed to be coming closer every second. If only there was a tree here to climb, or a pillar she could hide behind! In this open space, she was visible for all to see.

The sound of the men dragging the heavy lever up the steps was growing louder every second. They would be out any second now.

Her only hope of hiding from their sight was to get inside the temple. If only Swami Vaninanda and the person he was talking to would move a little further inside. Then she could slip in as well.

'No! You can't kill her.' It was Chitra's voice, sounding horrified.

So it was Chitra! Kaveri thought of Ramu, who had counselled her not to jump to conclusions. She had dismissed him each time. She sidled to the corner of the doorway, peering in. The temple was surrounded by a long corridor. Inside, she could see a pillared hall, and at one end, on a raised platform, the *garbha gudi* or inner sanctum with the main deity. Chitra was standing in the corridor with the Swami, both with their backs to her.

Kaveri slipped inside, crouching behind a tall wooden chest. The corridor was heavy with the scent of sandalwood. She looked around to see lit incense sticks, smoke rising from them. With an audible click, the last piece of the puzzle slipped into place.

Chitra had smelt strongly of sandalwood when Kaveri had met her in Cubbon Park – Chitra was a frequent visitor to the temple.

This must be where she met the Swami, at night time. The scent of the incense sticks was so strong, it pervaded Kaveri's hair and nostrils, just as it must have Chitra's. But Shanthi used a different Indian perfume – *attar*, with the aroma of roses and wet earth.

If only she had put these pieces together before now. But she had been so focused on Shanthi, so sure it was her despite the lack of proof, all because she disliked the way in which Shanthi seemed to have forced Chitra's marriage to Kumar. How judgemental she had been.

Kaveri came back to her surroundings with a start as she heard the Swami say, 'We can't afford to leave a witness. I'll ask Murali to kill her.' His voice was chillingly flat.

She raised her head as much as she dared above the wooden chest. The footsteps receded, as Chitra and the Swami moved out of the corridor. Swami Vaninanda pressed a switch on the wall, and the richly decorated pillared hall came into view. Kaveri squinted, waiting for her eyes to adjust to the sudden brightness. Then held her breath as she saw a pair of feet further down the corridor, beyond the entrance to the pillared hall. The feet were sticking out into the corridor, but the body was lying half hidden from sight behind another wooden chest.

It was Anandi, she was sure of it. Around her ankles was a delicate silver anklet which she always wore, and Kaveri could also see the toe rings that every married woman wore on her second toe. She squeezed her eyes to block out her tears, remembering how Anandi had confided in her the last time she'd seen her that she wanted to strip off her *mangalsutra*, her marriage chain, and the toe rings, but wasn't able to bring herself to do it yet. Kaveri had consoled her, saying there would come a time when she'd feel ready to strike out on her own.

She must have made a sound without realising it, for the Swami looked up sharply.

'Is someone there?' he demanded sharply, moving back into the corridor. Kaveri ducked back behind the chest, moving closer to the wall, making herself as small as she could. The Swami strode towards the entrance and looked out. Kaveri held her breath, not daring to breathe. If he turned, he would see her.

A small mouse darted out from the corner of the temple. The Swami turned and stared at it, his mouth breaking into a smile.

'There is our little eavesdropper.' He laughed, turning back to the door again. The sound of dragging had stopped, Kaveri realised, replaced by a noise of cranking.

'How long will you take to load the boxes?' Swami Vaninanda called out to the men.

Murali responded, grunting with effort as he cranked the lever, pausing between words to take deep breaths. 'Another . . . five . . . minutes . . . '

'Make it as fast as you can,' Swami Vaninanda called back. 'And then leave immediately for Kolar. I think you will be able to reach it by morning if you drive all night.

Remember to cover the crates with hay. No one should know that there are crates in the cart.'

'Don't worry,' Murali called back. 'They will only see a bullock cart laden with hay, and two men driving it. Nothing out of the ordinary at all.'

'Good. Once you arrive at our warehouse in Kolar, a bus will be waiting for you as arranged. You can send the cargo to Mangalore. From there it will make its way to Calcutta by ship.' The Swami's voice sounded regretful. 'It is a pity that we seem to have been found out – this woman must have been sent by the police to spy on us. But it had to happen one day. Ever since that woman detective started to snoop around, I knew this day was coming.' His voice sounded harder now. 'We will find a way to fix her, and re-launch our "business" in another city.'

'We will start again in Kolar,' Murali said. 'And don't worry about that woman. I can always slip back to Bangalore and attend to her.' He gave a coarse laugh.

Kaveri held her breath. Out of the corner of her eye, she saw a movement along the wall. What was it?

'Maybe. Or even in Mangalore. It is farther away, and people are less likely to know us there.' The Swami looked back at the corridor. From where he stood, if he turned his eyes even a fraction of an inch to the side, he would see Kaveri. But he was focused on the room inside.

He turned and walked swiftly into the room.

Kaveri waited for a moment, then exhaled the breath she didn't realise she had been holding. She saw the little mouse scurrying across the corridor again. Normally terrified of mice and rats, she felt like picking up the tiny creature and giving it a kiss.

She rose from her crouch cautiously, grimacing as she felt her circulation returning. She had held herself so still that her fingers and toes felt cramped. She worked them to

248

get the blood flowing, then crept noiselessly towards the temple hall.

Chitra and the Swami were standing near the inner sanctum, the *garbha gudi*. She tiptoed past the entrance to the pillared hall, hurrying towards Anandi's crumpled form lying against the wall. Kaveri's hands grew cold and clammy. Was she dead?

The young woman had a large lump on her forehead, and her hands and legs had been bound with rope. Kaveri felt anger filling the pit of her stomach and rising into her mouth. Anandi had so bravely volunteered to be the one who infiltrated the ashram.

She glared at Chitra and the Swami, then turned back, hearing a small whimper. She crouched down next to Anandi, her heart soaring with hope when she saw that Anandi's chest was rising and falling. Kaveri unclenched her fists. Anandi was alive then. There was still hope.

She quickly untied the ropes that bound her, and slowly massaged her hands. Anandi's eyelids fluttered, slowly opening. She looked at Kaveri, her eyes filled with confusion, then her expression slowly cleared. She opened her mouth to speak, but Kaveri hurriedly put a hand over her mouth, pressing a finger to her lips. She leaned forward, whispering in Anandi's ear, 'Can you get up and hide in a place of safety? They are going to come for you in a few minutes. You need to go before that.' Anandi nodded, and Kaveri got up, moving back towards the inner hall.

Chitra and the Swami were deep in conversation, and Kaveri strained her ears, but they were too far away for her to hear. The hall was filled with urns, pillars and other large objects. Perhaps she could use them to move closer? She moved swiftly, tiptoeing from the doorway to a large urn, then waited for a moment, wiping her sweaty hands on her sari. Chitra and the Swami were standing very close to each other, engrossed in intimate conversation.

Kaveri grimaced, thinking of her notepad of suspects – she should have taken the idea of a potential lover more seriously. Now all the fragments of her puzzle had fallen into place. Chitra and the Swami must have conspired together to embezzle the money and kill Mr Sharma, using Murali as a tool. She closed her eyes, suddenly feeling sickened. What kind of a woman must Chitra be, to have conspired to kill her own father, the man who had raised her from an infant and showered so much love on her – for the sake of an unscrupulous cheat like this man?

Kaveri crossed the room, hoping as she did that Anandi would be able to escape before Murali and his henchman returned. Moving from the urn to a large rosewood chest, she finally took shelter behind a large stone idol of Garuda. The Eagle God's wings were spread wide, a perfect spot for hiding, and Kaveri thanked him silently. She fumed at the thought of how the fake Swami had exploited the Eagle God for his own evil purposes. She hoped he would get his comeuppance soon in the same temple.

From this spot, she was close enough to hear the whispered conversation between Chitra and the Swami. Looking back, Kaveri saw Anandi stand up and slowly flex her arms and legs, stretching them to restore circulation to her body. Then Anandi starting edging sideways towards the main entrance of the temple. Kaveri held her breath. What was she planning to do? As she caught Anandi's eyes, Anandi gestured to the side. Kaveri's eyes widened as she saw a figure peering into the entrance. Ramu? How had he got in here? The walls were too high for him to scale without help.

She saw Anandi tiptoe out of the temple into the grounds. Ramu followed her, blowing a kiss towards Kaveri. Kaveri looked at the retreating figures longingly. She could not move now. The Swami and Chitra would be sure to see her. Besides, she needed to find out what they were saying to each other. But danger loomed thick and close in the damp confines of the narrow pillared hall, and she longed for Ramu's solid, reassuring presence.

'You should go now,' the Swami told Chitra, removing her arms from his neck and stepping back. 'Before they miss you at home.' He sounded brusque and impatient, not at all like a besotted lover, Kaveri thought.

Chitra gave a scornful laugh. 'She won't miss me. I put the sleeping medicine the doctor gave me in her water too.' She looked at the Swami again. 'What will you *really* do with Anandi? I cannot understand how or why she came here. My stepmother must have sent her to spy on me. Surely, you are not planning to kill her. You wouldn't do that, would you?'

Swami Vaninanda looked irritated when Chitra stepped close to him and tried to embrace him once again. Pushing her away, he said, 'You little fool. Are you really so thick-headed that you haven't yet figured it out? Just like I asked Murali to kill your father, I will ask him to kill her too. And you, if you don't stop.'

Chitra took a step back from him. Her voice sounded uncertain. 'Did you . . . Did you just say that you – that Murali – you both killed my father?' Her body trembled like a leaf in a thunderstorm.

Kaveri stepped back in surprise. Just a moment ago, when she had seen Chitra embracing the Swami, she had been so sure they were lovers who had conspired to kill Mr Sharma together. Now what was this? Could Chitra have been such a fool as to have helped the Swami to steal from her father and kill him, without realising what kind of a man he was?

The Swami spoke in his soft, musical voice, now edged with a jeering undertone, 'Oh Chitra, my dear, you are so gullible. Why did you think I got close to you in the first place? All I had to do was pay you a little extra attention – you were so thirsty for it that you practically handed me your father's money, helping to fund "our future together".' She flinched as he cruelly mimicked her voice. 'But once your father found out about the embezzlement, I realised the game was up. Your father was a dangerous man. Alive, he would have set that woman on the trail of the theft, persisting until he found out who had done it. He already suspected that you were too close to me. But with him dead,' the Swami shrugged, 'who was going to come after me? I admit, I was slightly worried when that woman took the account books with her. Who knows what she may have deduced from looking at them? But I think we stymied her once Murali sabotaged her car and we took the books back.'

Kaveri bristled behind the pillar. Her, stymied away from a case? He really didn't know her at all. But she kept quiet, biting her tongue, waiting to see how Chitra would respond.

'No!' Chitra whispered, extending her hands piteously towards him. 'I don't believe it. You killed my father? You sabotaged Kaveri's car? It was all you?'

'I sent Murali to do the dirty work, of course.' The Swami took out a shiny black revolver from his pocket, waving it at her. 'With the help of this little friend of mine.'

'I thought it was my stepmother!' Chitra's voice began to quaver. 'You told me it must be her too!'

'And that was a good thing, wasn't it?' The Swami picked up a length of rope from the floor and came forward. 'Because you suspected Shanthi, you told the woman detective that it was her, and she told the police. If only you had been a little more patient. First, you ought to have completed your marriage to Kumar. Then you would have

252

become an heiress. But no, you had to moan and complain that you could not bear the thought of his coarse hands on you. We could have arranged for him to die in his sleep, of a convenient heart attack.'

Chitra shrunk away from the Swami, but he waved the revolver, and she subsided. He tied her arms behind her back with the rope, anchoring her to one of the pillars.

Chitra struggled against the ropes, the sadness in her eyes flashing to anger. 'You monster! I trusted you. I *loved* you.'

'How touching, my sweet,' Swami Vaninanda said, looking at her coldly, then turning away. 'Whatever is taking the man so much time? Murali, is the cart loaded completely?' he called out loudly. Receiving no response, he irritatedly muttered, 'God give me patience. I am surrounded by fools on all sides. Do I have to do everything myself?'

He glanced at Chitra, who was standing stock still, tears running down her face. 'All of this is your fault. I told you not to come to the ashram every night. Someone must have seen you and followed you here. First, they sent that doctor to the ashram with a fake vaccination notice. Then they sent that woman as a spy. We need to get out of here before the police come rushing in.'

What an obnoxious man, Kaveri thought, getting angrier every minute. Where was Ismail? What was taking him so long?

She could hear a faint scraping sound in the distance. In a few minutes, Murali and the other man would be back with the crates, and would catch sight of Ramu and Anandi. Outside, there were few places to hide. What could she do? Kaveri fretted. It would not help if she got caught as well. They would just kill her too.

What could she do?

She looked around the room for a weapon. She could see a large bamboo cane lying in a corner of the temple. It had a dirty rag tied to one corner, clearly used to sweep the roof of cobwebs. Maybe she could use this to knock them both down, she thought. Her *kalaripayattu* teacher had taught her how to use a stick for self-defence, balancing it on her hands and whirling it around. This stick was about the size of the larger ones she had practised with. But how could she reach for it?

Just then, she heard the sound she had been waiting for. There was a heavy thudding at the front gate. 'This is the police. Open up immediately.' Ismail's voice – speaking through a megaphone, from the sound of it.

The Swami let out an impressive volley of oaths, then moved purposefully towards a heavy brass urn inside the inner sanctum, panting as he pulled and pushed the urn to the side, exposing a trapdoor.

The main gate shuddered violently, finally cracking open as something heavy thudded repeatedly against it. Ismail must have brought a battering ram, Kaveri thought.

This was her chance. It was now or never!

With a silent prayer to the Eagle God, Kaveri spat on her hands to moisten them, darted out from behind the shelter of the Garuda statue towards the corner where she had spied the bamboo stick. With a loud cry, she moved swiftly towards Swami Vaninanda, twirling the stick as she went. He looked up in surprise, raising his revolver and aiming at her. Kaveri fell to the floor, twisting expertly to avoid the gun, and countered his attack by sweeping the stick beneath his legs. Taken by surprise, he went tumbling to one side, hitting his shoulder against the wall. His revolver went spinning to the far side of the room.

The Swami came back up in an instant, his eyes glittering with rage. He lunged for Kaveri with his powerful arms, fingers outstretched like talons. 'You?! I should have known it was you. The nosy detective. Always interfering where you're not wanted. You should have died in that car accident.'

He was so focused on Kaveri that he did not see Chitra. Her hands were tied, but her feet were free. Sticking one foot out, she tripped him as he advanced. With a crash, he fell down, making an audible thud as his head met the hard stone floor.

'But I didn't,' said Kaveri coolly, putting down her stick as the police burst into the room, pinioning Swami Vaninanda's arms behind him and putting him in handcuffs as he lay on the floor spitting a volley of abuses at them. A young constable hurried in, rushing to Chitra and untying her hands. But Kaveri had eyes only for Ramu, who was running towards her. He hugged her tightly, as though he would never let go, mumbling endearments into her hair as Venu danced a triumphant jig next to them.

Ramu kept his arms around her as he spoke. 'Waiting outside was the hardest thing I have ever done. I felt as though the weight of the world pressed down on me, and I could not draw breath. I went into the coconut grove, with a foolish idea that perhaps I could climb one of the trees and try to jump over the temple walls from the top. But the trees were too far from the temple. Luck favoured me, though. I found a long coir rope wrapped around one of the trees, used for climbing. I removed it and tied a loose knot around one end, aiming for the spikes on top of the wall. I anchored the rope to the spikes, used it to climb up and squeeze past them, then jumped into the temple.' Ramu gave her a rueful grin, pointing to the deep scratches on his palms and feet. 'You feed me too well, Kaveri. If I was slimmer, I would have been able to squeeze between the spikes more easily.'

Anandi stood next to them, her voice shaking with excitement as Kaveri ripped off strips of cloth from the end of her sari, tying them around the bleeding gashes on Ramu's arms and legs.

'Do you know what we did? Murali and the other man had several trips to make with heavy loads. When they went back for the last load, Ramu *anna* and I unyoked the buffaloes from the cart. Ramu *anna* opened the gates, leaving them wide open. I slapped the buffaloes on their rear, and off they went, running towards the nice thick grass inside the coconut grove. When the men came back you should have seen their faces. They had the cart all loaded with the boxes, but no buffaloes to drive it away!'

She clutched her stomach, breaking out into helpless laughter. 'They cursed and yelled, finally bolting the gates again as they argued with each other, trying to figure out what to do. We hid near the women's rooms, and kept watch on them, enjoying the fun.' She glanced over at Ramu. 'Well, I enjoyed it. Ramu *anna* was so worried, he kept wanting to come to you. But I stopped him. Murali has a gun with him. If he had seen Ramu *anna* running towards you, he would have shot him.'

Kaveri shuddered as Ramu picked her up in his arms again, burying his face in her hair, refusing to let go. 'Never again, Kaveri, please God, never again. Every moment you were inside without a word to me was like several years of my life.'

32

A Meeting of Minds

The next day, Kaveri and Ramu sat at home with Shanthi, sipping tall glasses of spiced *majjige*.

'Why did you call me?' Shanthi asked. Then she paused, saying almost apologetically, 'I don't mean to sound so brusque, Kaveri. I owe so much to you for uncovering my husband's killer. I only worry about leaving Chitra alone at such a time. She is very fragile. I left her with Bhargavi *akka*, but I don't feel like leaving her alone for long.'

'Firstly, I owe you an apology,' Kaveri said, looking at her shame-facedly. 'I suspected you, not Chitra.' She cringed a little, remembering how quick she had been to jump to judgement on Shanthi. 'Next time...' she had told Ramu the previous night, as they lay next to each other. 'Next time, I will try to talk to people first, before I reach a conclusion. I won't rush to slot them into categories of good, or bad.' Ramu had nodded, gathering her into his arms as he comforted her.

Shanthi smiled at her a little wistfully. 'It's all right, Kaveri. Many people thought I had killed my husband for

his money, I am sure. Why would you be any different?
Don't give it any more thought. You found the true killer.
I will be ever grateful to you.' She turned to Ramu, pressing
his hands warmly. 'And to you. You both, and Anandi,
risked your lives to find the truth, and to save Chitra. I can
never thank you enough.'

'It was not that . . . ' Kaveri stammered, finding words
inadequate to express what was in her mind. She gave up,
and decided to turn to another topic that was puzzling her.
'I was wondering about your treatment of Chitra. I read
your article in *Saraswati*. It mentioned that you met your
husband at the women's suffrage meeting. I wondered, why
would a man be at a women's meeting? So, can you tell me?
How you and your husband met?'

Shanthi looked puzzled, and a little wary.

'I don't see what this has to do with the any of the recent
incidents. The theft, my husband's murder, your accident.
It is a private matter.'

'It is one of the last remaining pieces of the puzzle,'
Kaveri said. 'There are a few things I am still unable to
understand. And, if you believe so strongly in suffrage and
women's rights, why did you practically force Chitra to get
engaged to Kumar?'

'I will tell you,' Shanthi said, giving a helpless shrug.
'But, remember, this should not go anywhere. It is only
between the three of us.' She looked at Ramu. 'Even your
mother does not know. She cannot keep secrets.'

Kaveri agreed.

'We met at another meeting, *after* the meeting on
women's suffrage.' Shanthi lowered her voice. 'A meeting of
people calling for Indian independence.'

No wonder she was being so reticent! The British were
beginning to lean on the Mysore Maharaja to stem the
growing popularity of the civil disobedience movement

called by the Congress party. They wanted the Mysore government to ban the visits of well-known leaders like Gandhi to Bangalore and Mysore. The Mysore king had refrained from banning the visits outright, but the British had stationed guards at these meetings and kept spies in place to report on any seditious discussions.

'Tell me more,' Kaveri said.

Shanthi lowered her voice, so it was barely above a whisper. 'Do you remember Sarojini Naidu's visit to Bangalore, a couple of years back?'

Who didn't know the fiery Bengali poet? She was admired by women across India, even though some people still gossiped about how she had had a scandalous marriage with a doctor from another caste. She was now in her fifties, with grown children, and was a strong advocate for women's rights.

'I wasn't in Bangalore then. But I read about it when I was looking at the old newspapers,' Kaveri said. 'She gave a talk at the Women's Indian Association meeting arguing for women to have the right to vote in local elections.'

'That's right. I had volunteered to help organise the meeting, picking up Mrs Naidu at the railway station and escorting her to the venue. On the way, we fell to talking, and I told her that I was unmarried and had time on my hands since my mother's passing away. After the meeting, she pulled me aside and asked me if I would like to join her for another event that evening. She said she couldn't tell me more, as it would be too risky for me to know ahead of time. But if I wanted to learn something that would be of my interest, I could meet her at her host's house in the evening for tea.'

Kaveri exchanged a glance with Ramu. So much was going on in their city that they did not know!

'I thought we were going to have polite conversation

over high tea. But we went to an old godown used to store blankets – the storage area of Sampangi Mills.' Shanthi smiled at Kaveri's surprised face. 'Yes. My husband was a supporter of the movement.'

She continued, 'It was a Sunday evening, and none of the workers were around. We made our way to the shed in ones and twos, slipping in through a back door that led onto a relatively deserted street. There, after a long debate, Mrs Naidu asked me to speak up and share my views. There were very few women there, and she asked me to speak from a woman's point of view.'

Shanthi looked nostalgic as she gazed out of the window, clearly remembering the past. 'I don't know what came over me, but I think I was very influenced by Mrs Naidu's speech that morning. I spoke about how much our lives had changed because of the British presence. My father had visited Jallianwala Bagh just then, after the massacre of Indians by the British, and he was very affected by the sight of the massacre, with all the blood. Even though the place was empty, when he closed his eyes, he could hear the screams of people, mothers and children fleeing for their lives as they were mown down by a merciless hail of bullets. I told them of that incident, and how it had affected me. And I made an impassioned plea for women to join the cause in large numbers, rising up to overthrow these white strangers who came unasked to take over our land.' Shanthi spoke softly, but her eyes flashed fire.

Kaveri looked at her in admiration. 'That's when your husband fell in love with you,' she guessed quietly.

'How did you know?' Shanthi gave them a wistful smile tinged with heartbreak.

'I saw an older man, very distinguished-looking, with hints of white hair at his temples. He seemed so sad and serious. His eyes were fixed on my face as I spoke. I felt a bit embarrassed, and also, frankly, a bit annoyed. I looked pointedly away from him as I spoke. But after I had finished speaking, he talked about his experiences as a wealthy industrialist, and how difficult it was to work in the British regime. They took away all the raw material – cotton – from our country at cheap prices, and forced him to pay exorbitant rates for the spun fibre which he had to import from England. He also spoke of how he was determined that his workers should not suffer because of the rapacious greed of the British, and made sure he gave them decent working wages, also educating their children, especially their women.'

Shanthi had tears in her eyes now. 'He said that his dearest hope was that the daughters of his workers would grow up to fight for independence, not only from the British but also from the control of men, like he was training his daughter to do.'

She turned to Kaveri, reaching a hand out to her. Kaveri gripped her palm tightly in hers, as Ramu listened sympathetically.

'I fell in love with him instantly. I didn't know he was a widower. I felt sad, thinking a man like him would be out of reach for someone like me. But he walked me back home after the meeting wound up, and told me about the story of his life. He told me how his wife had passed away when his daughter was a young child, and how he was raising her to become a strong, independent woman who would take over the factory from him. We walked slowly, talking all the way.' Shanthi looked up. 'By the time we reached my house, I think we both knew. He asked me to meet him in the Lal Bagh park the next day, in the afternoon. We met at the zoo. It is very quiet there in the afternoons. Hardly anyone goes there.'

Kaveri spoke up. 'A few months ago, we went to the Lal Bagh zoo, to lie in wait for someone who we suspected to be involved in a murder.'

Shanthi gave a small laugh. 'Well, we certainly weren't plotting a murder.' She grew serious again. 'We did spend a lot of time speaking about how we could support the Quit India movement. Even after we married, we continued going to the zoo. It was the one place we could speak without people overhearing us.' She looked up suddenly. 'But why did you ask me all of this? How is it relevant to the theft at the factory or the murder of my husband?'

'I'm not sure,' Kaveri said, her brain buzzing furiously. 'But – some things don't add up.'

'Such as?'

'Kumar told me that around the time you and your husband met, Mr Sharma put in place a series of austerity measures. He reduced worker bonuses, stopped paying for their medical treatments, stopped supporting their children's education . . . '

Shanthi grimaced. 'That was not us, that was Chitra.'

'Chitra?'

'Yes. Her father has taken her to the factory since she was a small girl, encouraging her to dream that she would be the owner someday. She slowly started to take over the management of the workers, but around the same time, she met Swami Vaninanda. And that man . . . ' Shanthi grimaced, making a sour face. 'As we know now, that man is an impostor. A fake Swami. But he had Chitra eating out of his hands and he convinced her that the factory overpaid its workers.'

'So you were not a devotee of his?' Kaveri asked.

'Me?' Shanthi arched an eyebrow at her. 'I am an atheist, like my husband. Chitra's aunt was very religious, and raised her to follow her example. I don't know how she got into the clutches of this Swami. Even though I am not religious, that does not mean I disrespect others' beliefs. But I don't believe in according any respect to charlatans.

Swami Vaninanda played on the insecurity of others to manipulate them into giving him all their money. Look at how he influenced Chitra to reduce the salaries of workers. I am sure he also made her pass on the money she saved to him.'

'Chitra told me your workers were pampered like children.'

Shanthi gave a contemptuous laugh. 'Hardly! She instituted all sorts of cost-cutting measures, slashing their salaries and increasing their work hours. We almost lost the factory when the workers went on strike for a month. And when one of them set fire to our entire store of blankets, we feared we would never be able to recover from it.'

'Kumar told me this,' Kaveri said. 'But he did not tell me it was Chitra who made these changes.'

'Kumar is very fond of Chitra. That is why I suggested to my husband that he should get the two of them engaged.' Shanthi hesitated. 'Her father was furious with her when we returned from our honeymoon and found that the workers were on strike, and she had mishandled the entire situation. But I think he was mostly furious with himself, because he was so distracted and had lost sight of the factory during the time we had met and were seeing each other.'

She blushed, then continued. 'He wanted to disinherit her on the spot, but I suggested that he instead give Kumar greater control over the factory, not just as a hired employee but also as a member of the family, as his son-in-law. I thought that Chitra was unnaturally close to the Swami, who is supposed to be celibate after all. I felt she looked at him more as a lover than a spiritual figure. I think his decision only made Chitra hate me more. She resented me from the moment we met and was so possessive of her father. When we decided to get married, she was furious. She was convinced I was marrying her father only for his money. We had a simple, inexpensive honeymoon in Ceylon, staying at a plantation owned by my husband's friend. But she accused me – oh, out of my husband's hearing, she never said a word to me when he was around – of making him spend thousands of rupees on me and my fripperies.'

'Why?'

Shanthi pursed her lips. 'Chitra is hot headed, she shouts when she loses her temper, and has been that way since she was a child. Her father didn't want her to know about his involvement – *our* involvement – in the Independence struggle, she is too indiscreet and would leak it to everyone. But we wanted to help fund it in some way. So, my husband took me to Barton Centre, and bought me expensive jewellery – rubies and diamonds – which I then said I kept in the safe. But in reality, we gave it to the movement, to finance our brave young patriots who move from city to city in disguise, spreading the call.'

'And Chitra was confirmed in her views that you were a gold-digger, exploiting her father,' Kaveri said.

'She was frightened that she would lose her inheritance. She dared not confront her father and ask him to stop spending on me. She had tried to get him to donate money to Swami Vaninanda's ashram, but even though he was so indulgent with her, he refused to do this. So, she decided to squeeze the money she thought her family had lost on me from the workers instead.'

'How could she?' Kaveri said, getting fired up. 'To reduce the workers' wages to the point that they couldn't afford to take their elderly parents to the hospital, or send their children to school?'

'Chitra has always had an anger issue. She is stubborn and self-centred. Her father spoiled her, and so did her aunt, her mother's sister who raised her when she was little. When Chitra has a bit between her teeth, she doesn't think of anyone else. She just wants to go after what she thinks is hers.' Shanthi sighed.

'When we returned from our honeymoon, and found out what happened, my husband was horrified. Did you see the side gates? With the Garuda?'

Kaveri nodded.

'She had even got the gates replaced with the Swami's symbol and placed his portrait in the living room. My husband was furious, and wanted the gates to be taken out immediately, and to throw out the portrait. But I convinced him to leave them there. She was so angry with us already that this would only have pushed her over the edge. But we told Kumar to reinstate the bonuses and bring back the previous policies with instant effect. Even though we did, the workers have lost faith in our family. When we were away, one of the workers' sick father passed away because he couldn't treat him in time.'

'Oh no.' Kaveri turned her face away, biting her lip.

'They dislike us even now. There is an air of hostility that pervades the factory. But we have to somehow find a way to get them back on track.' Shanthi let out a deep breath. 'After all, the fault is ours. We cannot restore the life of the worker's father who passed away, but perhaps we can make a difference to other lives, to make amends for what we caused.'

33

The Ugliest Dog Comes Home

'Help! He's going to kill me!'

'Oh, Bhargavi. Don't be ridiculous. He's only a puppy.' Shanthi waved a dismissive hand at Bhargavi, grinning as she watched the Ugliest Dog in Bangalore slobbering on Bhargavi's slippers.

Bhargavi shuddered, kicking her slippers across the room. 'There, take them, you wretched beast. Take them and chew on them till they fall to pieces. Go ahead, make yourself sick. What do I care?' But there was affection in her voice, mingled with the annoyance. The pup, huge beast that he was, yipped joyfully and ran after the mangled chappals, crushing them further in his massive jaws. Bounding back to Bhargavi, he dropped them at her feet and gave a victorious bark.

'I give up,' Bhargavi said with a sigh, patting the dog absent-mindedly as she gazed at her slippers. 'Kaveri, you will have to lend me a pair of chappals. This little fellow has destroyed my footwear.'

'Her feet are much larger than yours, or mine. But you can take Chitra's slippers.' Shanthi pointed towards Chitra, who was sitting in a corner of the room, wrapped in a large shawl. Since that night at the ashram, the two women had largely made up their differences, uniting in their disgust and anger at the Swami. Chitra cursed herself for being his unwitting dupe, and was silent for much of the time. Kaveri had worried that Shanthi would also be angry at Chitra. But as Shanthi explained, Mr Sharma loved his daughter, and would have hated to feel that his death had torn the family apart.

Chitra gave Bhargavi a small smile. 'You can wear my chappals any time, aunty.'

They were sitting in Kaveri's drawing room, all of them gathered together a week after the incident at the ashram. The previous day had been Garuda Panchami, when the Eagle God was worshipped. Bhargavi had organised a special *puja*, prayers offered in thanks to Garuda for safeguarding Kaveri and Ramu. Kaveri still felt angry when she thought of how Swami Vaninanda had callously exploited his devotees' reverence for Garuda for his own evil ends, but she comforted herself with the thought that he was now behind bars – and would stay there for a long, long time.

It had been an anxious few days for them all. Chitra had been so affected by finding out that the Swami, whom she had trusted so completely, was the one who had killed her father. She had fallen to pieces when she'd realised she had unwittingly aided him by telling him that Kaveri was supposed to meet her father at the factory at 9 p.m. Worried that Kaveri, whose fame as a detective had preceded her, would find out the truth behind the embezzlement, Swami

Vaninanda had forged the typed note and sent Murali to kill Mr Sharma.

The Swami was now trying to pin everything on Murali, claiming that he was innocent, but Murali refused to take all the blame. Murali had confessed everything to the police, handing over the altered account books and typewriter to them as evidence against the Swami. Together with the revolver which the police had taken from Murali, and the statements given by Anandi, Chitra, Ramu and Kaveri, there was ample evidence to convict both men for murder.

Chitra had become very withdrawn for several days, feeling guilty about being the cause of her father's death. She spoke little, crying a lot of the time. It had taken her several days – a very anxious time for Shanthi and Kumar – to come out of her depression and take interest once more in what was going on around her. But once she did, the two women sat down and spoke, and arrived at a number of decisions. Chitra looked wan and thin, but her face looked much more peaceful than any of the previous times that Kaveri had seen her.

'I know now that my father loved me,' Chitra had told Kaveri when she had come to meet her. 'That is what brings me peace now. I thought my father transferred his affections to my stepmother and wanted to disinherit me. But my stepmother explained to me that he always put me first. It was only because he cared so much for me that he wanted to keep the factory safe for me.' She blinked back tears. 'He thought by marrying me to Kumar he would ensure my safety as well as the factory's progress. I know he made some tough decisions, but he meant well. And he died loving me.'

Kaveri had leaned forward and hugged her, meeting Shanthi's eyes silently over Chitra's head as Shanthi stood behind her. Perhaps the two women would never be as close as mother and daughter, but they seemed to have now united in their common cause of bringing the factory back on track, and in their love for the same man, a good man snatched from them in an unjust, untimely manner.

'We have much to tell you.' Kaveri came back to the present as Shanthi clapped her hands. All the women gathered in the room looked up expectantly. Only Kaveri smiled to herself. She knew what was coming. Chitra and Shanthi had discussed their plans with her, and Kaveri had approved, making a few additional suggestions.

'First, Chitra and Kumar's wedding has been called off.' Shanthi looked around the room, as if daring the women to object. But they all nodded approvingly, even Lakamma, who had joined them, bringing a packet of her most special coffee to celebrate the event they were all gathered together to discuss. 'They are not in love, and there is no need to force the wedding. Kumar can continue in the role of General Manager.'

Chitra took up the conversation, 'When the police searched the ashram from top to bottom, they found the account books that Kumar had given Kaveri, well hidden in the basement. Fortunately, they had not yet destroyed them. Murali has confessed to disabling her car, and to stealing the books from the car when she had the accident. He was worried that there would be something in them that would implicate the Swami. It was his foolishness, of course. The only person it would have implicated was me.' She paused, looking uncomfortable, then pressed on. 'We make enough profits that we should able to recoup our losses in a year, if we are careful. By next year we should be able to be in the black again.'

'How will you run the factory now, with a shortage of money?' asked Lakamma, of course.

'I still have some of the jewellery that my husband bought us. And there is a lot of silver and other valuables and artwork in this house that can fetch us some money.' Shanthi looked around the drawing room of Kaveri's house, which was much smaller than hers. 'In fact, our current house is far too large for two women. We plan to sell it too, buying a smaller and more manageable place like this one, and investing the money back into Sampangi Mills. This way, we can keep the mills running *and* pay the workers a generous wage.'

Lakamma applauded them. 'That is an excellent plan. After all, it is most important to get the workers back on board.'

Mrs Reddy spoke up, looking worried. 'I can understand why Chitra does not want to marry Kumar. But under the terms of the will, won't she lose access to her inheritance?'

Chitra smiled at Mrs Reddy. 'Yes. In a few days, once it has been a month since my father's death, I will lose all my inheritance and the house and factory go to my stepmother.'

'And once it is mine, I will draw up a deed giving half of it back to Chitra.' Shanthi gave them all a mischievous grin. 'But enough talk about us. Let us get to the matter that brought us all here today.'

The women gathered in the living room looked at the banner commemorating the event they were there to celebrate. Mrs Reddy and Mrs Ismail sat on the love seat in the corner, their heads close together, painting the final touches to a large banner that said 'Shanthi Women's Home'. Anandi sat with Mala and Narsamma on another sofa, embroidering another banner.

Bhargavi didn't know quite what to make of this mixed group of women. She had accepted the women's club meetings at their home only because she felt that Kaveri was doing a good deed by teaching women of the 'lower' classes. But to have these women sit on the sofas with them, eating the same food, from the same plates, acting like their equals? She pulled a face.

Shanthi nudged her, whispering in her ear, 'The world is changing, *akka*. Learn to move with the change. Leave behind your absurd prejudices. See how wrong you were to think that dogs are dirty, messy creatures? How much affection you would have missed out on, if you had clung to those beliefs.' Bhargavi's face softened as she caressed one of Putta's large ears. The Ugliest Dog was now lying on her feet. As Shanthi spoke, he let out a deep sigh, settling his head comfortably in Bhargavi's lap and settling in for a comfortable snooze.

Kaveri looked at her mother-in-law with affection. She had come a long way in the past few weeks, and so had their relationship. When Kaveri had first moved to Bangalore, she had been terrified of her mother-in-law's disapproval. But now, when she sometimes found Bhargavi turning to *her* for her opinion, she felt more included. It made her nice, to feel so valued.

'He helps me sleep better at night,' Bhargavi admitted. 'After my husband's death last year, I could not sleep at all. I started at every noise. Putta has ruined most of my slippers, but he sleeps on my bed at night, and I don't feel quite so alone.'

Uma aunty gave her an understanding nod. 'I used to feel alone too, when my husband passed away. But now my grandson sleeps with me, and I sleep better for the company.'

Kaveri's thoughts immediately went to Ramu. Even though a week had passed since she had been trapped in the Swami's temple, he still held her tightly at night. She could not imagine sleeping without him now. And yet, just a few months ago, she had been used to sleeping all by herself in a large bed that had once held her and her older sisters before they had got married and left, and she hadn't felt the slightest bit alone.

Anandi laughed, as did Mala. 'We are the opposite. We sleep better now that our men are no longer with us.'

They were all so different from each other, Kaveri thought, gazing around the room. And yet, similar at the core. The events of the past few days and months had forged a close bond between them. Closer than most sisters, her women's group.

'What are your plans for the Women's Home?' Mrs Ismail asked Shanthi, looking up with a satisfied smile as she showed them the completed banner.

'All the women are addicted to cocaine,' Shanthi explained. 'Ramu and the doctors at the hospital have designed a programme to wean them off the drug, by tapering down their doses. We have set up a tennis court in the open ground, and they do a daily round of *pranayama* and yoga, followed by a series of sessions with their racquets and balls. The exercise, fresh air and good food are slowly making a difference. Many of them seem more alert, less anxious than they were just a week back, when we first saw them.'

'What will happen to them once they are weaned off the drug?'

'Kaveri and I had many conversations about this. She told me about her friend and classmate Ambujakshi. Though a child bride like Kalyanamma and Coffeepudi Lakamma, unlike them she was not able to get her family's support to rebuild her life. I reached out to Kalyanamma, and she managed to trace Ambujakshi.'

Kaveri looked at her eagerly. She had been so attached to Ambu, who was her dearest friend in school. 'You have heard from Ambu?'

'I not only heard from her – I convinced her to take up the job.' Shanthi smiled at her.

'The job?' Mrs Reddy looked up from her banner.

'Yes, Kaveri gave me an excellent idea. We will set up a training school for these women. Ambujakshi will be the first teacher, and once they have learned how to read and write, we will employ them in our mills. Lakamma has also offered to hire some of the women we train in her coffee factory, and Kalyanamma is in need of more women journalists. It will take time, but with their support, we can help these women become independent and self-sufficient.' Shanthi beamed.

'Inspector Ismail also gave me some good news today,' Kaveri said. 'The government has seized the Swami's ashram, but are willing to give it on lease to a charitable cause. He has convinced them to give it to Shanthi, to use for the Women's Home. So the women can continue to live where they are, but in improved conditions. And even better, I have received a reward from the British government for breaking the cocaine smuggling ring. Ten thousand rupees! I am giving it to the Women's Home, of course. With this, they can build more rooms to house more women, get them better beds and clothes and the other things they need, and do so much more. Perhaps they can even take in some small boys.' She frowned, thinking of the raggedy-looking, half-starved boys she had seen catching rats. 'There are so many hungry boys in the city. They need education and training as well, so they can get jobs and help feed their families, just like these women.'

Shanthi got up, holding a glass of lime juice in her hand. 'I think it's an excellent idea.' She raised her glass. 'I propose a toast. To Mrs Kaveri Murthy, the best detective in Bangalore.'

She went to her purse, pulled out a box wrapped in colourful red paper and handed it to Kaveri. The women crowded around Kaveri as she opened it. Inside, in an ornate silver frame, was a hand-painted photograph of

Kaveri which Shanthi had persuaded her to have taken in the Picture House, the brand new studio on Brigade Road. The photographer, a young man who had seemed quite taken with the social cache he would get for having photographed Bangalore's famous woman detective, had placed Kaveri in a silver-painted chair, one knee crossed regally over the other, her foot resting on a velvet footstool. She wore a blue velvet blouse paired with a pale green French chiffon sari with blue sequins embroidered at the shoulder. The photograph showcased Bangalore's first lady detective to perfection, wearing her signature magnifying glass earrings and chain, and holding her magnifying glass in one hand as she gazed keenly out of the frame.

The women clapped and cheered. The Ugliest Dog woke, joining the celebrations with enthusiasm by contributing a long, loud series of barks.

'Thank you, but the real credit should be shared between all of us,' Kaveri said, as the women looked at her expectantly. 'To the Bangalore Detectives Club.' She gestured to them all as they clinked their glasses together.

'I propose the last toast,' Bhargavi spoke up unexpectedly, and they stared at her in surprise. 'To the next case!'

Kaveri's Dictionary

ajji – grandmother

akka – older sister, honorific used to address an older woman

almirah – cupboard

ammaavare – mother, honorific used to address an older woman

anna – older brother, honorific used to address an older man

annas – unit of currency – in British India, 16 annas equalled one rupee

appa – father

apsara – celestial Indian spirits famed for their beauty

ashram – hermitage

avallaki – parboiled, flattened rice

athe – mother-in-law

ayyo – flexible exclamation used to express shock, grief, disapproval, pity or allied emotions

barfi – solid, dense Indian sweet, usually served in rectangular or diamond shapes

bhayandanguli – colloquial, someone who is easily scared

bidi – hand-wrolled cigarette

chee – expression of disgust

dharma – duty

grahana – eclipse

hundi – money box for cash offered by devotees, usually found in temples

idli – savoury steamed cake made from a batter of fermented rice and lentils, traditionally eaten for breakfast

jamkhana – hand woven cotton rug used as a carpet

kamblihula – small bristly caterpillar that, when touched, causes intense itching

kalarippayattu – ancient Indian martial art from Kerala, believed to be thousands of years old

laddu – round sweet

lathi – large, heavy stick

lungi – loose piece of unstitched cloth worn around the waist by men

namaskara – respectful greeting

paan – betel nut leaf, with various additions, commonly eaten after meals

pallu – the loose end of a sari, usually draped over the shoulder

panchanga – Indian calendar which follows Indian systems of timekeeping. Used by many households to ascertain dates and times and dates of religious significance to Hindus

payasa – Indian sweet

pranayama – Indian breathing technique used in yoga

purdah – head covering for women, seclusion of women

prasada – sacred offering given to devotees

pravachna – religious exposition

pudi – powder

puja – Hindu rituals of worship

rangoli – a common household art, in which geometric
   patterns are drawn on the floor in front of a house
   every morning, using rice powder or chalk – considered
   auspicious, bringing good luck to the home
rava – semolina, coarsely ground wheat
sambhar – sour and spicy lentil dish with vegetables
saaru – sour and spicy watery dish made with lentils
swami – honorific title of a holy man or woman
thumba – extremely
tiffin – light meal of snacks
uppittu – savoury breakfast dish made from semolina –
   broken wheat
vada – savoury fried snack
yakshagana – traditional street theatre art form of south
   India, with performers wearing colourful costumes
   with masks and elaborate face makeup

Kaveri's Adventures in the Kitchen

Recipes for a mid-afternoon meeting of
The Bangalore Detectives Club

No meeting of The Bangalore Detectives Club is complete without food – lots of food. The women usually prefer to meet in the afternoon, once their household responsibilities are complete, and they can relax in the company of friends. Here is a typical menu that you might find them having, if you were to drop by Kaveri's house at about 3 p.m. during a meeting of the Club.

1. South Indian filter coffee

Every meeting begins and concludes with servings of hot, strong south Indian coffee. Coffee is usually passed around in small tumblers placed inside dabaras (flat-bottomed circular bowls). In Kaveri's times, these vessels were usually made of brass or silver, but today aluminium and steel are used. You can serve filter coffee in small cups or glasses, if those are easy at hand – but this is strong, so it's advisable not to serve it in a large mug. You might find yourself trying to climb the walls!

South Indian filter coffee is traditionally made in an Indian coffee press, which can be purchased in most Indian shops located overseas. This press, made of steel or brass, looks similar to a French Press or Aero Press. It consists of two long chambers that fit tightly together. The bottom of the upper chamber has a series of small holes. The powder is loosely packed into the top chamber. After pouring in boiling water, the chamber is closed with a tight fitting lid. There is no plunger – the water percolates into the bottom chamber, passing through the mix of coffee powder and chicory under its own weight. It is then mixed with boiled, frothing milk.

A South Indian coffee filter should be available in most Indian shops located overseas. But it takes a bit of experience to know how much coffee powder to add, and how tightly to pack it in the top chamber. An easier way to make it is using a regular French Press, or Aero Press. South Indian coffee powder usually contains anywhere from 10-20% chicory, but you can use pure coffee powder if you prefer. Use the press to make a strong decoction. Fill a small cup or tumbler about one-third of the way with decoction. Then take a small vessel of milk, and heat it until boiling. Pour the hot milk into the tumbler. Then pour the coffee-milk mix in a thin stream into a second tumbler, holding the first one as high as you can manage without spilling coffee all over the counter. Repeat this a few times, until the coffee is covered with a nice coating of froth. Vegans can use oat milk as a substitute.

If you prefer your coffee sweet, add sugar – or the sweetener of your choice – to the hot milk before pouring it into the decoction.

2. Musk melon rasayana

This recipe comes from the Udupi region of Karnataka. Take a very ripe musk melon/cantaloupe, and cut into small pieces, removing the skin and seeds. Add an equal quantity of coconut milk, and a pinch of cardamom powder. Sweeten with jaggery powder, honey, or sugar, and refrigerate for an hour before serving. This is delicious as an Indian alternative to fruit salad for dessert. If you prefer, you can blend the musk melon with the coconut milk, adding a bit of water to make it into a milkshake.

3. Maddur vada

This vada, a crisp fritter made from a mix of rice flour and semolina, derives its name from the small town of Maddur, located on the railway line between Bangalore and Mysore, where it is believed to have been first made by Ramachandra Budhya in 1917 to feed hungry passengers on the train. It is a popular snack at teatime. Always make a few more than you think people might eat, as these tend to disappear quickly!

In a large bowl, take ½ cup rice flour, ¼ cup semolina flour, and ¼ cup of all-purpose flour. Add ½ cup of finely chopped onion, 2 tablespoons finely chopped curry leaves, salt (to taste), and a few finely chopped green chillies to taste (omit this if you don't want it to be spicy). Mix well, using clean hands, and set this aside for about 15 minutes. Then, add a spoon of hot oil or ghee, and a couple of tablespoons of water, and mix the dough again. The moisture from the onions, released after mixing with the salt, should make the dough stick together, along with the tiny amount of water you add. Add another couple of tablespoons of water if you need to, but make sure the dough doesn't become too watery – it won't be as crisp when you fry it.

Take a shallow, heavy bottomed or non-stick pan, and add a couple of inches of vegetable oil (canola or peanut works well, but avoid olive oil for deep frying). Heat the oil until very hot. Test the temperature by dropping in a tiny amount of batter. If the batter sizzles and rises to the top, the temperature is right.

Lower the heat under the pan to medium. Using clean hands, shape the batter into small flat circles, about two inches in diameter and a quarter inch in thickness. Drop the circles into the oil and fry until medium brown, removing them with a slotted spoon, and placing them on paper napkins to drain the excess oil. This tastes delicious hot or cold, and can be stored for a couple of days in an air-tight container. The dough needs to be made fresh, and cannot be frozen.

4. Uppittu

In a medium-sized round-bottomed pan, take 4-5 tablespoons of any vegetable oil of your choice. Heat the oil, and when it is hot, add ½ teaspoon mustard seeds. Once they splutter, add a pinch of asafoetida, a teaspoon of freshly grated ginger, a couple of finely chopped green chillies, ½ cup finely chopped onions, ½ cup of finely chopped vegetables of your choice (capsicum/green bell peppers, peas, beans and carrots go very well with this recipe), and salt to taste. Roast on medium flame for a minute, and then add a cup of semolina. Roast for a few minutes, until the semolina starts to turn golden, releasing a toasty aroma. Add three cups of hot water. Cover the pan with a lid, and cook for about 5-10 minutes until the semolina swells up and absorbs the water, and the vegetables are cooked through, removing the lid and stirring every few minutes. You can add more water if you prefer a more porridge-like consistency. This dish goes very well with Indian pickle or coconut chutney.

5. Coconut barfi

Heat ¾ cup sugar with ½ cup water until the sugar dissolves, stirring it for a few minutes on medium flame until the mixture thickens slightly. Add a cup of grated coconut, and a pinch (¼ teaspoon) of cardamom powder. Mix well, and continue to cook on low flame until the mixture starts to slowly come away from the sides of the pan, ensuring that it does not burn. Take the pan off the flame and ladle the hot mixture into a greased cake pan, or a plate with a high rim.

Once it cools and sets, slice it into diamonds or squares. You can press a single roasted (unsalted) cashew or almond into each square for decoration.

This recipe is best made with fresh coconut, but if you have dessicated coconut at hand, soak it in a small quantity of milk overnight, to soften it before use.

Historical Note

The historical setting of Bangalore in 1921 is largely accurate, but I have taken a few additional authorial liberties. Sampangi Mills is fictional, loosely based on other mills that existed in Bangalore in the 1920s. Coffeepudi Lakkamma is modelled after Coffeepudi Sakamma, an inspiring woman who lived in Bangalore in the 1920s and ran a famous coffee industry. Married at sixteen, she was the third wife of a rich coffee planter in Coorg. When Sakamma's son was just a year old, her husband died of a sudden illness, with his other two wives. Barely eighteen, she was left in sole charge of a large plantation. She took over the plantation and moved to Bangalore, setting up a coffee shop and processing unit which supplied the rich and famous of the city.

Kalyanamma was a real personality, and her magazine, *Saraswati*, was well known. Married at nine, widowed in a few weeks – hers was an unfortunately common story of the times. Kalyanamma was an inspirational woman who returned to school after she lost her husband, completed her education, then started a magazine of her own. She began with an initial print run of one hundred copies, not only funding the magazine with her own money but also delivering it door-to-door. She went on to make substantial contributions to the cause of women and children's education, and her name is well known even today.

Swami Vaninanda is a fictional character, a figment of my imagination crafted to fit the needs of an equally imaginary plot. He bears no resemblance to any other Swamis, living or dead. In colonial India, there were a number of Swamis. Some of them were truly holy men, deeply spiritual, involved with works of charity and societal upliftment. Others were frauds and tricksters, twisting the real devotion of people and exploiting the weakness of the vulnerable for their own benefit.

The cocaine trade was widespread across north India in the early twentieth century, smuggled in from Japan, Germany and China. It was largely eaten in *paan* or betel leaves. There may not have been much cocaine use in Bangalore, which was in the south of India, but I have taken a writer's liberty to extend the trade to this city in the plot.

Lord Garuda is worshipped and revered across India, and in many parts of South and South East Asia. Garuda Panchami, the day when Garuda is worshipped across India, usually falls in August, but I have moved it back a month to September. There was no blood moon (lunar eclipse) visible in Bangalore in September 1921, although there was one a few months earlier.

Messrs Barton and Sons, who sponsored the silver cup at the dog show in the book, continue to sell fine decorative silver items in Bangalore. The Picture House where Kaveri's photograph was taken, is real, but was not established until 1955.

It is unlikely that Kaveri would have been able to openly learn and practise *kalaripayattu* in the 1920s. A martial art used in Wayanad for a revolt against the British, it was banned by the British government in the early nineteenth century – though it continued to survive as a form of covert resistance, encouraged by the Swadeshi movement against British colonial rule, passed on from teacher to student in secrecy. It is a lovely martial art, and one that Kaveri loves to practise.

Acknowledgements

This book would not be what it is without Venkatacha-lam Suri and Dhwani Nagendra Suri, my husband and daughter, who are ever-willing to brainstorm ideas with me, and have read and commented on multiple drafts of the book. Dhwani was not yet born when I started writing the Bangalore Detectives Club – it has been so lovely to watch the series come to life as she grew, started to read and added her strong feminist perspective. And without Cha-lam, who has been my support, inspiration and sounding board for ideas for thirty years, none of this would have been possible. They propel me along with their energy, en-thusiasm and love.

Since Bangalore's history is an area of professional research for me (as part of my day job as an ecologist), I benefited from a treasure trove of information on colonial Bangalore. I am indebted to a number of archives, including the Karnataka State Archives, the Mythic Society, the Indian Institute of World Culture, and the British Library – and to writers who investigate Bangalore's history like

Meera Iyer, to whom I am especially indebted for her fascinating article on polygonal domes in heritage buildings. Family stories, reminiscences and recipes shared by my mother Manjula gave me an intimate view into the lives of women and men who lived more than a century ago, impossible to get from books and maps alone. And special thanks to my aunt Lalitha, for her delicious recipe for muskmelon rasayana.

Priya Doraswamy, childhood friend and incomparable agent, is the best advocate for the book that I could ever wish for. And I truly lucked out with a dream team of publishers, with brilliant editorial inputs from Rebekah West and Krystyna Green at Little, Brown, Tom Feltham's insightful copyedits, and the terrific support provided by Claiborne Hancock, Jessica Case and Meghan Jusczak at Pegasus Books in the US, and Thomas Abraham, Riti Jagoorie, Naina Tripathi and Raghu Nandan at Hachette in India.

This book is a tribute to all the remarkable women who lived in times past, such as my great grandmothers Ammanithai Ammalu and Padmavati Bai, Coffeepudi Sakamma, Kalyanamma, and many others. Defying societal restrictions to forge their own path, they blazed the way for generations to follow – as Kaveri, Mala, Anandi, Uma aunty, Mrs Reddy, and the other women of the Bangalore Detectives Club are doing.

Finally, this book is for my father, CV Nagendra, who hooked me onto mysteries early. You would have loved reading about Kaveri and Ramu, Appa. I can imagine you're burning the telephone lines up in the sky, calling up all your friends to tell them your daughter wrote this book!

Harini Nagendra is a Professor of Sustainability at Azim Premji University, Bangalore, India, and the author of *Nature in the City: Bengaluru in the Past, Present and Future*. She received a 2013 Elinor Ostrom Senior Scholar award for her research and practice on issues of the urban commons, and a 2007 Cozzarelli Prize with Elinor Ostrom from the Proceedings of the US National Academy of Sciences for research on sustainability. *The Bangalore Detectives Club*, the first book in the Detective Kaveri mysteries, is her first fiction novel, and was featured on the New York Times list of 100 notable books of 2022.

Harini lives in Bangalore with her family, in a home filled with maps. She loves trees, mysteries, and traditional recipes.